"I DON'T
   SAID HE

"I'm afraid of you, Steve, of that pragmatic mind of yours. You have the power to hurt me—and I'm sick of being hurt."

"It doesn't have to be that way. We can work it out. Maybe you could start therapy with a—" He broke off, his eyes stricken. "I didn't mean that. I don't know why I said such a stupid thing. My only excuse is that I'm half out of my mind with fear that I've lost you for good."

When she didn't answer, he made a helpless gesture. "It's no go, isn't it?" he said. "I blew it again. Well, you don't have to worry. From now on, I'll leave you alone. Just remember that I do love you, that I always will...."

ABOUT THE AUTHOR

Superromance readers need no introduction to California-based author Irma Walker, who is also a successful writer of mainstream fiction. Irma's sixth Superromance features a clairvoyant heroine, and Irma tells us she definitely believes in "second sight" because her mother had it, usually in the form of dreams. Apparently even Irma's practical-minded father learned to disregard his wife's visions at his own risk! Irma didn't inherit her mother's gift, but the subject has always fascinated her.

Books by Irma Walker

HARLEQUIN SUPERROMANCE
104—SONATA FOR MY LOVE
147—THROUGH NIGHT AND DAY
163—SPANGLES
210—GAMES
247—MASKS

Don't miss any of our special offers. Write to us at the following address for information on our newest releases.

Harlequin Reader Service
901 Fuhrmann Blvd., P.O. Box 1397, Buffalo, NY 14240
Canadian address: P.O. Box 603,
Fort Erie, Ont. L2A 5X3

Irma Walker

CRYSTAL CLEAR

Harlequin Books

TORONTO • NEW YORK • LONDON
AMSTERDAM • PARIS • SYDNEY • HAMBURG
STOCKHOLM • ATHENS • TOKYO • MILAN

Published January 1989

First printing November 1988

ISBN 0-373-70339-2

Printed in U.S.A.

To my mother,
Edith Nethery Fields,
who had the gift of second sight.

CHAPTER ONE

IT WAS SPRING, and the first really warm day after what had been an unusually cold winter for northern California. As Marma stood at the open window of the apartment she shared with Angie D'Marco and stared at the aquamarine waters of San Francisco Bay, she made a discovery. She was happy—happy and at peace, now that the demons of the past that had haunted her for so long had finally been banished for good.

"Awesome," she murmured, borrowing one of her roommate's favorite expressions.

Her euphoria, she suspected, also originated from such simple things as the warmth of the San Francisco sun, which really was as golden as the song said, and the fresh, moisture-laden breeze that drifted in from the Marin County highlands across the bay, ruffling the freshly laundered window curtains she'd hung just that morning.

That her lighthearted mood had something to do with her recent promotion at work, she was also aware. And at least part of it probably stemmed from having had a three-day weekend, her first since Christmas, which had given her the precious gift of time—time for the handicraft projects she found so satisfying, for girl talk with her roommate, for put-

tering around the apartment and for putting things
back in order. Order was necessary to someone whose
life had so often been uncertain and chaotic.

With a start, she realized that Angie had been talking nonstop for the past few minutes, that she'd been
so preoccupied with her own thoughts, she hadn't
taken in a word. A little guiltily, she forced her attention back to her friend.

"—good thing you have such a strong nesting instinct," Angie was saying.

Angie was comfortably plump and sunny- natured.
Her strawberry blond hair and green eyes were a sharp
contrast to Marma's own ebony hair, dark blue eyes
and petite figure. At the moment, Angie was sitting
cross-legged on the floor, lazily sorting through a stack
of old magazines, stopping often to browse through an
issue that caught her interest. With secret amusement, Marma noted that the pile to be saved was twice
as tall as the one that was to be tossed out.

"If it were up to me," Angie went on, "we'd always be knee-high in dirty dishes and old newspapers. How come a career type like you is such a demon
housekeeper?"

"I guess clutter makes me uncomfortable," Marma
said. "When I was growing up, Papa was so strict
about keeping the house neat. Our home was always—" She broke off, angry with her loose tongue.

"Home being Tennessee—right?" Angie said.

The question was casual; the curiosity in Angie's
eyes was not.

"Right," Marma said, then added quickly, "and I
could use a cup of coffee right about now. How about
you?"

"Uh-huh. In other words, mind your own business," Angie said. "Okay, subject closed. Who am I to intrude upon your precious privacy?"

Marma studied her with troubled eyes. Angie wasn't just her roommate. Angie was her best friend and, under her nonchalance, Marma sensed a real hurt.

"It isn't personal," she said reluctantly. "It's just that—well, when I left home, I turned my back on—on a very painful situation. I try not to think about life before Brown."

Angie's eyes softened. "Good ol' Brown U. Talk about cultural shock. Me from laid-back California, you with a Southern accent you could cut with a knife, and both of us homesick enough to die—or at least, I always thought homesickness was why you were so out of it that first year."

"Well, if you were homesick, it didn't show. Thank God you took me under your wing. I don't know if I would have survived my freshman year without you."

"Yeah. Well, you did learn quickly. You even lost your accent—with amazing quickness, come to think of it."

"I did a lot of practicing on the sly," Marma said, smiling at her. "I was determined to change my—" Again, she broke off. What was *wrong* with her today? She never talked about the past, not even with Angie. Could it be spring fever?

"You were determined to what?"

"Lose my accent."

"Uh-huh. That wasn't what you started to say but never mind. Someday you'll open up and tell me what the devil caused those nightmares you used to have so often. I can still hear you yelling in the middle of the night about, of all things, mice. Rats, I could have understood, but mice? They must have been super big ones. You know—the mice that ate San Francisco?''

Marma forced a smile at Angie's teasing, but inwardly, she was cringing. How strange that Angie had used those particular words—*the devil*. Marma had often suspected that the devil had something to do with the nightmares that destroyed her sleep and wrecked her peace of mind. But she hadn't had any lately. Not since she'd come to San Francisco two years ago to take a management trainee job with Flagg Banks, Inc.

Hoping Angie would drop the subject, she stood back from the framed quilt she'd just hung on the wall, her head tilted to one side. It was a little off-center and she straightened it carefully, then stood back again, this time to admire her handiwork. The quilted wall hanging was a riot of rich colors, her own interpretation of the classic Star of Bethlehem pattern, and it created a splash of cheer against the cream-colored wall.

''There—is it straight?'' she said aloud.

''As a ruler. It's really awesome, Marma. No way should those colors go together and yet they form, y'know, a perfect whole.''

''Good phrase, that—very good, Angie,'' Marma teased. ''Maybe you should have been a poet instead of a kindergarten teacher.''

''Poet? Not this practical gal. You're the artist around here. What you've done to jazz up this apartment is pure magic—and it didn't cost an arm and a leg, either. Why did you go for a business degree, Marma? You should have opted for the arts.''

"And starved to death? No, thanks. Besides, working with statistics and mathematics is very satisfying," Marma said. "It makes me feel safe."

"From what?"

"Just . . . safe."

"Well, money wise, you certainly chose the right career, although I can't honestly say I envy you. I love working with kids. Not that I'd hesitate a moment to quit teaching to marry Danny and stay home to raise a houseful of my own kids."

A houseful of my own kids. . . . How easily, how confidently Angie said those words. For a moment, envy stabbed Marma. What wouldn't she give to be able to take for granted such things as someday having a husband and children—and how impossible such dreams were to a freak like her. . . .

Freak. . . . Another hurtful word. When would they stop, those little flashes of pain from the past?

"And once you catch your guy, what am I going to do for a roomie?" she said aloud.

"Oh, you can swing the place alone now that you've got that promotion. Besides, I'd see that Uncle Louie gave you the same break on the rent that he gives me. And I'll still be around. We'll always be best friends—" Angie jumped up and gave Marma an exuberant hug, almost knocking her down "—even if you won't confide your deepest, darkest secrets to me."

Marma hugged her back, a little gingerly. She envied Angie her ability to be demonstrative, to say extravagant things without weighing their effect, to be generous with her hugs and her confidences. But then Angie came from that kind of people: a warm, wonderful Italian family. The D'Marcos were always kissing and hugging each other—and squabbling and arguing just as often. At their family get-togethers, the noise level was sometimes so high it was impossible to think, much less make yourself heard. Wasn't it odd, Marma thought, that even though they had opened their hearts to her, accepted her as one of their own because she was Angie's friend, she still felt so lonely and set apart, even in the midst of all the feasting and talking and laughing?

Unexpectedly, an image of her own family crept into her mind: Papa, her sister, her three brothers and herself, grouped around the old pine trestle table in the kitchen, eating supper in almost total silence, the only conversation an occasional, "Pass the gravy," or, from Papa, "Go fetch some more of that johnnycake, Marma."

She took a long shaky breath to calm herself, but something of what she felt must have shown on her face because Angie asked, "What is it, Marma? You look like you've just seen a ghost. Something bothering you?"

"Nothing a little coffee won't cure," Marma said and went into the kitchen to plug in the electric kettle.

Later, as they sat at the kitchen table, sipping coffee and nibbling at the cookies Marma had baked that morning, Angie gave a contented sigh.

"I love San Francisco this time of year, just before the tourists start pouring in," she said dreamily. "What's Tennessee like in the spring?"

Marma searched her memory. Duncan Hollow—better known as Duncan Holler—in the spring—oh, yes, she remembered it well....

"Right about now," she said, smiling, "the red-buds and cherry trees have almost stopped blooming and the dogwoods and apple trees are just beginning to show color. In a few weeks, the rhododendron will turn the valley floor deep purple. Already, the yellow pines on the mountain behind the house are showing new growth, and there's bound to be a fresh litter of kittens in the barn. Since it's three hours later at home, Papa is—" She broke off because her voice had suddenly thickened.

"Papa is what?" Angie said.

Marma took a deep breath. "Papa is in the spring-house, separating the milk. He keeps Jersey cows, which give the richest milk, because he gets a premium price for cream from a Nashville dairy."

"And your mother—what was she like, Marma?"

Marma looked at her friend with bleak eyes. "I don't remember her. I look like the picture of her Papa keeps by his bed. Black Irish, he called her once. I'm the only one of the kids who has blue eyes like the McCanns, my mother's side of the family. My sister and brothers are all dark, like Papa."

"Have you broken off with them completely, Marma? Don't you ever get the urge to go back home for a visit?"

"I wouldn't be welcome. Papa made it clear that he had washed his hands of me. That first year at Brown, I wrote him several letters but they all came back marked 'refused'—in his handwriting. I stopped writing because it was so painful when my letters were returned."

"What about your brothers or your sister? Did you ever write to them?"

"No. We were never very close. We didn't have much in common." Marma's voice was stiff. To forestall any more questions, she added, "If you want to be ready for your date with Danny, we'd better get back to work."

Angie groaned. "Slave driver! But you're right. I'll need gobs of time to get ready. Maybe this will be the night he proposes. Spring doth bring out the romance in men—some men. So I want to look really great—and sexy—tonight, which takes time. If I looked like you, I'd just run a comb through my gorgeous black hair, put on some lip gloss, and away I'd go. Honestly, I must be crazy, sharing a flat with you. Danny practically drools every time he comes by to pick me up."

Despite her teasing tone, there was a wistful note in Angie's voice, and Marma felt a sudden impulse to give her friend a good hard shake. Didn't Angie know that her roommate would have traded almost anything for Angie's social ease, her infectious, happy-go-lucky ways and her warm and loving family?

Silently, Marma rose and began clearing off the table. With a sigh, Angie got up, too, but before she returned to sorting magazines, she gave Marma a long, thoughtful look.

"You work too hard, Marma. You should get out more often and have some fun. How about letting me fix you up with that friend of Danny's—you know, that tall blond guy you met at Mama and Papa's anniversary party? Danny says he keeps asking questions about you."

Marma shook her head. "Not tonight. Maybe some other time."

She turned away, wondering what had happened to her euphoria. Talking about her family had been a mistake. It still hurt, after all these years, remembering that last terrible row with her father when he'd told her that she was no longer his daughter, that he was taking her name out of the family Bible.

And now Angie knew too much about her private business. Being the inquisitive person she was, she was sure to bring it up again, ask more questions....

With a sigh, Marma decided to put the whole business out of her mind. She washed and rinsed the cups they'd used, left them on the sink mat to dry, then went to help Angie finish sorting magazines. For a while, they worked in companionable silence, and then Angie disappeared into the bathroom to get ready for her date.

Marma switched on the TV, changed channels several times and then switched it off again because she wasn't in the mood for early evening game shows or news commentators. She slipped a cassette, chosen at random, into the tape player, and when the soft, insinuating voice of Johnny Mathis filled the room, she curled up on the wicker sofa with a book she'd been meaning to start reading. Her cat, a stray female Siamese who had recently adopted Marma, jumped into her lap and settled down for a nap.

It was a good book, a Dean Koontz thriller, and Marma was soon absorbed in the hero's perils, which was why she was so surprised when the print suddenly blurred in front of her eyes and a familiar grayness fell around her, draining the color out of the room.

The book slid off her lap and fell to the floor with a soft thud, startling the cat, who jumped to the floor.

Marma gripped the arms of her chair with both hands, as if by holding on to something solid she could thwart the hateful thing that was happening to her.

But it didn't work—not this time. There was a roaring in her ears, and weakness invaded her whole body, making it hard to breathe. A frightening dizziness struck her and forced a gasp from her throat. As streaks of gray swirled around her at an ever-increasing speed, she hung onto the chair's arms, afraid she would black out and fall.

Then, as though someone had switched on a powerful spotlight, an image formed in front of her. Indistinct at first, it slowly became clearer, and suddenly she was looking down at the sleeping face of a woman. No—*not* a woman. The person asleep on the bed was little more than a child, probably in her mid-teens. Her face was a pale ivory oval under a mop of dark hair that tumbled over her forehead, and although Marma couldn't put a name to her, her face seemed hauntingly familiar.

The image lasted only a few seconds—to her intense relief—before it began to dissolve into grayness. Marma opened her eyes and discovered that her sight had returned, that she was still sitting upright in the old lounge chair, still gripping its arms tightly with numb, bloodless fingers. Although she knew she was safe, that the vision wouldn't come again—at least not soon—the realization did nothing to comfort her.

Her old nemesis had returned to torment her. Just when she thought she was finally safe, the curse that had made her childhood a nightmare and had turned her into an object of shame to her family was back. Fighting nausea, she drew a shuddering breath of air into her constricted lungs as words from the past flooded her mind: taunting, hurtful words flung at her from across a country school yard.

"Crazy Marma...she's a witch...a witch...a witch...."

And the thing that was so frustrating was that this particular vision made no sense—none at all. Usually the visions heralded danger to someone she knew, but the girl she'd seen today was a stranger, and had been sleeping peacefully. So why, after such a long time, had the visions returned?

Was she being punished for letting down her guard and daring to be happy?

CHAPTER TWO

PRAISE FROM OTHERS, especially in connection with his job, always made Steve Riley uncomfortable. After all, doing the best he was capable of for *World Beat*, the national newsmagazine he worked for, was what he got paid for. Which was why, for the past couple of days, he'd been staying away from the magazine's office on Polk Street, doing research, conducting interviews and following up leads for a new series of articles. He knew it wouldn't be long before the exposé that had earned him the prestigious Wilcoxon Award for Journalism fell into the category of yesterday's news.

He was proud of the award, of course, but being named one of the country's top investigative reporters by the *Washington Post* was an embarrassment. Talk about overkill....

Not that he wasn't good at his job. An earlier exposé he'd done on nursing homes had earned him a hefty raise and an offer to take over as west coast editor of *World Beat*, an offer he'd promptly turned down because he wasn't quite ready to be trapped behind a desk. But as confident of his abilities as he was, Steve was uncomfortably aware that much of his success had been based on luck, just as it had been pure luck to have been transferred to San Francisco, his hometown, where the west coast offices of *World Beat* were located.

As Steve entered one of the elevators in Flagg Towers, a high-rise office building located on New Montgomery Street in downtown San Francisco, he reflected that a very important benefit of his recent transfer was that he was once again living near his uncle, Arnold Flagg, who was president and majority stockholder of Flagg Banks, Inc., the banking firm he'd founded. Since Steve's return to the west coast, they had had lunch together every Tuesday, an event Steve always looked forward to.

He got off the elevator on the top floor, where the executive suite was located. His uncle's personal secretary, a marvel of svelteness and understated elegance, greeted him with her usual deference. If Steve hadn't know that Arnold wasn't a chaser, he might have suspected she'd been chosen for her spectacular looks. As it was, he knew she had to be a whiz at her job; Arnold was a perfectionist, especially where his business was concerned. Come to think of it, Steve mused, so was he. Maybe there was something in genes, after all.

Steve smiled to himself, liking the idea that he'd inherited some of his uncle's qualities. For Arnold was more than his uncle; he was also his mentor and best friend. After the death of Steve's parents in a freak boating accident had made him an orphan at fourteen, Arnold had taken him in and given him not just a place to live, but a real home. Steve's aunt, although in frail health, had also made him welcome, and after his time for grieving had ended, he had come to regard Uncle Arnold and Aunt Laura as the parents he'd lost.

Laura had died while Steve was a junior at Stanford, and he'd grieved as deeply as he had when he'd lost his real mother. Later, when he'd graduated with an MBA degree, he could have gone to work at Flagg Banks, but instead he had turned down his uncle's offer of a job. His inquisitive nature, his restlessness and his desire to see the world had made banking seem a dull way to earn a living, so he'd utilized the journalism courses he'd taken at Stanford and had gone to work as a cub reporter at the *New York Times*, eventually becoming an investigative journalist with his own column.

When, a few years later, he had become restless again, he'd moved to *World Beat*. That he'd never regretted his choice of career was proof that his instincts had been right.

The secretary—her name was Sylvia, he remembered now—spoke into the intercom on her desk, and the high-powered smile she flashed Steve as she told him to go right in, his uncle was waiting for him, communicated a personal interest that he pretended not to understand. He wasn't turned on by sleek, sophisticated women with predatory eyes, and Steve's own smile was cool as he went into Arnold's office, closing the door behind him.

Arnold Flagg was sitting behind a priceless Queen Anne desk that blended well with the other antique furnishings of his chestnut-paneled office. Even before the door closed, he was on his feet, coming toward Steve, his hand outstretched. He was a trim, slightly built man with alert young eyes that belied his deeply lined face. His hair, which had once been as rusty as Steve's, was now iron-gray.

"You look like hell, boy," he said by way of greeting as they shook hands. "Why don't you try sleeping alone at night and maybe you'd get some rest?"

It was a running joke between them that Steve was a playboy, which wasn't even remotely true, but Steve played along with his uncle, as always, retorting, "And spoil my fun? You're only young once, you know."

Arnold groaned. "How did you make it as a journalist, using those tired old chichés?"

"I don't write 'em. I just say 'em." Steve said, grinning.

"Uh-huh. You're a tad late—which is okay. I got tied up with my lawyer and it threw my schedule off."

"Nothing wrong, I hope?"

"No, I was signing a new will. Or rather, I should say that I just added a codicil to my old one." He glanced at Steve, then quickly looked away. If it hadn't been so ridiculous, Steve would have guessed that his uncle was embarrassed. "There's something I think I should tell you, just to clear up any—well, questions that might arise in the future when my will is probated."

Steve didn't say the polite thing: that since Arnold was obviously in perfect health, the probating of his will would undoubtedly take place at a time far off in the future. Instead, sensing the seriousness behind his uncle's words, he nodded agreeably and settled himself in a tapestry-covered chair. He tried to hide his curiosity. His uncle was a man of strong opinions that he seldom changed, the very opposite of impulsive.

Adding a codicil to his will seemed out of character. And what had Arnold meant by clearing up any questions that might arise when his will was probated?

"You've probably guessed that you're one of my principal heirs," Arnold said. At Steve's start, he smiled slightly. "No, I see you haven't. Well, you are, and if you're wondering, yes, Millicent knows all about it and thoroughly approves of her favorite—and only—cousin being remembered in my will. After all, she's married to a very wealthy lawyer who will see that she and my granddaughter are always well provided for. She also knows about the codicil—that I'll be leaving a tidy legacy to a—a friend."

"Someone I know?"

Arnold hesitated briefly and again Steve wondered if he was embarrassed. "Her name is Marma Duncan," his uncle said finally. "And no, I'm sure you don't know her. But since I'm obviously of sound mind and body at present, and since you happen to be one of the executors of my will and can so attest— well, I just don't want any misunderstandings to occur when the time comes."

"Oh?" Steve managed to sound only mildly worried. "Are you planning on going somewhere soon?"

"Not for another couple of decades." There was a glint of amusement in Arnold's shrewd eyes now. "I just wanted you to know that I'm depending on you to see that everything goes smoothly when the time does come."

Arnold's lips closed with a snap that was almost audible, which meant, Steve knew from long experience, that his uncle had said all he intended to on the subject of his will—and the mysterious Marma Duncan. Steve nodded as if he understood, which he didn't. Although he remained silent, there were a dozen questions he wanted to ask, starting with, "Who the *hell* is Marma Duncan?"

He knew for certain that she wasn't a relative. Arnold's only living relatives were his daughter, Millicent, his granddaughter, Lisa, and his nephew. And Steve doubted this Marma Duncan was the daughter or wife of an old friend; he knew almost all Arnold's friends.

Which left another possibility: that Marma Duncan was Arnold's mistress. After all, Arnold had been widowed for almost a decade. What was more, he was in good health and, as far as Steve knew, still a virile man. He was also a responsible person who paid his debts and took care of his own. It wasn't too farfetched to assume that he'd added that codicil to ensure that the mistress he felt responsibility toward would be financially secure in the event of his death. The fact that no rumors about such an alliance had reached Steve's ears was immaterial. Arnold was a very private person, a man who kept his own counsel. If he had a mistress, he would, no doubt, be discreet about it.

And more power to the old guy, Steve thought, repressing a smile.

They ate their lunch, which had been sent up from a nearby restaurant, on a small terrace that overlooked New Montgomery Street, the core of San Francisco's financial district. It was solid, hearty fare, what Arnold called "men's food," and as they lingered over their wine—a fruity Sonoma County Beaujolais—they conversed on a number of eclectic and wide-ranging topics. Arnold, always keenly interested in anything that concerned Steve, finally got around to his nephew's prizewinning series of articles in *World Beat*.

"You really came down hard on mediums and psychics, didn't you?" he remarked. "I was surprised that you didn't take at least a token stab at presenting the other side of the story."

Steve's face tightened. "There is no other side," he said shortly. "I interviewed a dozen or more victims of so-called psychics and it's incredible how persuasive those scam artists can be. They know every trick in the book about extorting money from the gullible. I talked to one elderly woman who had been bilked out of her life's savings. She was left destitute after one of those bastards cleaned her out. He convinced her that her dead husband was speaking to her from beyond the grave, advising her on how to invest her insurance money."

"Which proves only that charlatans will always take advantage of the unwary," Arnold protested. "It doesn't prove that ESP and other psychic powers don't exist."

"Maybe not, but during my research, I checked out numerous psychics and fortune-tellers, attended readings and séances, posing as a client with personal problems. Nothing happened that couldn't be explained away by reason and logic."

"Have you thought about the possibility that your being a skeptic might have inhibited their powers?"

"Hogwash. It either works or it doesn't. And I saw nothing to convince me that such a thing as ESP, clairvoyance, second sight—call it what you want—

exists. And there's something else that's even more convincing: if precognition really does exist, why aren't there a lot of rich clairvoyants in the world?''

Arnold considered Steve's question, frowning. "I may have an answer to that. According to a friend of mine, who just happens to be a psychic, and other experts I've read on the subject, true clairvoyance is a hit-and-run thing, so erratic it can seldom be called up at will. And if perverted for personal gain, it soon becomes unreliable and can even disappear.''

Steve gave a disbelieving snort. "With all the recent interest in ESP, it would surely manifest itself during some of the bona fide investigations into the phenomenon. But I couldn't find any convincing evidence that this has happened, at least not when laboratory conditions using scientific methods were used.''

"Are you saying you believe all psychics are fakes?''

"Oh, I have no doubt that there are people who believe they have metaphysical powers, but it's obviously self-delusion. I did a thorough survey of those predictions that psychics make each New Year, and the accuracy rate is not only poor, it's worse than the law of averages would allow. Even the few predictions that seemed to have come true were worded in such a vague, general way that the meaning could have been twisted in a dozen directions.''

"But suppose the very act of trying to produce proof in a laboratory environment inhibits the talent? And what about the cases where psychics have helped police find lost children and other missing people?''

"I checked that out, too. Some cases seemed promising, but on close investigation, they all proved to be inconsistent, or the facts had been twisted, the wording of the prophecy open to several interpretations. For every success there are dozens of failures. Naturally, the failures don't get any press coverage. The frustrating thing is that my exposé will have little effect. The superstitious will always believe in mumbo jumbo, regardless of the evidence. Which is a pity because these people, whether deliberate fakes or honestly deluded, do so much harm."

Arnold regarded him thoughtfully. For a moment, Steve thought his uncle was going to continue the argument, but he must have reconsidered because he changed the subject to politics and they were soon squabbling over San Francisco's recent mayoral election. Since Arnold was a conservative and Steve a liberal, it was a lively argument.

Later, as Steve was leaving his uncle's suite, he paused by Sylvia's desk. "Would you happen to have Marma Duncan's address?" he asked pleasantly.

From the blank expression on her face, he knew the answer even before she said, "That name isn't familiar. Perhaps it's listed in Mr. Flagg's private files. I can ask him—"

"It's not that important. I'll look it up in the phone book," he said and moved away quickly, aware that she was staring after him.

As he took the elevator down to the lobby, his thoughts were on his next assignment. With the psychic articles finished, he was doing research on a series about the homeless, a consistent and worrisome problem not only in San Francisco but in all large cities. Deep in thought, he barely noticed when the elevator stopped at the eighth floor and two women got on. He paid no attention to their conversation—until he heard one address the other as "Marma."

Since their backs were turned, Steve wasn't certain which woman had spoken. Was it possible that one of them was the mysterious woman Arnold had written into his will? How many women named Marma could there be in San Francisco—and riding an elevator in Arnold's office building to boot?

He studied what he could see of the two women with interest. One of them was tall and willowy in a well-tailored suit, with silver-blond, smoothly coiffed hair. She turned her head to say something to her companion, and he realized that despite her careful makeup, she was in her early forties. The other one laughed, an infectious, young sound, and he dismissed her immediately; with her slight, youthful figure, she was obviously little more than a teenager.

Which meant the older woman was Marma Duncan, Arnold's "friend." What exactly was going on between this woman and his uncle? An affair, as he had suspected earlier? There was something about her aggressive, too-abrupt voice that rubbed him the wrong way. It was hard to believe that Arnold could be so smitten with this woman, that he would alter his will for her.

Motivated by curiosity, he followed the two women off the elevator on the fourth floor and down a long, thickly carpeted hall. As Steve trailed after them, he noticed that the older woman was doing most of the talking. When they turned into an office, Steve paused long enough to read the brass plate on the door— Home Mortgage Division, Flagg Banks, Inc.—before he followed them inside.

He found himself in a large room that held a couple of dozen desks and hummed with activity. To his surprise, the older woman was just disappearing through a door marked Charlotte Everett, Director. He watched, frowning, as the second woman headed for another door. The sign on this one read Assistant to the Director. By the time he reached the door, which she'd left open, the black-haired woman was putting her purse away in a desk drawer.

A nameplate on the desk read Marma Duncan.

Steve sent a quick look around the small room; besides the usual office equipment, there were some bright wall hangings and an assortment of plants. The office was surprisingly homey and informal. The woman glanced up; she looked startled when she saw him standing in the doorway.

Steve surveyed her with the observation skills he'd honed during hundreds of interviews. He took careful mental notes.

Her eyes were wide-set, darkly lashed, and so deep a blue that they looked almost black. He groped for a color, came up with midnight blue and then changed it to lapis lazuli. Her clothing consisted of a well-cut, classically simple gray suit, and a tiny rosebud in her lapel that added an informal touch to an outfit that would otherwise have been too austere for a woman her age. Thick, ebony hair—a startling contrast to skin the color of rich cream—swung to her shoulders. Piquant features included a short, straight nose, a well-rounded chin, smoothly planed cheekbones and a generous, sweetly curved mouth that was—his throat was suddenly too dry—incredibly kissable....

"Yes? May I help you, sir?" the woman said, as he detected a hint of a southern accent. She wasn't from Texas or the deep south, he decided. Tennessee or Kentucky, maybe—possibly West Virginia....

Steve fought off the desire to say something inane, like, "What's a nice southern gal like you doing in a place like this?" or, "Didn't your mother tell you to stay away from older men?"

The expression on her face changed from polite inquiry to wariness, and Steve finally found his voice. "Sorry—I seem to have taken the wrong turn. I was looking for—uh, the personnel department."

Her frown vanished; it was surprising what a smile, even an impersonal one, could do for that incredible mouth. "You got off on the wrong floor, sir. Personnel's on seven."

Steve thanked her and started for the door.

"Good luck," she said, so softly that he was already through the door before her words registered and he realized she had assumed he was a job seeker.

Good luck indeed, Marma Duncan. Do you realize that this is your lucky day—that Arnold Flagg, who may or may not be your lover, just added a codicil to his will naming you as one of his heirs?

Steve's thoughts were bleak as he got back on the elevator and pushed the lobby button with unnecessary force. Marma Duncan was a real charmer, and he couldn't really blame Arnold for going overboard for her. But Steve couldn't feel good about the situation. He would have approved of an older woman; even that sharp-voiced blond woman he'd followed from the elevator would have been a better choice for Arnold. But the age spread between Arnold and Marma

Duncan had to be at least forty-five years, which put a different light on the whole business. Arnold, he was convinced now, was making a mistake—a serious mistake. Not only was the woman young enough to be his daughter, she was young enough to be his granddaughter.

Suddenly Steve's reportorial instincts were working full blast....

CHAPTER THREE

MARMA WOULDN'T HAVE GONE to the bank's annual promotion and retirement banquet if her superior, Charlotte Everett, hadn't made such a point of telling her she was expected to attend.

Charlotte had called Marma into her office just before lunch. She was signing letters when Marma came in, and when she finally glanced up, she examined Marma carefully, as if looking for flaws. Marma had been glad that she was wearing a smart summer suit, and that her hairstyle, while very simple, would pass muster with Charlotte. She was also uncomfortably aware that she probably shouldn't have given into temptation and pinned the rose she'd bought at a Market Street flower stand that morning to her collar. But then it *was* spring....

"You do plan to go to the company banquet, don't you?" Charlotte asked. "It's really *de rigueur* to attend once you join the management ranks." She smiled, her austere face taking on a wintery warmth. "It comes under the heading of company loyalty."

"I hadn't really thought much about it," Marma answered doubtfully, thinking of her wardrobe. "It's pretty formal, isn't it?"

"I'd say so. If you don't have anything suitable to wear, why don't you take the rest of the afternoon off and go shopping? Sally can cover for you."

Charlotte turned back to the letters on her blotter, and Marma returned to her own office, not a little disgruntled. It seemed that she was going to the banquet—and that she'd be wearing a new dress. Well, she could use a new dress, even though she seldom had use for anything too fancy.

That afternoon, Marma looked carefully through the sales racks in one of I. Magnin's better dress departments, but there was nothing in a size seven that didn't look shopworn or wasn't exorbitantly priced, despite a sale. Even so, a feeling of excitement stirred inside Marma. When was the last time she had shopped for a party dress? Her clothes were the best quality she could afford, but were mostly for office wear. So why not consider this a treat—and just enjoy it?

She was heading for a less expensive dress department when her eyes fell on one of the wax models that flanked the entrance. The dress on display was a deep midnight blue, and was made from a fine, shimmery material that looked like real silk. The cut was deceptively simple—Marma was sure those flowing lines would be devastating in motion. She checked the price tag, made a face and was turning away when a saleswoman came up.

"Lovely, isn't it?" The woman inspected Marma, smiling. "Do you realize it's the same color as your eyes? That dress was made for you."

Marma shook her head. "Unfortunately, it costs more than I want to pay. I'd wear it so seldom—"

"Oh, but the style is classic! It would never go out of fashion. You'd be wearing it ten years from now."

Marma started to shake her head again, and then heard herself say, "I guess I *could* try it on."

A few minutes later, she knew she would be taking the dress. Not only did it seem custom-made for her petite figure, but she'd been right about the cut of the dress. The silky material fell free from one shoulder, baring the other, and touched her body in subtle, exciting ways before it ended in a froth at the ankle.

"See? I told you it was made for you," the clerk said smugly. "Think of it as an investment."

"If I don't take it, I'll probably regret it," Marma said, sighing. "Okay, wrap it up—but I'll have to brown bag my lunch for the next three months."

When she got home, she couldn't resist trying on the dress again. She was whirling in front of the mirror, admiring the way the skirt swirled around her ankles, when Angie spoke from the doorway. "Wow! You look like a princess, Marma! That *is* you inside that awesome dress, isn't it?"

"Keep it up and I'll throw something at you," Marma said, but she flushed at the admiration in her roommate's eyes.

"So what's the big occasion? Don't tell me you've finally found a man you want to impress?"

"What I've found is a small kicker that goes along with my promotion," Marma retorted. "It seems that management, even at the lowest level—to quote my boss—is expected to attend the bank's annual banquet. I'll probably have to wear this dress for ten years to get my money's worth out of it."

"Oh, lighten up! Go with the flow and you'll have a wonderful time. In that dress, every guy there will be panting after you."

Marma groaned. "Now I know I don't want to go."

"You're a real hard case, roomie. I've introduced you to the most gorgeous men I know, including all my unattached cousins and my rich Uncle Russ, and you haven't gone for one of them. What kind of man does it take to get your attention?"

Marma was silent, thinking. "Oh—someone kind," she said finally. "Someone tolerant and nonjudgmental, who really cares about what I think and who I am."

"That's a hard bill to fill. What else are you looking for—physical description this time, please. Maybe I've overlooked a second cousin or two."

"Since you're related to the entire Italian community of San Francisco, that wouldn't be hard to do," Marma teased.

"Don't change the subject. Physical description, please—in detail."

Marma thought a moment. An image formed in her mind. "Well, I'm partial to auburn-haired men, especially if they have brown eyes. Height and age aren't too important, although I'd prefer he be at least a couple of inches taller than I, and in his late twenties or early thirties. I feel uncomfortable with large, muscular men, so try to find someone with a rangy build—long and lean, please! He doesn't have to be handsome, but if he has the kind of smile that can light up a room, that would be—"

She stopped, suddenly uncomfortable. How weird; she'd just described the man who had wandered into her office by mistake a few days earlier, looking for personnel.

"Hm . . . that doesn't fit any of my unattached relatives, but I'll do my best—"

"Please don't, Angie!" Marma said in alarm. "I was just kidding. I can find my own dates—and besides, I'm not really interested in men at this point of my life. It's just not the right time."

Angie's eyes widened. "It's always the right time for men! If you keep on isolating yourself, you won't have a chance when you finally fall for someone—Mr. Right *or* Mr. Wrong. I've seen it happen before. Better you get some experience or you're going to be a sitting duck for the first good-looking guy who comes along and takes your fancy."

"Oh, I think I can handle it," Marma said. "I'm not exactly a recluse. I do my share of dating."

Angie snorted. "You never date a man more than a couple of times. What kind of learning process is that? I hate to think of the broken hearts you left behind at Brown. You had quite a reputation with the male students for being—" She stopped, looking embarrassed.

"For being what?"

"For being particular," Angie said, then added hurriedly, "Who's taking you to the banquet?"

"I'm going alone."

"Marma, Marma, what am I going to do with you?" Angie moaned. "Surely there's someone you could invite?"

"I prefer to go alone," Marma said firmly, not telling Angie that she'd already had two invitations to the banquet, one from a young lawyer in the bank's legal department, the other from the recently divorced head of security, who'd been bombarding her with invitations lately.

"Why on earth would you want to do that?"

"So I can leave whenever I like and not be accused of being a spoilsport."

Angie groaned, but to Marma's relief, she let the subject drop and went to get dressed for a date with Danny, leaving Marma to wonder if her roommate was finally giving up on her matchmaking attempts.

And what had Angie meant to say about her reputation at Brown? That she was thought to be a cold fish? She wasn't . . . or maybe she was. She'd always been careful not to put her sexuality to the test; she seldom allowed her dates even the most rudimentary intimacies.

But she couldn't tell Angie that, any more than she could tell her friend that the real reason she never dated a man more than a couple of times was her fear that some day one might come along who would break down the barriers she'd erected and present a real danger to her resolution to never marry. . . .

A WEEK LATER, Marma was sitting in front of a gilt-framed dressing-table mirror in the women's lounge of the Mark Hopkins hotel ballroom, repairing her lipstick and thinking that her decision to go to the banquet alone had been the right one. The Mark Hopkins was one of San Francisco's finest old hotels, but dinner had seemed interminable. Not only had the speeches been long-winded and the toasts repetitious, but the food, although delicious, had been much too rich for Marma's taste. She had changed drastically since she'd left Tennessee—as Angie was always pointing out—but she still preferred the plain, simple food that Angie called "down-home vittles."

"So how come you stuff yourself with everything I cook?" Marma had asked her once.

"Because it's *there*," Angie said dramatically, clasping her hands and rolling her eyes.

Marma smiled at the memory, but she sobered quickly, remembering that Angie was taking advantage of her absence tonight to cook dinner for Danny at the apartment. If she returned home too early, she was sure to spoil Angie's plans for the evening. Which meant that after she'd hid out in the women's lounge as long as she decently could, she still had to kill more time. Well, she could go to the hotel coffee shop and linger over coffee for a while, she thought. Then maybe she'd catch a cab and take in a late movie.

One thing she knew for sure—no one would miss her if she left early. The people at the table where she'd been seated during dinner were not from her department. They'd probably assume that she was out on the dance floor or that she'd joined a group from her own department—if they thought about her at all. It wasn't that she would lack dance partners if she returned to the ballroom. She'd been approached twice on her way to the women's lounge, and had turned down both invitations with the excuse that she had to powder her nose.

It wasn't that she didn't dance. As part of an attempt to make herself more socially adept, she'd taken dancing lessons and had discovered that not only did she love to dance, she was a natural at it. The main reason she seldom did—and one reason she was hiding out right now—was because large crowds intimidated her. When she was in a crush of people, she felt boxed in, so much so that she sometimes broke out in a cold sweat and found it hard to breathe—which was why she avoided people en masse, including crowded dance floors, as much as possible.

She was running a comb through her hair when the door flew open and Charlotte came bustling in. She looked Marma over, taking in the midnight-blue dress and silver sandals, and the silver filigree hair clip that held her hair back from her face.

"You look very nice," she said—a bit grudgingly, Marma thought. "You'd better come back in now. Mr. Flagg makes it a point to personally congratulate everybody at the home office who's had a promotion during the year. As your immediate superior, I'm expected to make the introduction."

Marma stared at Charlotte in bewilderment. She'd heard nothing about being introduced to the firm's president. After all, her promotion was relatively unimportant, considering that there were three thousand or more employees working at the home office. Besides, Mr. Flagg was noted for his diplomatic disappearances early in the evening at the annual party; she had assumed that he'd already left for home. Even if he hadn't, it wasn't likely he would notice if one newly promoted, very minor employee wasn't introduced to him.

But in the interest of not making waves, she gathered up her purse and followed her superior out into the hotel's elegant ballroom with its crystal chandeliers and fluted support pillars. Charlotte hustled her toward a group of men, most of whom Marma recognized as being top management. They were clustered around a small, elderly man with iron-gray hair, and Marma took a deep breath to steady her nerves.

"This is my new assistant, Mr. Flagg," Charlotte said, her voice honey-sweet.

Mr. Flagg's appraisal of Marma was so thorough that hot blood rushed to her face. There was nothing she could do about the blush, but she did manage to murmur a polite greeting without stammering.

"Congratulations on your promotion, Miss Duncan."

Mr. Flagg's voice was surprisingly deep for such a diminutive man. Although he looked every year of his age, which she knew from office gossip to be in the mid-sixties, his smile was unexpectedly young—and warm. As she returned it, she wondered how it was that he knew her name when Charlotte had introduced her simply as "my new assistant." She was even more surprised when Mr. Flagg dismissed the others with a smile and a nod, then took her elbow and led her toward a small table that had been set apart from the others that surrounded the dance floor.

For the next few minutes, Marma was the recipient of Mr. Flagg's full attention. Later, she would think it strange, considering the fact that their table was the center of attention, that she had so quickly forgotten her embarrassment at being singled out. Mr. Flagg's questions were so sympathetic, his interest in her answers so obviously genuine, that she found it easy to talk freely about herself.

"There's no way I could have gone to a top college like Brown without a scholarship of some kind," she said in answer to a question about her choice of colleges. "I couldn't even have managed a state school without also holding a full-time job because of—of circumstances at home."

"What kind of circumstances, Miss Duncan?"

"My father doesn't believe in higher education for women. In fact, I was very lucky to finish high school."

"And yet he allowed you to accept the scholarship?"

"He had no choice. I had already turned eighteen and was of legal age," she said, and for a moment, her father's cold, condemning voice rang in her ears. "A few days before my graduation from high school, my school adviser contacted me and told me that he'd just received information about a scholarship for Brown University that was custom-made for me. It was like—well, it was like some kind of miracle."

She went on to explain that the scholarship was funded by a private foundation that had been set up to provide higher education for female high-school graduates from her county, then added, "The directors prefer to remain anonymous, so I've never had a chance to thank them personally for giving me such an opportunity."

"How fortunate that you met all the requirements." There was a note in Mr. Flagg's voice that Marma would have read as amusement, except that it seemed so out of place.

"Yes, I was fortunate. One requirement was that the recipient had to have had a religious background, and as it happens, my father is a lay minister of his—our church."

"You obviously did quite well at Brown or you wouldn't have been recruited for our company," he observed.

"I worked very hard," Marma said, and didn't tell him that she'd made the dean's list every term except one. "There were personal problems at first—I'd never been farther away from home than Bradyville, our county seat. So it was quite a cultural shock, being exposed to a different set of standards." Again, she didn't go into specifics—her terrible homesickness that first year, the crushing guilt and despair of knowing that by defying her father, she had burned all her bridges and could never go home again.

"And now you're living in San Francisco, which also must be a cultural shock," Mr. Flagg observed.

"I was delighted when I was recruited by your representative," she said, giving him a shy smile. "I understand, sir, that Brown University is your alma mater?"

"It is, indeed," Mr. Flagg replied, returning her smile. "Which is why I send a recruiter there every year—sort of a sentimental gesture."

"It was very lucky for me. I wanted that management trainee's job so badly that I didn't sleep a wink the night before the interview," Marma confessed. "My roommate at Brown was returning to San Francisco, her hometown, after graduation, and she wanted me to settle here, too, so we could share an apartment. Knowing that I already had a good job waiting for me—well, it was another miracle." She hesitated briefly, then added, "My recent promotion falls in the same category."

"I hope you'll be with us for a long time—or is there a boyfriend waiting in the wings, ready to carry you off into marriage and motherhood?"

"No boyfriend at all," she said, shaking her head.

"I find that hard to believe, Miss Duncan."

"My first priority is work, not men—" Marma stopped, flushing. Why had she said that? It was true, of course, but it sounded so—so self-serving, as if she was trying to convince him that she'd still be around when future promotions were given out.

"I'm sure that will change—in time," Mr. Flagg murmured. "Most young women, even those who are career-oriented, eventually marry and have children."

"I'm afraid that doesn't apply to me. I doubt I'll ever marry," she said without thinking. "There's a heredity factor in my background that makes me leery of having children. And since it wouldn't be fair to any man I might marry—"

She stopped abruptly, aware how much she was revealing about herself again. How strange that Mr. Flagg, of all people, had drawn a confidence out of her that she'd never discussed with anyone, not even Angie....

Mr. Flagg didn't seem to notice her silence. "I'm sure there are many men who don't want children who would be delighted to marry you."

Marma hesitated, then said honestly, "I don't think I'd be interested in that kind of man. I've made the decision to remain childless, but it isn't something I prefer. I'd love to have children."

"I see." Mr. Flagg studied her with thoughtful eyes. Just when she was braced for another personal question—and why was he so interested in her personal life, anyway?—he surprised her and asked her opinion of the new computer system the bank had recently installed in its home office.

A few minutes later, when one of the bank's directors came up to the table with a question, Marma realized that she'd monopolized Mr. Flagg for far too long. That their preoccupation with each other had been noted—and not happily—by others, she was made aware of when she caught Charlotte's hard stare. Feeling embarrassed, she rose, saying, "I'm sorry. I've taken up too much of your time, Mr. Flagg—"

"On the contrary. I'm the one who should apologize for keeping you from dancing with some lucky young man." He stood and shook her hand. "One of these days soon I'd like to have you join me for lunch so we can continue our conversation."

Marma mumbled something polite and eased herself away. Mr. Flagg was just being polite—or so she hoped—but somehow she wished he hadn't extended that lunch invitation. She started toward the cloakroom to retrieve her coat; as she rounded one of the ballroom's fluted pillars, she crashed headlong into a very solid body. If a pair of masculine hands hadn't snatched her out of the air, she would have landed on the floor.

"I'm sorry," a man's voice said. "Wasn't watching where I was going."

She looked up a few inches into a pair of amused eyes. They were the color of dark chocolate, a shade that went beautifully with the man's rust-colored hair and lightly tanned skin. Marma's breath caught in her throat as she recognized the man who had lost his way

and wandered into her office a few days earlier. *How
odd,* she thought. *Just this afternoon I was thinking
about him and wondering if he got the job....*

The man snapped his fingers suddenly. "I remember you—you work in home mortgages." At her start,
he smiled widely, and again her breathing seemed re-
stricted. She hadn't been wrong about his smile. It
really did light up a room. Moreover, it improved a
face that was already devastatingly attractive. "I
blundered into your office by mistake last week—remember? What a coincidence, meeting you again."

"So you did get the job," she said, smiling back.

"Job?"

"You *were* looking for work that day, weren't you?
Since you're here at the banquet tonight, I assume you
were hired."

"Very logical reasoning—for a woman," he said
wickedly.

"Oh, dear—are you one of those?"

"No, I'm not a chauvinist. I was teasing you—and
right now, the band happens to be playing one of my
favorite songs. Why don't we take advantage of it?"

Before she could protest that she was just leaving,
she found herself in his arms, on the dance floor.
Somehow she wasn't surprised at how light and
graceful he was on his feet, how easy it was to follow
his lead.

"That gown must have been custom designed for
you. It's hard to tell where it leaves off and your eyes
begin," he said, his warm breath stirring a tendril of
hair near her ear.

Marma had always distrusted extravagant compli-
ments from men, but she was pleased with this one

because it seemed sincere. His arms tightened around her slightly as he guided her between two couples, and she discovered that she liked the firm pressure of his hand against her back, the warmth of his body touching hers, the lemony scent of shaving cream—or maybe of soap—and the musky odor of a healthy male body. The music finally registered, and she realized the band was playing "Send in the Clowns," one of her own favorite songs.

"Send in the clowns...there ought to be clowns," the woman on the bandstand sang.

As the man shifted his position slightly, settling her even closer against his hard body, she thought—as she often seemed to these days—about how seldom she allowed anyone to touch her. She found it difficult to respond to Angie's impulsive hugs, and she was careful never to put herself in the position of having to ward off a physical pass from a man—which was a wise habit for a woman who never intended to marry or even have an intimate relationship. So why did she feel so comfortable, so at ease in the arms of this stranger whose name she didn't even know?

"My name is Steve—Steve Riley," he said, as if he were reading her thoughts. "And I have a perfectly good job, but not with Flagg Banks. I'm here tonight at the invitation of an old friend who works at Flagg. He's an early-to-bed type and had already left or I'd ask him to introduce us properly so you'd know that I'm unmarried and otherwise unattached, and that I'm reasonably harmless to lovely ladies like—what *is* your name, anyway?"

Marma hesitated, then said, "Marma Duncan."

"Marma—that's an unusual name. What does it stand for?"

"It stands for Marma," she said, her tone short, but when his eyes twinkled, she sighed and said, "Very well. It's short for Marmalade—and no jokes, please. I had to take enough teasing about my name when I was a youngster."

"And where was that? From that accent, I'd guess you were raised somewhere in the South."

Marma pulled away a little to frown up at him. "I don't have an accent," she said.

"Not one that most people would notice," he said. "It happens to be a hobby of mine, placing the birthplace of people from their speech patterns. There's a sliding quality about the way you end your sentences that gives you away. And why does the idea of having a slight accent bother you?"

"It doesn't *bother* me. I did think I'd lost my accent, though."

The band began a medley of Cole Porter songs, and Steve swung her into a fast fox-trot, ending the conversation. The music pulsated against Marma's ears, and she put everything else out of her mind except the pure enjoyment of moving in time with the beat, of being so expertly guided around the floor that she felt no responsibility except to follow her partner's lead. How safe she felt, how rootlessly content. Was this kind of thing getting to be a habit with her? Well, she'd think about the dangers of letting down her guard later. Right now, she wanted to go on dancing with Steve Riley forever—or at least for the rest of the evening....

This time there was no warning at all: no preliminary dizziness or leaching out of color, no alarms of any kind. One second she was enjoying the music and the novelty of being physically close to someone else, and in the next, it was as if she'd been transported to another place. She was hovering near a strange bed, looking down at the same teenage girl she'd seen in her earlier vision.

But something had changed. Now the girl was awake, and her face was pale, glistening with sweat, as though she'd just awakened from a nightmare. She was sitting up in bed, hugging her chest with her arms. Her mouth, soft and young, opened and her throat muscles moved, but what she said was lost in a sudden rush of static-like sound.

Vertigo struck Marma. A gray vortex opened up around her and she felt herself falling, falling, falling. At first there was only the swirling mist, and then she had slipped into total darkness. Just when she was sure that she was lost, that this time she'd never find her way back to reality, a voice called out her name.

"Marma? Can you hear me, Marma?"

She opened her eyes and met the concerned stare of Steve Riley. The dance floor, the bandstand and the other dancers were gone, and it was only when she felt the cold night air against her face that she realized she was sitting on a bench on the terrace outside the ballroom, leaning heavily against Steve's hard chest. She had no idea how she'd gotten there.

"What happened?" she asked thickly.

"You had a fainting spell. It was too warm in the ballroom, I guess. I brought you out here to get some fresh air. Are you okay?"

She wanted to tell him that no, she wasn't okay. As always after she'd had one of her visions, she felt debilitated, drained of energy, as if she'd just finished running the Bay to Breakers marathon. When she tried to pull away, Steve pressed her head back against his shoulder.

"Not yet. Rest a while and then I'll take you home."

"That won't be necessary. I can catch a taxi. And I'm fine now. I just—well, it must have been the heat in the ballroom."

"Or something you ate. Or the onslaught of the flu. Which is why I intend to see that you get home safely. And if you're wondering if I'm to be trusted—" He fumbled in a pocket, took out a slim wallet and flipped it open to a driver's licence. "See? Steve Riley, just as I said."

She had to smile at the formality in his voice, and suddenly she lost the will to refuse his offer. What harm could come of it, especially since she was so exhausted that she wasn't sure if she could make it on her own?

"Thank you," she said, and earned a brief smile.

Steve's car, to her surprise, was a late model station wagon, not the sports car she'd expected. When he helped her into the front seat, she sank onto the leather cushion with a sigh of relief. As he fastened her seat belt, saying it was a bit tricky, his face was so close that his breath fanned her cheek. Even after she was belted in, he didn't move right away. In fact, he looked down at her so long, his stare so intent, that she was sure he meant to kiss her. But then he was closing the door, circling the car, and she couldn't decide if she was relieved or disappointed.

"Where do you live?" he said, his voice decidedly stiff now.

Piqued by what seemed to be a sudden coolness, she spoke impulsively, choosing a town two hours north of San Francisco. "Ukiah," she said.

At his consternated stare, she cocked her index finger at him. "Gotcha!" she said with satisfaction. "And not to worry. You don't have a four-hour round trip ahead of you. I live on Russian Hill."

He threw back his head in a laugh, and she stared with fascination at the strong, masculine lines of this throat. Not handsome, no, but God, he *was* attractive....

"You 'gotcha' me, all right," he said. "Do you live with your family?"

"With a roommate."

"Male or female?"

"Female. Any more questions?"

"Sorry. I'm a very curious fellow," he said.

Marma felt a sudden discomfort. This was the second time tonight that someone had shown unusual curiosity about her personal life. First Mr. Flagg, and then this stranger—and he *was* a stranger, even though she found it hard to reconcile this with the ease she felt with him. Had she accepted him so quickly because she'd met him once before, however briefly? Or did he seem familiar because she'd thought of him so often afterward? One night she'd even dreamed about him—which should have been a warning to be wary. After all, what did she really know about Steve Riley?

"I saw you earlier—talking to an older man," Steve said abruptly.

"That was Mr. Flagg. He's president of Flagg Banks."

"Oh? Are you old friends?"

"We're not any kind of friends. Tonight was the first time I've met him," she said.

Steve took his eyes off the traffic to give her a quick glance. In the soft glow of the dashboard, she was sure she read disbelief in his eyes. He started to say something, then stopped. For the rest of the trip across town, he concentrated on his driving.

Marma told herself she was relieved that he seemed disinclined to talk. She was having a hard time keeping her eyes open and she also felt unaccountably depressed. Once, when they came to a cross street, a gust of wind rocked the heavy car, and she shivered a little, even though the heater was on. She wished she were already home in bed, the covers pulled up around her shoulders, the world, with all its complexities, shut out for the night.

"How about having dinner with me tomorrow evening?" Steve said, breaking his long silence. "If you like seafood, we could drive over to Sausalito."

Marma's first impulse was to say yes, she'd love it, but her own eagerness, the sudden lift of her spirits, rang a warning bell in her mind. "I'm going to be busy tomorrow night," she said.

"Then how about Friday evening or—"

"I'm sorry. I'm afraid I'll be busy for the next few weeks."

Steve was silent. She stole a glance at him and took in the tightness of his jaw. It was obvious that her refusal had disappointed him. Why was that? A man that attractive probably had hordes of women eager to date him. How could it possibly matter to him that a woman he barely knew had turned down his invitation? Maybe it was simple male pride. Well, at least he wasn't trying to change her mind. That was what she wanted, wasn't it? Well, wasn't it?

When they reached the tangled web of streets that was Russian Hill, she was glad for the chronic shortage of parking space. Steve was forced to double park in front of the pre-earthquake Victorian house where she lived, thus obviating the possibility that he'd expect to be invited in for a nightcap.

She was ready, purse in hand, when the station wagon came to a stop; she thanked him quickly and was out of the car, shutting the door firmly behind her, before he had time to answer.

Only when she'd reached the lobby door did she look back. Steve Riley was still there, staring straight at her, his expression grim. Although he did the gentlemanly thing and waited until she had unlocked the lobby door and was safely inside, he didn't return her wave before he drove away.

CHAPTER FOUR

STEVE DIDN'T REALIZE that he was driving too fast until a car he passed honked a warning at him. He slowed down immediately, irked with his own recklessness. He was usually a careful driver. What the hell was wrong with him, anyway? Was his nose out of joint because a woman he'd known such a short time had turned down his dinner invitation? Okay, it was a little more than that. What really bothered him was the way she'd worded her rejection.

"I'll be busy for the next few weeks," she'd said, which had to be a lie. She worked for a banking firm, for God's sake. No matter how overloaded or ambitious she might be, nobody, including department heads' assistants, worked overtime every night and on weekends and couldn't take time off for meals. And the way she'd fled from the car, as if she were afraid of him—what was that all about? Had she sensed his suspicions?

Earlier, he would have sworn that she enjoyed his company. While they had danced she'd been relaxed, following his lead with obvious enjoyment. And later, after she'd had that fainting spell, she'd readily agreed to letting him take her home. So what had happened during their short trip across town? Had she suddenly remembered that she had a rich lover who might not appreciate her dating other men?

An image formed in his mind of Marma's fresh young body in his uncle's aging arms. He grimaced, but then he told himself not to be stupid. He had no personal interest in Marma Duncan. Maybe if things had been different...but as it was, she was his uncle's affair, not his.

He smiled painfully. An appropriate choice of words. His uncle's affair—yes, he was more sure than ever that his earlier suspicions had been right. The lie she'd told him about her relationship with Arnold had come easily to her lips; she was obviously a practiced liar. The proof was in that little tête-á-tête he'd witnessed. It had been a long time since he'd seen his uncle so animated and young looking. Yet she'd claimed that tonight was the first time she'd met Arnold.

Well, it made some sense that they'd want to keep their relationship quiet. If it became known that Arnold Flagg—who was so well known in banking and financial circles that he'd appeared on the cover of *Time* during the Black Monday debacle—was having an affair with one of his employees, a woman a third his age, it would cause one hell of a lot of gossip. Bankers were by nature conservative, and his uncle was an exceptionally private man. But at least he hadn't married the woman. California *was* a community property state, with all those ramifications to consider.

There were other things that fueled his suspicions. That outfit she'd been wearing tonight, for instance. It looked like a designer's gown, which certainly didn't match her income. Although most people thought of banking as a well-paid industry, he knew for a fact that bank wages were not particularly generous until employees reached the top ranks—and Marma wasn't exactly in a high management position.

Then there was that handsome Victorian apartment house she lived in. He'd done his share of apartment hunting in San Francisco before he'd bought the condo on Nob Hill, and he knew the rent in her building had to be exorbitant. Charm and a view didn't come cheap anywhere, much less in San Francisco. So how could she afford to live there unless someone was paying her share of the rent?

Of course, the roommate—he had to take Marma's word that she really had a female roommate—didn't fit into the picture of a kept woman. Maybe Arnold maintained a cozy little love nest for them somewhere else and the roommate was camouflage. Somehow Steve doubted that they held their rendezvous at the Pacific Heights mansion where Arnold had lived with his wife for so many decades.

One thing was clear to him after having met Marma for a second time, and that was the reason why his uncle was so enamored of the woman. She was a genuine beauty with that husky voice and enticing figure, that black, black hair and those unusual lapis-colored eyes. If he hadn't known better, he would have been taken in by the aura of innocence she carried around like a protective mantle. He even might have believed that she had no idea how attractive she was. No wonder Arnold, for all his shrewdness and knowledge of human nature, had fallen for her.

As for Marma's feeling for his uncle, it didn't seem possible that she was genuinely in love with him. A woman just out of her teens didn't fall in love with a man hitting seventy, no matter how great a guy he was. Oh, she might respect him, even love him, but surely not in a sexual way. So what was she up to? What was she after? His money? Career advancement?

Steve suddenly felt uncomfortable with his own thoughts. What right did he have to mess around in his uncle's private life, anyway? He would resent it no end if the tables were turned and Arnold tried to interfere in his business. So maybe it was time to butt out of the whole thing. Period.

In fact, he was beginning to wonder why he'd asked Marma out to dinner. Curiosity? A desire to find out what made the woman who had become so important to his uncle tick? The latter seemed the most likely explanation. After all, he'd been interested enough in Arnold's welfare to wangle an invitation to the banquet, using the excuse that he wanted to talk to some of the bank's employees for an article he was researching. Steve felt a sudden twinge of guilt. Had Arnold taken his request as the prelude to a career change? Whatever he'd thought, Arnold had asked no questions. A couple of days later, the invitation had appeared in the mail, and during the banquet, Arnold had made a point of ignoring him, as he'd requested.

When Steve had managed to bump into Marma Duncan as she'd come around that support pillar, he had only hoped to get a better look at her and maybe draw her into conversation. He certainly hadn't planned to ask her out for dinner, for God's sake.

Well, she'd put him in his place quickly enough. At least she seemed to be faithful to his uncle. That should be reassuring, he told himself. Why, then, having decided to drop the whole thing, was he still thinking about her? Why couldn't he put the way she'd felt in his arms—supple and soft and exciting as hell—out of his mind? Why did he keep remembering that her breath against his cheek had been sweet as wild mint, and that her perfume, a light, elusive floral scent that reminded him of an old-fashioned English garden, had filled his nostrils as they'd danced?

There was no answer to that, none that was acceptable. She was his uncle's lover, and even if he wanted to carry this thing further, he wasn't about to compete with someone who was like his own father. And who was he to begrudge Arnold some personal happiness during the autumn days of his life? His only honorable course was to put the whole thing, including his dangerous physical attraction to Marma Duncan, out of his mind.

MARMA WAS SO EXHAUSTED she should have fallen asleep right off, but she felt so tense she couldn't get comfortable, couldn't relax. Bits and pieces of the evening played themselves out in the theater of her mind, and when she found herself wishing that she'd accepted Steve's invitation, she gave up, turned on the lights and went to heat a glass of milk, even though she disliked milk, hot or cold.

And then, when she went back to bed and finally did doze, the nightmare started.

She dreamed that she was walking down a long dark tunnel and was unable to move quickly, even though she knew something terrible was behind her, stalking her. She held her breath; the flesh on her body crawled; she heard a rustling behind her: a sly, stealthy sound that wasn't human. She forced her head around, but all she saw were dark shadows. Then, in the darkness, something moved. She tried to scream, but her throat muscles tensed, choking off the scream and adding pain to her terror.

The rustling, like a thousand corn husks rubbing together, was closer now. She fixed her eyes on the light up ahead that promised safety and an end to her terror. It seemed brighter—surely she was almost there. But now she couldn't move because there was a barrier, like a wall of wooden slats, beyond which she could not pass. The sound, like claws scrabbling, was so close that she was sure she felt hot breath against her neck. In a minute the thing that had been stalking her would touch her and then—she screamed, kept on screaming....

"Marma, Marma—wake up," Angie cried. Her warm hand shook Marma's shoulder. "You're having a nightmare. Are you awake?"

"Yes," Marma said, her tongue so stiff that her voice sounded thick and muddled. "I'm awake. Sorry I bothered you."

"Not to worry. Look, do you want something—a glass of water, some warm milk, some scintillating conversation?"

That made Marma smile. Her fear quickly eroding, she was ashamed now that she'd been scared by a mere dream.

"Was it the mouse that ate San Francisco again?" Angie asked.

Marma thought of her nightmare, of the small clicking sounds; she managed not to shudder. "Something like that. And I'll be fine. Guess I was overtired—"

"Uh-huh. You looked like you-know-what warmed over when you came in from the banquet. And thank you for your diplomatic retreat into your bedroom."

There was something, a smugness, in her voice that made Marma stare at her. "How did your evening go?" she asked.

Angie's green eyes sparkled. "I thought you'd never ask. Danny proposed! He didn't exactly get down on his knees, and it was a little on the 'Hey, I think we should get married' side, but it was a genuine proposal, all right."

"He didn't!"

"He did, and I accepted promptly although I should have played it coy and made him suffer a little because it took him so long. But anyway, it's all settled. The wedding will be in August, when Danny gets his vacation and my school is out for the summer. We'll honeymoon in Hawaii and then it will be domesticity for the rest of my life."

And then Angie, who was perpetually cheerful and who never cried, burst into tears. "I'm so happy!" she wailed.

Marma put her arms around her friend and hugged her, murmuring both reassurances and congratulations. She was truly glad for Angie, but felt a little sad, too. Her roommate's happiness made her own future seem—flat and dull.

After all, what lay ahead for her? A career she found satisfying and stimulating, yes. But would it be enough? Angie, who had such a generous heart, would share the children she and Danny were sure to have, just as she'd shared her parents, her grandparents and the rest of her family with her friend. Marma would be Aunt Marma to Angie's kids—but she'd still be perpetually on the fringes of other people's lives, vicariously enjoying something that might have been hers except for an incident of birth.

Why me? Why was I the only one in my family who inherited Mama's curse? she thought.

The question echoed through the hollow depths of her heart, but she heard no answer. Even later, when she was back in bed, trying to sleep, the question still haunted her.

On Monday, she went in to work knowing she looked haggard and pale despite the blush she'd applied liberally. Her nerves were so finely drawn that when Charlotte reprimanded her for mislaying a report, she had to fight hard not to snap back.

Marma was clearing off her desk, getting ready to go to lunch, when her phone rang. She muttered, "Dammit," under her breath and picked it up.

A woman's voice, cool and crisp, said, "Marma Duncan, please."

"Speaking," Marma said, half her attention on Charlotte, who was approaching her desk, a Manila envelope in her hand. "This is Mr. Flagg's secretary," the voice said in her ear. "He'd like you to come to his office immediately."

It took Marma a few seconds to recover from her surprise. "Do you have any idea what he wants to see me about?"

"He'll discuss it with you when you get here. Shall we say—in ten minutes?"

Marma hung up, frowning. Charlotte, who had been waiting, said, "I hope that wasn't a personal call. You know department rules."

"It wasn't personal—at least, I don't think it was."

"What an odd thing to say. Who was it?"

"It was Mr. Flagg's secretary," Marma said reluctantly. "He—wants to see me."

The corners of Charlotte's mouth twitched. "Indeed. Then I think you'd better get a move on. You don't want to keep him waiting, do you?"

She dropped the envelope she was holding on Marma's desk, turned on her heel and stalked away. Marma put the Manila envelope into a drawer without looking at it. Before she headed for the elevators, she ducked into the women's rest room to run a comb through her hair and to repair her lipstick, her thoughts chaotic.

Why would Mr. Flagg want to see her—and on such short notice? Surely this wasn't what Charlotte obviously believed. He had been kind at the banquet, interested enough to draw her out, but there hadn't been anything—well, sexual in his attitude. She would swear to that. So what was this all about?

When she got onto the crowded elevator and pushed the button for the penthouse floor, she felt as if everybody else in the elevator was staring at her. Which was ridiculous. Even so, she was glad when the elevator emptied out on the eighth floor, where the employee's cafeteria was located, so she could relax and concentrate on putting Mr. Flagg's summons into perspective.

No matter what he wanted, she was sure she could handle it. After all, she wasn't the naive girl she had been when she'd first left Duncan Holler. If Mr. Flagg had something unacceptable in mind, she would make it very clear that she wasn't interested. And if worse came to worst—well, she could always quit. Yes, she loved her job, and would hate to leave, but if she were forced to, she was prepared to change jobs. It wouldn't be a disaster. There were plenty of jobs in San Francisco. It would probably take a while to find something, but she had saved money these past couple of years, and with the excellent training and experience she'd had at Flagg Banks, she was bound to find something suitable. Who could tell? Maybe she'd even better herself....

When she got off the elevator, she paused a few moments to look around. She was immediately impressed by the subtle luxury of the reception hall with its thick, bronze-colored carpeting, rich-looking paneled walls and tall, potted palms. The elegant plants flanked a recess in the wall that held a small white marble statue of a Greek runner.

She'd heard rumors about the statue, one of which held that it had been found during a dig in Greece that Mr. Flagg had financed. Another rumor claimed the statue was not old at all, that a famous sculptor whose work Mr. Flagg sponsored had created it as a gift of gratitude. As Marma headed across the reception hall she decided that either rumor about the statue, which was breathtakingly beautiful, was believable.

The woman who greeted her outside the door of Mr. Flagg's executive suite was as elegant as her surroundings. Marma was self-confident enough not to feel intimidated, but she couldn't help noting how thoroughly Mr. Flagg's secretary looked her over before announcing that Mr. Flagg was waiting for her, to "go right through that door."

Mr. Flagg's office, she saw at first glance, was filled with antiques and looked more like a living room than a business office. To her relief, his greeting was courteous and friendly, but not overly so, allaying any suspicions she might have had.

"It occurs to me that you probably haven't had lunch," he added. "Would you like to have something sent up from the cafeteria?"

"No, no, that won't be necessary," she said and was sure he looked relieved.

He gestured toward a sofa with a gracefully curved back, part of a conversation grouping in front of a white marble fireplace. "Why don't you sit down, Miss Duncan? I'll have my secretary bring us some coffee—or would you rather have tea?"

She chose coffee, and as they waited, they engaged in a pleasant, impersonal conversation covering such topics as the weather, the state of the economy and a new show at the Golden Gate Theater that Mr. Flagg recommended highly, but there was a barely suppressed tension behind his casual words that added to her curiosity—and anxiety.

Even so, she tried to relax and enjoy the mysterious interview. After all, how often did she capture the attention of a man as distinguished as Mr. Flagg?

It was after his secretary had brought them coffee, then left discreetly, that she noticed the slight tremor in his hand as he raised his cup to his lips. In the light from the windows that opened onto a terrace, the skin on his face seemed to sag. He looked as though he'd lost weight since their last meeting, and his eyes had a sunken look that made her wonder if he was an insomniac. Surely he hadn't looked this old two nights ago at the banquet. Of course, the diffused light from the ballroom's crystal chandeliers had been flattering, but even so—had he been ill since the banquet? If so, why wasn't he at home, in bed?

Mr. Flagg's cup clattered against its saucer as he set it back down, and her muscles tightened with apprehension. She knew, in the way she sometimes did, that she wasn't going to like what he had to say next.

"You're probably wondering why I invited you here today," he began.

She nodded. "I also wondered about your—your curiosity about me at the banquet."

His face relaxed slightly, and for a moment there was a glint of humor in his eyes. "Surely that was obvious. You're a very interesting and intelligent young woman."

"I hadn't spoken more than a word or two before you took me aside. How could you possibly know if I was—uh, the things you just said?"

"You're right. I couldn't have, not if you were a stranger. But as it happens, I knew quite a bit about you, Marma Duncan, long before the banquet."

"I don't understand—"

"There was no need for you to understand, not then. But it's important now that you—that I be totally honest with you. Are you willing to hear me out?"

"Of course, but I still don't understand—"

"You will in just a minute." But having said this much, he fell silent again. He seemed uncertain how to go on. "I'm a widower, Miss Duncan," he said finally. "I guess you know that from the company's very efficient rumor mills?"

"Yes, I have heard that."

"Do you also know that my daughter's married name is Millicent Montgomery?"

Marma shook her head, wondering where this was leading.

"Don't you recognize that name, Miss Duncan?"

"I'm afraid not. I don't know a—" She broke off, staring at him. Of course she knew a Millicent Montgomery. It was a name from the past, one she'd managed to block out of her mind.

"You're her—Mrs. Montgomery's father?"

"And Lisa's grandfather." His voice had thickened; she studied the strain on his face as she struggled to make sense of his words.

A realization came to her, and she blurted, "The job recruiter who hired me—you told him to, didn't you? Because it's too much of a coincidence otherwise."

"He had orders to solicit your application. You passed the interview and the tests on your own."

"There were a hundred other well-qualified business-major graduates at Brown," she protested. "I'd hate to think I got the job through patronage."

"Since you're the kind of management trainee the bank tries to attract, I assure you it wasn't patronage. I would have wanted you on our team under any circumstances."

"But if I hadn't been approached by your recruiter, I wouldn't have known to apply for the position. I hope you don't think—look, you don't owe me anything, Mr. Flagg. I'm sure they would have found Lisa anyway.''

Mr. Flagg rubbed his left eye as if it stung. "I'm not convinced of that. And if you're wondering—no, I had nothing to do with your job progress. You earned your raises and your promotions. For a person who started out with substantial handicaps, you've done remarkably well.''

Marma didn't ask him what handicaps he was talking about, she already knew the answer to that question. Instead, she said, "I've been working for the bank for over two years. Why did you choose today to tell me all this?''

"I didn't want your gratitude—or maybe your censure for interfering in your life. But now—God, I need your help desperately, Marma. If it takes gratitude to get it, so be it.''

His eyes had taken on a sheen. She was sure he was close to tears. When he leaned toward her abruptly and took her hand in his, she was so startled she didn't pull away.

"Lisa—my beautiful Lisa—has been kidnapped and I don't know what to do. You're the only one who can help the police find her before it's too late.''

Marma felt a chill that seemed to penetrate her bones. She must have shivered, because Mr. Flagg's hand tightened around hers. His skin felt cold, very dry. *An old man's hand,* she thought. *How quickly he's aged under pressure....*

"Was she kidnapped for ransom?'' she asked.

He nodded. "She disappeared from her bed Saturday night. There was a note on her pillow, addressed to both me and her father, asking for a million dollars in small, unmarked bills, and warning us not to call the police. I had the money ready by Sunday noon." He smiled mirthlessly and added, "There are advantages to owning your own banking company." His attempt at humor only made Marma wince.

"Lisa's father made the drop this morning," he continued, "following the kidnappers' orders to the letter. But something went wrong. The police were tipped off—I still don't know how that happened—and they put a stakeout at the pickup spot near Land's End. The kidnappers must have been watching because the money was still there two hours later. There's been no further word, not even a threat. The police are sure they recognize their MO—the crime pattern. If they're the ones under suspicion, they have a record of—" his voice broke suddenly "—of killing their victims if something goes wrong. And now those monsters have had Lisa for thirty-six hours. God knows what kind of hell she's going through. Our only hope is you, Marma. I'm asking—no, begging you to help us."

Panic filled Marma. The air in the room seemed to thicken, to press down upon her. She gasped for breath, but that didn't help. Her lungs refused to cooperate, and she realized that she was having a panic attack.

She tried to rise, only to have her legs give out on her. She fell back against the sofa, making its aging legs creak in protest. To shut out the anguish, the pleading on Mr. Flagg's face, she closed her eyes. That this proud and respected man had been driven to humble himself to her hurt badly. And yet, under her pity, another emotion stirred, one that she was ashamed of: resentment.

Arnold Flagg had intruded into her life, had stirred up the past, reminding her so painfully of her long struggle against the very thing he wanted to exploit again—and she resented it bitterly. She had put that all behind her and had gained a little peace. Wasn't it enough that she'd gone through hell seven years ago because of his granddaughter? How much more did he and the Montgomerys want from her?

She felt Mr. Flagg's hand on her arm, and reluctantly, painfully, she opened her eyes.

"I can't help you," she said dully.

"You saved her once before. Won't you try again—for Lisa's sake? She's so young, so vulnerable. Even if she comes through this thing alive, I'm afraid—her parents and I are afraid how it will affect her. It might already be too late, but if so, we have to know, even if—" he paused, fighting for control "—even if, God help us, she's already dead."

"You don't understand. It isn't that I don't want to help you. It's that I *can't* help you. I have no control over the—the visions. They come or they don't come. It's out of my hands."

His eyes bored into her, as if he was trying to see into her brain. When his shoulders sagged, when the hope died in his eyes, she knew he believed her.

"Then God help her," he said heavily. "God help my lovely Lisa."

CHAPTER FIVE

AFTER MARMA LEFT Arnold's suite, she took the elevator to the lobby, bypassing her own floor, not even stopping to tell Charlotte she was going home. Later, she would call her boss, apologize and make some excuse. For now, she was in such mental turmoil that she was sure she couldn't talk coherently to anyone.

Rather than board a crowded bus, she walked the four miles home, fighting her own unbridled emotions every step of the way. Who or what she saw during the time it took her to walk to her apartment, she couldn't remember afterward, only that she had covered so much ground so quickly that she was out of breath most of the way. The past, never as far away as she wished, had crowded in on her and demanded her attention. She could keep it at bay only by falling into a near stupor, even though she knew she was only postponing the inevitable reckoning.

She let herself into her apartment and went immediately to the kitchen to plug in the electric kettle. She didn't really want tea—she felt a little nauseous, in fact—but she needed the warmth, the comfort that she hoped a cup of one of Angie's exotic herbal teas would bring her. While the water heated, she sat at the kitchen table, her face buried in her folded arms, fighting the memories that kept surfacing like jetsam after a wreck at sea. It had all been so long ago, she thought in despair, but now Arnold Flagg had stirred up all the old misery, guilt and self-doubt. And wasn't it strange how much anger was still there, festering inside her?

Sluggishly, her natural honesty stirred. No, Arnold Flagg hadn't been the one to bring back the past. It had reared its head even before her encounter with him today. Twice in the past week, she'd had visions—and they'd had nothing to do with him. As far as she could tell, they'd had nothing to do with *anything*. Were they simply phantoms of visions—echoes from the days when they had come to her so often?

An image of Arnold Flagg's face, so deceptively calm until you caught the anguish in his eyes, surfaced. If she could have helped him, helped the girl she'd saved from a terrible death once before, she wouldn't have hesitated, no matter what the cost to her own peace of mind. But there was no way she could summon the second sight. It came in its own time, for reasons unknown to her, and nothing she did seemed to change that.

One of the few times she'd tried to look into the future, she'd been driven by fear. Her youngest brother, always the reckless one, had failed to come home one night from a trip into Bradyville, and she'd been so worried that she'd attempted to summon a vision. Not only had she failed, but she'd ended up with a splitting headache that had lasted long after Mark had straggled in the next morning, having spent most of the night sleeping in Papa's truck because he'd forgotten to fill the gas tank.

But thinking about her brother, the one she'd cared for the most, was a mistake. Because now the wall she'd erected against the past came tumbling down and memories poured into her mind. She fought them, but it was no use. As she sat there, trying futilely to cleanse her mind of all thought, the past slowly, relentlessly, overwhelmed her....

MARMA HAD JUST TURNED six when she realized for the first time that her father hated her. Until then, she had only known that he was kinder to and less critical of her brothers, Luke, Matthew and Mark, and her sister, Louise, who was the oldest.

For a long time, she'd had dreams—awake dreams, she had thought of them. She would be playing in the yard, making dolls out of the Queen Anne's lace that grew so profusely at the edges of the fields, or doing one of the chores Papa had assigned her, and suddenly she would be caught up in a dream so vivid that it was hard to tell what was real and what was not. The people in the dreams were usually familiar to her, although at times it was strangers she saw. Sometimes, they were doing ordinary, everyday things, but most of the time they were in some kind of danger.

She never spoke of her dreams to anyone. For one thing, they were over so quickly that there was rarely anything interesting to tell. Besides, Papa didn't hold with story telling. The only stories he approved of were those from the Bible that taught a lesson. Also, there was little time in her life for casual talk. Like the other Duncan children, she had her chores: feeding the chickens, setting the table, making the beds, helping Louise with the cooking and cleaning, and weeding in

the truck garden that gave the family its only income
except for the cream Papa sold to a Nashville dairy.
Besides, she'd learned not to say anything that might
unduly attract her father's attention. Sometimes the
most innocent remark could bring his wrath down
upon her head.

But today was different. It was her sixth birthday.
She knew it was her sixth because Louise, who was
twelve, had told her so. When her brothers and sister
had birthdays, there was roast chicken stuffed with
sage dressing for supper, followed by a sponge cake
with chocolate icing, a rare treat in a motherless home
where the cooking was plain and very simple. There
were no presents, which were forbidden by their
church, but after they finished eating the cake, Papa
would get out his father's old fiddle and play and sing
hymns and even some of the old-time mountain songs,
with everybody joining in.

Sometimes, there would be company, one of the
other families that belonged to the fundamentalist
church around which their lives revolved, and then
Papa and the other man would swap stories that had
come down from their grandparents—and this Marma
liked almost as much as she did the cake.

Papa was a lay preacher. Their church was very
small, a plain frame building with a congregation of
only twelve families. Since the church couldn't support a paid preacher, Papa led the congregation in
prayer. It was a rigid, black-and-white religion, something Marma fully realized only after she'd left home.
No frivolity of any kind was allowed on Sunday—not
even a game of hide-and-seek. There was no running
or laughing out loud, no dancing or playing Old Maid,

and no reading—not even schoolbooks. Only the Bible was permitted.

On Sunday mornings and at Wednesday prayer meetings, Papa stood before the congregation and gave thundering lectures on the evils of the world. He talked fervently of fighting the devil with prayer and godliness, and it often seemed to Marma, sitting on a hard, backless bench with her brothers and sister, that Papa's words were aimed directly at her. At those times she would freeze in her seat, afraid to move for fear she would attract the attention of the devil.

When the last prayer was over, and Papa gave the signal to his family that it was time to go home, her short legs would be asleep from having dangled so long over the hard edge of the bench, and when she stood, the prickly pain of returning circulation would make her bite down hard on her tongue to keep from crying and disgracing herself—and Papa.

Although she always looked forward to the birthdays of her sister and brothers, Marma had never wondered when her own turn would come. Maybe that was due to her age; being only six and not yet in school, she measured time in terms of weeks, not years. Until now, she had hardly noticed that she was the only child never to have had a birthday celebration....

But on that Sunday morning, as they did the breakfast dishes, Louise told her that it was her sixth birthday and even held up six fingers to show her what that meant. Because of this rare attention from her sister, Marma made the mistake of expecting a celebration, and thus committed the sin of greediness: the birthday child always got two pieces of birthday cake.

Even more than that, she looked forward to being the center of attention, to have Papa ask what she, as the birthday child, wanted him to play first on his fiddle.

But the afternoon passed and there was no smell of cake baking in the kitchen's old iron range. Even then she wasn't worried. Sometimes Papa got a neighbor lady to bake the birthday cake instead of having Louise do it. Foolishly, Marma expected the cake to appear in all its chocolate glory after the last of the supper plates had been scraped into the slop pail and Papa was drinking the cup of hot water he allowed himself as a substitute for the coffee or tea that was forbidden by their church.

But supper came and went and still there was no cake. Nor was there any mention of the day being a special one, of Marma being a birthday child. She held her tongue until long after supper, hoping against hope that the treat was merely late, that Papa was teasing her, and the rest of the family was in on the joke.

But when Papa rose from the old morris chair in which he'd been reading his Bible, and went to wind the twenty-four-hour Seth Thomas clock on the mantelpiece—a signal that it was bedtime—she couldn't hold out any longer, and asked Papa if he'd forgotten that it was her birthday.

Papa was a man of strict rules and inflexible beliefs, but he wasn't a violent man. In fact, she'd only seem him whip one of her brothers once, and that was when Matthew's carelessness had caused one of the milk cows to get mired in mud and suffocate. He was kind to the farm animals—kinder, she secretly thought, than to his youngest daughter. But she accepted this, knowing her own imperfections and failings, knowing that to spare the rod—in this case, Papa's tongue-lashings—would surely spoil the child.

So she wasn't prepared when his face turned dark red and he rose and stalked toward her.

"There'll be no celebrating of *this* day in my house," he roared.

He struck her across the face, but at the last moment, he pulled the blow and it was a slap rather than a hard punch. Even so, it stung, and she cried out and backed away. Papa stood there, staring at his own hand. There was a strange expression on his face, as if he'd suddenly seen the devil he was always talking about. Abruptly, he wheeled and went to bank the fire in the big iron cook range that provided their heat in the winter.

"Get along to bed, girl," he said gruffly. "And I don't want to hear no more about birthdays. Envy is one of the sins the Bible warns us about."

Her misery and disappointment was almost too much to bear. She didn't cry, nor did she put her hand up to hide her stinging cheek. Without looking at the others, she ran out of the kitchen and upstairs to the unheated room she shared with her sister. She undressed in the dark and put on the cotton nightgown that was a hand-me-down from Louise and crawled under the bed covers. But she was still awake when her sister joined her a few minutes later. Louise whispered her name, but she didn't move, not until her sister's breathing grew deep and regular.

During that long night, she soaked her pillow with silent tears, but she also came to terms with life the way it was, rather than the way she wanted it to be.

She even came to accept as truth Papa's frequent remarks that she, of all his children, had to pray the hardest because she had been born under an evil cloud.

Once, when her brother Matthew had been sulking because Papa had punished him for getting a D in English, his worst subject, he'd told Marma that if it wasn't for her, their mother would still be alive. At the time, Marma hadn't understood this. But as she had lain with her face buried in her pillow, her father's words had come back to her. "There'll be no celebrating *this* day in my house," he'd said, and then he'd struck her across the face.

So Matthew had been right. Somehow she had caused her mother to die, and that was the reason that Papa seldom spoke to her, never looked at her directly or praised her—no matter how hard she tried to please him—and never called her by name.

After that, because she loved Papa and wanted his approval so desperately, she spent long hours on her knees praying, not really understanding what she was paying penance for. She only knew that if she cast out the evil inside her, then Papa would surely love her as he did the others.

She had always been a quiet child; now she spoke only when necessary. In her fear that Papa would find out about the awake dreams, which she knew instinctively were unnatural and therefore evil, she fought unsuccessfully to banish them. When they only came more often, she tried to put them out of her mind, and she never told anyone about the things she saw, even when they foretold disaster—like the time the creek below the house overflowed in the middle of the night, ruining the bumper garlic crop that Papa was planning to harvest the very next day.

Then, when she was seven, she made another mistake, this one with disastrous results. It happened so quickly, with such innocence on her part, that it was a long while before she realized what she'd done wrong.

Papa, who discouraged conversation at the supper table, had broken his own rule that evening to inform the boys that it was time they started digging a new well. Not only was their cistern dry because of a summer drought, but the water level in their old well had suddenly dropped so low that quick sponge baths had replaced weekly tub baths, and to save what little well water was left for cooking and drinking, they'd had to haul water from the creek for the stock and for household needs.

Marma listened as Papa and the boys tried to decide where to dig the new well. That was when, seeing a chance to get into Papa's good graces, she spoke up rashly.

"Why don't you dig along the root line of that old water oak 'round in back of the house, Papa?" she asked.

Papa's eyes narrowed. "What you talking about, girl? There ain't no water there. It's too far uphill from the creek."

"But there is, Papa. There's a big pool of water on top of the limestone, about thirty feet down," she said eagerly. "If you dig there, it ain't likely the well'd ever go dry, even in a drought year."

Even now, almost two decades later, Marma remembered the silence that had filled the kitchen. No one spoke; no one moved. Louise had just raised a forkful of fried potatoes to her lips, and she froze, her eyes fixed on Papa. Her brothers' expressions ranged from alarm on Mark's face, to dark satisfaction on Matthew's.

Marma knew then that she'd said something bad and would be punished—and that there was nothing she could do to stop it.

Her punishment was swift. Papa's gaunt face was like granite as he rose, hauled her from her chair by the scruff of her neck and dragged her from the kitchen, across the yard to the corncrib. Still silent, he lifted her inside, fastened the Yale lock on the door and left her there alone in the dark with only the rustling of mice among the corn husks to keep her company.

Marma was afraid of the dark. She knew, from the stories her brothers told when Papa wasn't around, that terrible things lurked there—ghosts and demons and ghouls that ate human flesh. As she cowered on a heap of corn husks, her arm shielding her face, she became sure that someone—something!—was watching her through the slats of the corncrib. Was that the wind, moaning through the slats—or was it something else, something ugly and hungry and filled with hate?

She burrowed deep into the pile of corn husks, trying to hide herself. The husks rustled and squealed under her, setting her nerves to jumping, but at least she was warmer now—only what if the monsters were already inside the corncrib? What if they had buried themselves deep under the corn husks to keep warm, too?

With a cry, she surged up from the corn husks. She huddled against the door, even though the draft was worse there. The night that followed was interminably long; the hours crept by slowly, second by second, minute by minute. The wind dropped; now she could hear other sounds—scrabbling and furtive stirrings—even though she kept her hands pressed against her ears to shut the noises out. Once a mouse ran over her foot and she moaned with loathing and dread.

Finally, numbed by sheer exhaustion, she slept, and in the morning, Louise came, but only to take Marma to the outhouse. Louise didn't speak, not even when Marma begged her to tell Papa that if he'd only let her back into the house, she'd never be bad again.

Later, Louise brought her a quart mason jar of water, an empty pail with a cover and one of their mother's old quilts. Just before she fastened the Yale lock again, she thrust a triangle of warm, buttered corn bread stuffed with fried ham and wrapped in a dishcloth into Marma's hands.

"Don't tell Papa," she said and turned away before Marma could thank her.

That evening, Papa came. He knelt beside the corncrib and began to pray out loud for the Lord to cast out the devil inside his daughter and wash her soul clean so she was fit to live with decent, God-fearing people.

Marma knelt on the corn husks, with her head bowed, but she didn't join him in the prayer. Her stomach was too empty—and besides, something rebellious inside her kept asking why her punishment was so great when all she'd done was try to help Papa find water.

For three days and nights, she stayed in the corn-crib. Every morning, Louise brought her water and a piece of meat in a hunk of johnnycake or hush puppy, wrapped in a feed-sack dishcloth that she took away the next morning. And every evening, Papa came to pray that Marma would see the light and put away evil. He seemed not to hear her promises to be good, or see her tears. Only on the fourth day, when she developed a bad cough and a fever, did he relent and allow her back in the house.

Marma never forgot those nights alone in the dark. In some ways, they'd toughened her. She had been quiet before; now she spoke only to answer a direct question. When she did speak, her voice was husky, as if all the tears she'd shed alone in the dark had rusted out her vocal chords. She never cried again, either, not in front of people—not even when, after a tussle with the county school board, Papa was forced to let her go to school when she was nine, and the other children teased her unmercifully.

Louise had taught Marma to read and write and do sums, and after she'd been tested by school authorities, she was placed in the third grade. In her eagerness to make friends, she forgot to be careful. On the third day of school, she told the girl who sat next to her that she was real sorry their teacher, Mrs. Brownlee, had broken her leg when she had fallen down her root-cellar steps. The girl asked her crossly what she was talking about. Marma looked up and saw that Mrs. Brownlee had come into the room and there was nothing wrong with her leg. Too late she realized that their teacher's fall hadn't happened yet.

The next day, it was announced by a substitute teacher that Mrs. Brownlee was in the hospital with a broken leg, that she'd fallen down her cellar steps. The girl in the next seat gave Marma a scared look and raised her hand to ask the substitute teacher if she could move to another seat because "Marma Duncan was acting funny."

The story spread, and no one would play with Marma during recess, or even talk to her. And sometimes, when the teacher wasn't around, the older kids called her names like witch and Crazy Marma.

In her hurt, she retreated into her shell. She wanted to explain that she wasn't crazy; it was just that she sometimes had dreams about things that were going to happen. But she held her tongue, knowing that would only make things worse. She filled the void in her life with study, with voracious reading from the meager supply of books in the school library—and discovered a solace that, for the rest of her life, would never disappoint or fail her.

The teasing, which was all it was at first, gradually became something worse, maybe because she never fought back. She was soon going home with bruises and cuts and once with a black eye. If Papa noticed, he never questioned her. Only Mark, her youngest brother, who was in junior high school, took her aside and told her bluntly that if she didn't want to be picked on in school, she would have to learn to fight back.

The next time the school bully knocked her down, she did just that; fought back so fiercely that although he was a husky boy, two years older than her, he ended up, to his surprise, with a scratched face and bite marks on his arm. It was inevitable that he would win the fight, of course. He pushed Marma into a puddle of mud, then sat on top of her until the recess bell rang because she wouldn't give in and cry "uncle."

She refused to tell her teacher why she had a cut lip and was covered with mud, not because she didn't want the bully to be punished but because experience had taught her that she would be blamed for starting the fight. After that, the other children still teased her and called her names, but from a safe distance. And occasionally someone would speak to her, if only to borrow a pencil or an eraser.

Things got better as she grew older. By the time she was attending one of the county's high schools, an hour's ride in a school bus from Duncan Holler, she had earned, if not the friendship of her schoolmates, at least their respect. Or maybe, Marma thought now as she sat huddled at the kitchen table, looking back from a distance of ten years, they had simply gotten tired of teasing her.

The boys changed first. As her narrow body developed curves, and the too-thin face she saw in the mirror above the kitchen washstand took on a maturity, they began hanging around her locker at school, vying for her attention. She didn't make the mistake of letting her newfound popularity turn her head; she treated the boys as she always had—with wariness. The girls, too, changed, and Marma even developed a casual relationship with one girl who lived in another part of the county. It was only a school friendship, but at least now she had someone to eat lunch with. It gave her hope that someday things would be different and she would finally fit in.

And then, when she was seventeen, everything changed again. The world that had finally become tolerable collapsed and she was back where she had started.

Or was that a fair way of putting it, Marma wondered as she poured boiling water over the tea bag in her mug. Hadn't it really been a new beginning, however painful? Would she have had the courage to break away when the opportunity presented itself if she hadn't been made to realize, once and for all, that nothing was ever going to be different for her unless she left Duncan Holler—and Papa?

It was a Friday, and she was a senior, at the top of her class. It wasn't that she was that much smarter than her classmates; it was just that she had a hunger for knowledge that served as a substitute for other things she'd been denied.

She was in study hall when it happened. Usually, her waking dreams—she's learned to call them visions by now—were so brief that she could explain her occasional blackouts by pretending she'd fallen asleep or had been deep in thought. But this particular vision lasted for several minutes, and when it was over, she found herself slumped in her chair, her cheek resting on the top of the desk. Even though her eyes were still closed, she heard whispers and knew the other students were watching her, but there was nothing she could do about that. Even to raise her head from the desk would be to court nausea or even a fall.

In the vision, she had seen a young girl, about seven or eight years old, lying at the bottom of a mine shaft.

She didn't know which one, because dozens of old played-out mines honeycombed the mountains of the area, but she sensed that this one was located in or near her own valley. The girl was dark-haired, very small and fragile looking, and she was hurt so badly that she couldn't move.

"Mama, Mama," she cried out as Marma watched, horrified and full of pity.

Usually, Marma would have put the whole thing out of her mind, but this time the vision intensified, grew clearer, and now she realized that a piece of wood was lying across the lower part of the girl's body, pinning her down. The plank was shaped like a half circle, and Marma wondered if it was the shaft's seal, which had split in two when the girl had fallen down the shaft. The light was so bright now, she could read the few letters that had been burned into the cover.

"—ilton Mining Company. No. 4," it read.

The vision faded, leaving her so dizzy that she couldn't answer when the study-hall teacher, finally noticing that she was resting her head on her desk, asked if she were sick. The teacher assigned two students to help her to the dispensary, where the nurse gave her an aspirin and made her lie down. In a short while, Marma was back to normal, but she pretended to be asleep, wondering what to do next. If she told anyone about the vision, the old stories about her would start up again. And besides, what could she say that made any sense? That she'd had a vision about a little girl who had fallen down a mine shaft?

Still undecided, she went home. If she was even quieter than usual that evening, no one seemed to notice. It was after supper, when Papa turned on the radio to listen to the evening news, that she finally had to face the truth, something she'd only suspected until now.

She heard the words, "Lisa Montgomery, age seven, lost in the area of White Hawk State Park . . ." and the blood rushed from her head, leaving her dizzy and weak. She didn't doubt, even before the news commentator described the missing girl as being dark-haired and small for her age, that it was Lisa Montgomery she'd seen in the vision.

And now she fought a battle with herself. She had never told anyone about her visions—except that once—but she'd often suspected that Papa was aware she had them regularly. If she spoke up now, he would be furious. And yet, a child's life was at stake. How long could she survive, badly hurt, lying at the bottom of that mine shaft without food or water? The commentator had said that Lisa had wandered away from her parents' campsite during the night, or early in the morning. She could have covered miles before she'd been missed. What were the chances that the search crews would find her without help?

Marma discovered her heart was beating too fast, that her mouth was trembling. Afraid that Papa would notice, she grabbed up the slop bucket that held their table scraps and took it outside to pour into the pig's feeding trough. She didn't go back inside immediately. Instead, she stood there, leaning against the pigpen railing, watching their greedy sow and trying to decide what to do.

If she told Papa about her vision, he was sure to call it the work of the devil, and then he'd forbid her to ever mention it again. But if she remained silent, the little girl might die—and how could Marma live with something so terrible on her conscience?

Again, a childish voice echoed in her ears. "Mama, Mama," it said.

Marma stirred finally, her mind made up. There was little chance that he would believe her, but she had to talk to the sheriff, no matter what the personal cost. Feeling better for having made the decision, she returned to the house and, a few minutes later, went up to bed.

When Louise—twenty-three now and soon to be married to Charlie Burleau, the son of a neighbor—was asleep beside her, Marma slid out of bed, dressed quickly in the dark and crept downstairs. She got a sweater off a hook in the mudroom and went outside, silently shutting the door behind her. Luckily, there was a nearly full moon, but she took Papa's Coleman lantern with her anyway, more for comfort than from need.

As she hurried down the road, the beam of light from the lantern bouncing in front of her, she wondered if Lisa Montgomery was staring up the mine shaft at the moon—or was she lying there in total darkness? Marma shivered, and for a brief moment, she was seven years old again, locked in Papa's corncrib, seeing demon shapes in the dark, hearing demon voices in the wind.

It was almost four o'clock before she reached Bradyville. Although the sheriff's office normally would have been dark this late at night, light poured out through its windows. She heard men's voices as she drew closer and somewhere a radio was squawking.

Even when she reached the building, it was a long time before she summoned up the courage to open the door. When she finally went inside, she was relieved that no one paid much attention to her. With the exception of one woman, all of them were men; they were milling around the office, drinking coffee and talking. Some of them she recognized: Jesse Small, the county sheriff; Arnie Breckenridge, one of the sheriff's deputies who had come to her school to give a speech on career day; two farmers she'd seen around town; Mr. Fields, who owned the big feed and grain store at the edge of town, and Dr. Campbell, who had once set her brother Mark's broken leg.

The others were strangers, but she picked out the father of the missing girl at once, even before he stopped pacing long enough to squat beside the woman and pat her hand. The man was short with a husky build; in his jeans and plaid shirt, he could have passed for a local man except for the thick gold watch on his wrist and his fur-lined jacket, which he wore indoors as if ready to leave at a moment's notice. There were other things, such as the way his hair was styled, and the unconscious authority in his manner when he stood up to exchange a few words with the sheriff, that marked him as an outsider, a city man.

The woman was younger than her husband and very pretty, despite her swollen and puffy eyes. She perched on the edge of a splintery oak chair, holding a full mug of coffee between her hands. No steam rose from the ironstone mug, and Marma wondered if she'd forgotten she was holding it. Her pallor and the lost look in her eyes touched Marma deeply, and she wanted to rush up to the woman, tell her about the vision and what she'd seen. But she turned away without speaking, knowing it was the sheriff she had to convince.

She waited until he was alone. He was studying a county map that was spread out on his desk when she approached him.

"Can I talk to you, Sheriff Small?" she asked, and despite her determination to sound confident, her voice shook a little.

The sheriff gave her a curious look. "You're one of Dan Duncan's kids, ain't you?"

"Yes, sir. I want to tell you about—"

"I appreciate you Duncan Holler folks lending us a hand, even if you are jumping the gun a mite. The search parties can't start out till sunup. It's too dangerous, fooling around in them mountains at night, but we're gonna need all the help we can get, come morning."

"Papa and the boys didn't come with me. I—I came alone."

"I didn't know you was old enough to drive."

"I'm seventeen. I know how to drive Papa's truck but I don't have my license yet, so I had to walk into town—"

"You mean you walked all the way from Duncan Holler alone in the middle of the night? How come you did a fool thing like that?"

"That's what I want to talk to you about."

"This is important?"

"Yes, sir. Real important."

"Well, I was about to grab a few winks before the folks start pouring in, but I can spare you a few minutes. We can talk back there in the cell block."

Marma followed him through a door. To her relief, the cells were all empty. Sheriff Small sank down on the edge of a bunk with a tired sigh.

"I don't know the last time there's been such a fuss about something around here," he said fretfully. "Seems this fellow Montgomery and his wife are real important people in California, where they come from. They even got contacts with the governor. Not that it makes no difference. We'd do all we could to find that little gal even if they was hippies."

He paused to yawn so widely that his eyes watered. "Okay, what's so all-fired important that it couldn't wait till morning? What's your name, anyway? Louise, ain't it?"

"Louise is my sister. My name is Marma," she said.

"Marma, you say? So you're the youngest, the one that's—" He paused to scratch his nose, looking embarrassed. "What's on your mind, Marma?"

Marma wasn't sure where to begin. "You'll think I'm crazy, I guess, but I had to come," she said slowly. "I saw something—I guess you'd call it a vision."

"This got something to do with the Montgomery kid?"

Marma nodded. "That's who I saw in the vision. She was laying at the bottom of a mine shaft." She thought she saw skepticism in his eyes and she hurried on, not giving him a chance to speak. "The girl had dark hair and was wearing jeans and a jacket, only her shoes—she wasn't wearing gym shoes like I heard on the radio. She was wearing—well, they looked like slippers—bedroom slippers, a sort of greenish blue."

The sheriff stared at her, but she had the feeling that he wasn't really seeing her. "This mine—did you see where it was located?"

She shook her head. "There was something written on a wooden plank that may help." She described what she'd seen, spelling out the letters of the incomplete first word for him. "Does that mean anything to you?"

She watched him expectantly, but the expression on his face didn't change. Her heart sank when he asked, "What did your pa have to say about this?"

Marma swallowed hard. "I didn't tell him. That's why I came alone. He has strong opinions about—about some things."

"Yeah, I've heard about your pa." His voice was dry. "Well, I've seen some strange things in these mountains. If this business can help us find that little girl, it's worth a try."

"You mean you believe me?"

"Enough to check it out. My own ma had second sight. Your pa, being such a religious man, probably calls such things devil's work, but Ma helped a lot of people, never harmed anyone." He stood up and stretched his back, wincing. "You get some rest, and I'll see what I can find out about the old mines around here. And you stay put, you hear? I don't want you going off again on your own. Too many crazies running around loose, even in a backwoods place like this. And don't worry about your pa. I'll call Lester Moore—he's got a phone and he lives up your way. He can get word to your folks that you're okay."

He handed her a musty-smelling pillow and a rough wool blanket and pointed to a bunk. "You can sack out here. Nobody'll bother you."

He was gone before she could ask permission to join one of the search parties in the morning.

Marma was sure she wouldn't be able to sleep, but as soon as she'd wrapped herself in the blanket, stretched out on the bunk and rested her head on the pillow, she was gone. When she awoke, it was morning. For a while, she lay there, getting her bearings. She had dreamed during the night, and although the dream had already faded, she knew it had been pleasant. From the front of the building, she heard men's voices, but only a few. Did that mean the search parties had already left? If so, would they find Lisa Montgomery in time?

She shivered suddenly and pulled the scratchy blanket Sheriff Small had given her over her shoulders. No matter what else happened, she was in trouble with Papa—big trouble. Even if the girl was found—*please God, let her be found alive!*—he was bound to be mad. He wouldn't banish her to the corncrib this time because she was too old for that, but he would pray for her and make her sins the subject of his sermons for weeks to come....

Papa arrived a couple of hours later. Marma was sitting at one of the desks, finishing off the coffee one of the deputies had put into her hands, even though it was bitter—and forbidden by her church. When Papa came through the door, he spotted her at once. He took the mug away from her, his eyes the color of cold slate. Ignoring the two deputies who'd been left behind to monitor the radio and coordinate the search parties, he seized Marma's elbow, jerked her to her feet and propelled her toward the door. When one of the deputies asked him if he knew about any abandoned mines in Duncan Holler, he gave the man a long, cold stare and didn't answer.

Marma knew it would be a mistake to try to explain, so she was silent on the ride back to the valley. Somehow, she wasn't surprised that Papa didn't turn off at their own road, but stayed on the county highway for another couple of miles.

She knew where he was heading, of course, even before the truck shuddered to a stop in front of the church she'd attended all her life. When she saw the cars and trucks already parked there, she realized why Papa hadn't come earlier. When he'd found out where she was and what she'd done, he had summoned the whole congregation to assemble at the church. Indeed, they were all there, down to the last baby in arms. Even her oldest brother, Luke, and his pregnant wife, who lived over on White Hawk Mountain, a good hour's drive away, had come. Louise, sitting with her hands folded in her lap, looked as if she had been crying, but after one quick glance at Marma, she stared down at the floor as if she were ashamed of her sister.

As Papa led her down the aisle, nobody made a sound, not even the children. When a baby started crying, it was quickly hushed by its mother. Marma reached the front of the church and turned to face them; her shame was so great that it was only pride that kept her from bursting into tears.

Papa began to speak. At first, his voice was low, but it increased in volume as he told them that his daugh-

ter, who had always been a problem child, had sinned
and turned her back on everything she'd been taught.
God knew he'd tried to raise her in a righteous way,
but all his efforts had been in vain because she'd
turned her back on the Lord.

In her pride, her vanity, she'd given in to temptation. She had listened to the voices, the images the
devil had put in her mind, and now he was asking for
their help to cast out the devil within her and save her
from damnation. That was why he had summoned
them, he went on, his voice ringing with conviction.
They were all good people who lived God-fearing
lives. Surely, their prayers would weigh heavily in the
Lord's eyes.

And then he forced Marma down to her knees and
told her in a thunderous voice to repent her sins and
pray for forgiveness—it was the only way she could be
saved.

The others joined Papa in prayer, and Marma suddenly understood that these people who had known
her all her life had already made up their minds. No
matter what she said or did in the future, they would
always believe that she was possessed—and she would
live with that stigma for the rest of her life.

Something stirred under her shame and humilia-
tion, and suddenly she was angry, more angry than
she'd every been before in her life. Yes, she had
shamed Papa when she'd gone to the sheriff on her
own last night. But what other choice had she had?
How could it possibly have been wrong to try to save
the life of an innocent child? Didn't that mean anything to these righteous, God-fearing people—to
Papa?

They were still praying when the sheriff came through the door. He was a portly man, shorter by several inches than Papa, but he looked very tall as he stood at the back of the church, listening to the babble of praying voices, his gray eyes cool and considering. For a moment longer he stood there, and then he was stalking down the aisle.

At first, she was sure her father would ignore him, but when the sheriff had almost reached the pulpit, Papa held up his hand for silence.

"You are interrupting God's work," he said.

"I don't think God has anything to do with what's going on here," the sheriff said. "Your daughter saved the life of a little girl today. We found Lisa Montgomery an hour ago at the bottom of one of the old Hamilton mines, just like Marma said. If she'd held her tongue, Lisa would be dead now. Is that what you want? To see a child die rather than have your daughter use the God-given gift she was born with?"

Papa's face darkened, but he didn't speak.

"I can't do nothing about this—this business here," the sheriff went on. "Religions have got a right to follow their own ways in this country, and I got no quarrel with that. But I'm telling you, Dan Duncan, not as a law officer but as one father talking to another, that what you're doing to this girl is a crying shame."

He turned his attention to Marma. "If you want to come into town and stay with my missus and me, you're welcome. We got an extra bedroom now that our oldest boy's off at college in Knoxville. I promise you'll be right comfortable there. If you've a mind to, you can help the missus with the younger kids to pay for your keep while you finish high school. It's up to you."

Years later and two thousand miles away from Duncan Holler, as Marma relived that day, she remembered how long she had hesitated, how tempted she'd been to take Sheriff Small up on his offer. Why she hadn't gone with him, she wasn't sure, not even now. Had she hoped that if she didn't, Papa would change, forgive her for causing the death of her mother in childbirth—learn to love her as he did Louise and her brothers? Or was it something else? Had she stayed with Papa because she couldn't bear to shame him before his congregation, before the whole county?

Whatever the reason, she had thanked the sheriff and then told him she'd be okay, that she'd better stay with Papa.

Sheriff Small studied her a while, then nodded. He didn't try to change her mind. Maybe he was relieved that she had refused his offer. "It's your choice. Just remember that you're always welcome to come stay with the missus and me."

He turned and gave the silent congregation a long, hard look; a few of them met his eye but most of them looked away.

"I think you folks had better get along home now and tend to your own business," he said.

Papa started to say something, but the sheriff's voice overrode his. "As for you, Daniel Duncan, I want you to think about this. Your girl's getting to a legal age where she can do what she wants. You keep on the way you've been headed, and the day'll come when you'll wish you'd done things different."

He nodded to Marma, and stalked off down the aisle. There was a long silence after the door closed behind him. When Papa thanked the others and told them he'd see them come Sunday, she knew that the sheriff's visit—and maybe his offer to give her a home—had accomplished one thing. The meeting was over—and she was sure that it would never be repeated.

Papa seemed thoughtful rather than angry as he drove the family home in his truck. He didn't speak to Marma until they reached the house, and then he told her that since Louise had done her chores that morning, she was expected to make it up to her sister.

That evening, he didn't turn off the radio when the new announcer talked about the miraculous rescue of a lost child from an abandoned mine near White Hawk State Park where her parents had been camping out. Her physical condition was described as good. There was no mention of Marma's part in the rescue, and she knew she had another reason to thank the sheriff.

It was a month later, just before graduation, that Marma's school adviser called her into his office to tell her he'd just received information about a four-year scholarship to Brown University. It had been set up by a New York-based charitable foundation to provide higher education to eligible female seniors who attended Lawson County high schools—and it could have been custom-made for her.

The rest was history, including her final alienation from her father and family. It was also the beginning of a new life for Marma.

And now, just when she'd been so sure that she'd finally succeeded in burying the past, the visions had returned—and Arnold Flagg had asked—no, begged—her to use her clairvoyance to find Lisa Montgomery, who was once again in terrible trouble.

CHAPTER SIX

MARMA WASN'T EXACTLY SURE how long she had sat there, nursing a mug of tea between her elbows, lost in her own thoughts, but it must have been an hour or so; when she became aware of her surroundings again, she noticed the sun had moved lower in the sky. A weight resting on her knees, told her that her cat had taken advantage of her preoccupation to commandeer her lap. She scratched the cat on a favored spot at the tip of her spine, and Magic closed her eyes in feline ecstasy and began purring loudly.

"Lucky Magic," Marma told her. "You don't know what it means to have regrets—or rotten memories. You even have a willing slave to provide you with plenty of tender loving care, a steady supply of cat food, including liver once a week, and a warm lap."

She gently disengaged Magic's claws from her skirt and set the cat on the floor. She got up, intending to dump the cold tea into the sink, but she never got the chance. One minute she was thinking that she should surprise Angie with a home-cooked meal—Danny was out of town—and the next she was caught up in a by-now-familiar vision.

As before, the dark-haired teenager was in bed, lying on her back, a blanket tucked under her chin. Her face was without animation and her eyes were blank, as if she had fallen asleep with them open. She was so still, in fact, that Marma's heart skipped a beat, until she saw the barely perceptible rise and fall of the girl's chest.

Something else had changed, too. This time, she wasn't alone.

Two people stood at the foot of the bed—a man and a woman. The man, who looked to be in his late thirties, was whippet thin; his hair was already thinning on top, and his face was too narrow for the bushy mustache that graced his upper lip. The woman was younger, and at first Marma thought she was pretty—until she caught the coldness in the heavily made-up eyes.

The girl on the bed moved restlessly, capturing Marma's attention. She studied the teenager's softly rounded chin, the slight indentation near her mouth that was probably a dimple when she smiled, and her thin, narrow nose, and suddenly—as if a veil had been ripped from her eyes—she knew who the girl was.

Lisa Montgomery, Marma thought, seven years older than the child she had seen in that earlier vision, but still the same girl. Why hadn't she made the connection this afternoon when she had first learned that Lisa had been kidnapped? It seemed so obvious now. Was it because she hadn't wanted to face the truth, to become involved in another potentially painful incident? In her desire to insulate herself from anything that might stir up old self-doubts and fears, had she become selfish, totally wrapped up in preserving her own well-being?

The suspicion was painful. Another thought came to her. If this *was* Lisa, then the couple standing by the

bed had to be the kidnappers. Marma returned her
attention to them, trying to fix their faces in her mind,
only to find that the vision was fading. As she strained
to recapture the image, sweat broke out on her forehead and pain arched through her head, threatening
to split her skull in two. She set her jaw, ignoring the
pain, trying to bring the image back in focus. But now
there was only a gray mist, billowing like a theater
curtain caught in a strong draft.

And then, deep within the grayness, she saw something move. A number—no, several numbers—appeared, etched in black against the gray: first the
number one, followed rapidly by a four and a nine,
and then, much fainter, a forty-five. The figures wavered against the mist for a few seconds and then dissolved into grayness again.

A new onslaught of pain jolted her back to reality.
She blinked several times and the ache gradually subsided enough that she could rise to her feet and stag-
ger into the bathroom. She swallowed two headache
tablets, washed them down with tap water, and then,
knowing that two wouldn't be enough, not for what
looked to be the granddaddy of all migraines, she
swallowed two more, reasoning that being a little
groggy was better than enduring the pain.

She wanted desperately to lie down while the pain
reliever did its job, but of course she couldn't. Not
only had the vision verified that Lisa was still alive,
but now she could give Mr. Flagg a description of the
kidnappers. She had to relay the information to him
as quickly as possible, tell him every detail of what she
had seen. The numbers—149 and 45—meant nothing

to her but perhaps they would to him—or to the police.

She winced at the thought of trying to convince the police that she wasn't some kind of crackpot, but resolutely, not allowing herself time for second thoughts, she went to the phone and quickly dialed the number of the bank. It took a few minutes and a small white lie—that Mr. Flagg was expecting her call—to get past the switchboard operator.

"Mr. Flagg's office," his secretary's brisk voice said.

"This is Marma Duncan. I'd like to speak to—"

"Mr. Flagg isn't here," the woman interrupted. "He left shortly after his—uh, appointment with you."

"It's very important that I reach him. Could you give me his home phone number?"

There was a long silence. "I'm sorry. That's confidential information. Why don't you leave a message? He'll get it in the morning when—"

"No—no, that won't do. I must contact him immediately." Marma paused to take a long breath, realizing how hysterical she must have sounded. "Look, will you at least call him at home and tell him that—that I have the information he needs? That I'll be waiting at home for his call?"

"I'm sorry. I couldn't possibly disturb Mr. Flagg at home." She sounded a little shocked at the idea. "And I'm already late for a dental appointment."

The phone clicked in Marma's ear. She mumbled an epithet she rarely used, then dialed again with frantic fingers, only to have the switchboard operator tell her this time that no one was answering the phone in Mr. Flagg's suite.

She spent the next few minutes trying to coax his home phone number out of the switchboard operator. Not even her insistence that she was an employee of the bank with urgent information for Mr. Flagg helped, and she was finally cut off again.

Her head throbbed; the pain, although dulled by the tablets, kept time with her pulse. She sat there, staring at the phone in her hand, aware that she'd made a mess of the whole business. She should have told the secretary that it was a matter of life and death, and if that hadn't worked, she should have said she had information about the whereabouts of Mr. Flagg's kidnapped granddaughter. It might have broken through the woman's officiousness—or it might not have. She was obviously very protective of her employer, and who could blame her, Marma asked herself. She'd feel the same way herself if she worked for someone like Arnold Flagg.

Marma replaced the phone and stood, still uncertain what to do. The obvious move was to go to the police—but how long would it take to convince them that she wasn't some psychopath or publicity seeker? Her only other course was to contact Mr. Flagg directly. Yes, that made sense. As to where he lived, that was no problem. Everybody at the office knew that their president's home was a designated historical landmark, the grandest of the old Victorians in Pacific Heights.

Marma went into the bathroom to run a comb through her hair, but she didn't bother renewing her makeup. Time was too important, and besides, her hands were so unsteady she suspected she'd make a mess of it. But she did take time to scribble a note to Angie, saying she had to go out on an errand and not to wait to eat dinner with her, that she'd be back as soon as possible.

A cold wind whipped her hair into a frenzy as she left the lobby for the street. She shivered and pulled the collar of her jacket up around her neck, and looked around for a taxi. Just as she thought she'd have to go back inside and call for one from the lobby pay phone, a black-and-white cab pulled up at the curb to let off a passenger. Relieved, Marma hailed it quickly, and after she'd slid onto the back seat, she directed the cab driver to the old Flagg mansion.

"Sorry, but I don't know the exact address," she added. "And I'm in a terrible hurry."

The taxi driver only nodded, and she settled back and tried to relax. But the urgency was back, and it was all she could do not to urge the driver to go faster. Since he was already exceeding the speed limit, she restrained herself and concentrated on planning just what she would say when she finally reached Arnold Flagg.

Fifteen minutes later, she paid the driver in front of an imposingly large house that had survived not only the earthquake and conflagration of 1906 but also decades of changing styles and modernization fads since. As she climbed the mansion's broad front steps, it occurred to her for the first time that Arnold Flagg might not be at home. Wasn't it more likely that he was at his daughter and son-in-law's house, waiting for further instructions from the kidnappers? And even if the kidnappers had made contact directly with

Lisa's multimillionaire grandfather, there would surely be police officers in the house. How much would she have to tell them before they let her see Mr. Flagg?

As it happened, she had no problem getting in. As soon as she gave her name to the stolid-looking man who answered the bell, he searched her purse and scrutinized her from head to toe, then admitted her.

After he identified himself as Sergeant Cummins of the San Francisco Police Department, he told her, "Mr. Flagg's secretary gave him your message. He's been trying to contact you. Come along, miss—he's in the library."

As she followed his broad back down a long, deep-carpeted hall, Marma silently prayed that the information she was bringing would be helpful. At the end of the hall, Sergeant Cummins opened double doors that were richly carved with Chinese figures, then stood aside so she could enter a large room that seemed to hold more books than a public library.

Mr. Flagg was seated behind a graceful writing table, his eyes fixed on the ivory-colored French phone at his elbow. His face seemed even grayer than it had just a few hours earlier. Two men stood in front of a blue-tiled fireplace, talking quietly together. One was a stranger—a tall, thin man with incongruously ruddy cheeks. The other was Lisa's father, looking much as he had seven years ago.

As she watched him listen to the thin man, Marma's heart throbbed with pity. There was such weariness in the slump of his stocky shoulders, such anxiety in his deep-set eyes as he turned his head to look at the woman who was huddled in one corner of a large damask-covered sofa.

Marma's breath caught as she followed his glance. The years might not have changed Lisa's father all that much, but this wasn't true of Mrs. Montgomery. Marma knew the woman was only in her early forties, yet she looked like an old woman. Had the years been unkind to her, Marma wondered, or had the change occurred recently—say, within the past two days? How unfair that these two people should have been forced to go through the same kind of hell twice in their lives, Marma thought, and prayed to God that this latest crisis would end as happily as the first one had....

As if Millicent Montgomery felt Marma's eyes watching her, she looked up. When she saw Marma standing in the doorway, she half rose, her hands clasped tightly together, he eyes filled with hope.

It seemed strange to Marma that she'd only seen Mrs. Montgomery once—that time in the sheriff's office—and had never exchanged one word with her. The day after Lisa's rescue, the Montgomerys had come out to Duncan Holler to see Marma, only to be turned away by Papa. She had heard his voice, ordering them off his property, but she hadn't dared go outside.

They must have written her because Papa had come in from the mailbox two days later, his face like a thundercloud, to inform her that from now on, he would collect the mail. Soon after that, she'd found a scrap of cream-colored stationery lying in the ditch near the mailbox. It had smelled faintly of perfume, and there had been a few words written on it, enough to tell Marma that it had been a thank-you letter.

The woman started to say something, but then, to Marma's surprise, she sat back down, biting her lower lip, and it was Mr. Flagg who spoke first.

"What is it, Marma? Have you remembered something?"

"I had a—a vision. I saw Lisa with two people, a man and a woman. She was a little pale, but I don't think they had harmed her."

"Thank God," Mrs. Montgomery said, and Marma realized that she hadn't spoken earlier because she'd been too afraid the news would be bad.

"Were they wearing masks?" the thin man asked.

"Masks? No. Does that matter?"

The man exchanged a glance with Sergeant Cummins. "It could mean—" He broke off.

Marma finished the sentence in her mind. *It could mean the kidnappers don't intend to let Lisa live....*

Her face must have lost color because Mr. Flagg rose and came toward her. He took her arm and led her to a chair. "What else can you tell us? Can you describe the couple—or the place where Lisa's being kept?"

For the next few minutes, Marma did her best to describe the room and the couple she'd seen, even though she was sure her description of an ordinary bedroom and two people who looked like a thousand others couldn't possibly help. But her description of Lisa, of the nightgown she was wearing, did accomplish one thing.

For the first time, the tall, thin man's skepticism, which she'd sensed even before Mr. Flagg had introduced him as Police Captain Wilson, seemed to subside slightly.

Lisa's father leaned forward, his eyes boring into hers, reminding her that he was a lawyer. "And you're sure Lisa's nightgown was blue?"

"Yes—light blue. With an elaborately embroidered yoke. It looked like a very fine cotton—you know, the kind that's imported."

Behind her, Mrs. Montgomery spoke, her voice high-pitched and uneven. "Oh, God, Phillip! That's the nightgown Lisa was wearing when they took her from her bedroom—"

Captain Wilson gave her a warning glance. "And that's all you can tell us, Miss Duncan?" he demanded.

Marma rubbed her forehead with her fingertips; she winced as pain lanced through her skull. In addition to the headache, which had subsided only briefly, she felt sick to her stomach and bone tired.

"There is something else, but I may have imagined it. I wanted so badly to help, you see."

"What is it, Marma?" Mr. Flagg asked. "What did you see?"

"Just as the—the image was fading, I thought I saw several numbers, but they didn't make any sense to—"

"Let us be the judge of that, Miss Duncan," Captain Wilson said. "What were the numbers?"

Marma closed her eyes, trying to recall exactly what she may or may not have seen. "One—I'm sure it was a one—and then a four and a nine. And then forty-five."

She opened her eyes and looked at him. "Does that mean anything to you?"

Captain Wilson grunted; he didn't answer her. He snapped shut the notebook he'd been jotting in, then took Sergeant Cummins aside. They conferred briefly, their voices so low she only caught a word or two. There was a muffled sob from Mrs. Montgomery. Marma wanted to go to her, comfort her, but she sensed that it would take little to send the woman over the edge into hysterics. Marma pressed her hand against her diaphragm and swallowed hard; there was a burning pain in her stomach that she blamed on the headache tablets. *Or maybe I'm getting an ulcer,* she thought wearily.

She rested her head against the back of the chair and closed her eyes. She felt dazed, disoriented, as if the whole world was out of focus.

"She's exhausted," she heard Mr. Flagg say. "Paranormal incidents burn up a lot of energy."

"You've made a study of the subject?" The skepticism was back in the captain's voice.

"I researched the subject after my granddaughter's experience in Tennessee. I know you find this hard to believe, but Marma really did save Lisa's life that time. It's possible there's a special affinity between them. It happens, you know. And I'm sending Marma home now. She needs to rest."

"So do you, sir," the man said, and now there was a touch of warmth in his brusque voice.

"I'll rest after we find Lisa," Mr. Flagg said.

What happened next was a blur. Marma was aware that she was thanked by a tearful Mrs. Montgomery, that Mr. Montgomery pressed her hand and that Mr. Flagg kissed her on the cheek. And then she was being escorted by a silent Sergeant Cummins down the hall, out the door and into a long, silver-gray limousine. She was conscious of giving directions to the driver, but she must have slept during the trip across town because she didn't remember it later. When they reached her apartment building, the driver helped her up the stairs, used the key she gave him to open the door, tipped his cap and was gone. She remembered going into her bedroom and turning down the Texan star quilt she used as a spread, but later, when she awoke from a dreamless sleep, she couldn't remember having taken off her clothes and gotten into bed.

She saw by the clock radio on her nightstand that it was almost eight o'clock, which meant she'd slept two hours. She switched the radio on, turned it to a news station, and it was then she learned that Lisa Montgomery, the kidnapped granddaughter of multimillionaire banker Arnold Flagg, had been found alive and unharmed in an apartment in the San Francisco neighborhood called "The Avenues," that the kidnappers were still at large.

The address where she'd been held was 149 Forty-fifth Avenue.

STEVE HEARD THE NEWS at the same time that Marma did, by way of the TV behind the bar of the Irish grill he'd stopped at after work for a quick corned beef on rye and a beer. The news stunned him. It also angered him, and not just because his young cousin had gone through such an ordeal. He left his sandwich and beer untouched, dropped a bill on the table and sprinted for the door.

It took him half an hour to reach his uncle's house and another five minutes to talk his way past a truculent police sergeant, who not only made him show every piece of identification in his wallet, but insisted on searching him before escorting him personally to Arnold's den.

Steve forgot his anger as soon as he saw his uncle. Arnold was sitting in the big leather chair he favored. He was wearing a robe, a silk paisley one that Steve recognized as one of his own Christmas gifts, and he had obviously come right out of the shower because his iron-gray hair was still damp. He was holding a half-full brandy snifter, a bottle of brandy at his elbow, and from the high color on his normally pale face, it was obvious this wasn't his first brandy of the evening. Arnold waved airily and invited Steve to help himself to a drink, but since his uncle wasn't a drinking man, Steve knew how deceptive his outward calmness had to be.

"Why didn't you let me know?" Steve asked bluntly.

Arnold rubbed his jawline. "I forgot to shave this morning," he said with an air of surprise. He caught Steve's scowl and shrugged. "It all happened so quickly, there wasn't time to contact you—or anyone else. Besides, it was imperative to keep my phone line open because their note said this was where they would contact us. Then the police got involved, and they insisted the whole thing be kept under wraps. Besides," he added a little belatedly, "what could you have done?"

"I could have stood by. I could have held Millicent's hand. Good Lord, Arnold, she must be devastated—"

"She was—until we got Lisa back. Now she's so busy fussing over her chick that she hasn't time for anything else, not even a nervous breakdown."

"And Lisa? Is she okay?"

"She's fine. Still a little scared and very weak. Those bastards dosed her with barbiturates to keep her quiet. But the doctors say she'll be good as new in a few days. She looks so fragile but the truth is she's pretty damned tough. I'm really proud of that granddaughter of mine."

"A chip off the old block—and you still haven't told me why you didn't contact me. The reasons you gave are hogwash and you know it."

"You never give up, do you? Which makes you a good reporter, I guess. Okay, it seems the man in charge of the case, a Captain Wilson, knew you were my nephew and he was adamant that no newspaper men—especially you—be involved." He gave Steve a thin smile. "I understand you two have locked horns on more than one occasion in the past?"

"Yeah, he's been on my case ever since my article on police brutality." Steve grimaced suddenly. "God, I hope they catch those bastards. Any news along those lines?"

"Nothing yet. They were gone when the police raided the apartment, but Captain Wilson assures me it's only a matter of time until they're caught. You know the law: kidnapping for ransom is a federal crime so now the FBI is in on it. I'm confident they'll find them eventually."

"I hope so. The sooner they're behind bars, the better. You know, I think I underrated Captain Wilson. I had him figured as an opportunist more interested in advancement than in police work, but the speed with which he found Lisa is impressive. I'll have to give him a call and apologize for calling him a politician in my article."

Arnold took his time responding. "It wasn't good police work that saved Lisa—although the police did all they could with the little they had to go on," he said. "If I told you that a psychic told us where to find Lisa, I suppose you'd make some smart-aleck crack about a sucker being born every minute?"

"You said it, not me. And you're right. That's just what I would say."

"And I tell you that Lisa was saved because a woman with paranormal talents saw her and the kidnappers in a vision, along with several digits that spelled out the address of the place Lisa was being held at. You can believe it or not. As for me, I have no doubts, and neither do her parents. Even that hardheaded Wilson is reserving judgment." He paused to study Steve's stiff face. "This isn't the first time it's happened, Steve. Lisa wouldn't be alive today if the same woman hadn't saved her life seven years ago."

Steve frowned at him. "Wait a minute—are you talking about the time in Tennessee when Lisa fell down a mine shaft? What has this business got to do with that?"

"The same woman saw Lisa lying at the bottom of that shaft in a vision. That's how the search party knew where to find her. Marma was little more than a girl herself at the time it happened." He didn't seem to notice Steve's shock. "She went to the local sheriff and—well, Lisa was found in time to save her life. And now Marma came forward again and we're doubly

obligated to her. I'm trying to find a way of rewarding her, the way I did the first time, but she's fiercely
independent, and I suspect all she'll accept is our
heartfelt thanks."

"What do you mean by 'rewarding her' the way you
did the first time?"

Arnold took a long drink from his brandy glass; it
was empty when he set it down. "If I answer your
question, it must remain a secret."

"I know how to keep a secret," Steve said shortly;
he hoped Arnold wouldn't notice that he hadn't exactly made a promise.

"After Lisa was found in that mine shaft, I offered
to put Marma through college, but her father—a
sanctimonious bastard if I ever saw one—refused. I
knew that any other offer would get the same treatment, and yet I couldn't just walk away as if nothing
had happened. So I had my lawyers set up a dummy
charitable foundation and offer a four-year scholarship to Brown University that was tailor-made for
Marma. It helped, of course, that she was at the head
of her senior high-school class."

He paused for a moment, then continued. "As it
happened, she could have qualified easily for scholarships to other colleges, but according to her school
adviser, her father pulled every trick in the book to
discourage her from applying. For one thing, he
claimed their religion forbade accepting charity of any
kind. Even without the religious angle, most of those
mountain people are stiff-necked as hell. Which is
why, I suspect, she's been paying the foundation back
her grant money. She's already returned a fair portion of the money, far more than she can afford on her

salary. That's why I decided to add that codicil to my will. She can hardly refuse to honor the wishes of a dead man.''

Steve fought hard to conceal his dismay. His uncle was an unusually shrewd businessman. Couldn't he see how cleverly the woman had roped him in?

"Why haven't you told me the whole story before, Arnold?"

"Because—well, it was a promise we made the sheriff. He wanted to protect Marma from any publicity."

"I see," Steve said. He was having a hard time keeping his voice even. "Tell me—why are the police here?"

"Because the kidnappers are still at large—and possibly furious because their plan went sour. Captain Wilson isn't taking any chances. I'm hoping it won't take long to round them up, now that the FBI is in on it. Neither of the couple has an arrest record, so there are no photographs, but one of the police artists is drawing up some sketches. With two witnesses, they should be pretty accurate."

"You think their descriptions will match?" Steve said, trying to keep his cynicism from showing.

"Lisa was drugged most of that time, and Marma only caught a glimpse of the kidnappers during the psychic phenomenon, but the police seem to think they can put together a good likeness."

I'll just bet, Steve thought. "How are you going to reward Marma Duncan this time?"

"Oh, I'll think of something. Maybe I'll increase her legacy."

"Which means the payoff will be years away. Doesn't that bother you?"

"It bothers me. Maybe I can come up with another idea."

"Oh, I'm sure you'll think of something," Steve murmured and earned a hard look from Arnold.

"You have a problem believing this, don't you? If you knew the woman—well, you wouldn't be so skeptical. In fact, I'm sure you'd decide, as I have, that she's just what she seems."

The phone on Arnold's desk rang. He went to pick it up and spoke into the receiver. His face tightened. "No comment!" he snapped and slammed down the phone. "Dammit! I might have known," he muttered as he returned to his chair.

"What's the problem?"

"It seems one of your colleagues, a reporter from the *Chronicle*, just received a tip that a psychic helped the police find Lisa. Which probably means the story will be on the eleven o'clock news tonight."

Silently, Steve agreed. The story had too many provocative angles not to be exploited by the press. A beautiful, very rich kidnap victim miraculously saved by an even more beautiful psychic; yes, it would be on the local news this evening and on the wire services by morning.

"It'll blow over," he said, hiding his doubts. "These days, the public's attention span is only about two days long. By next month, it will be forgotten and the family can get back to living normally again."

Arnold shook his head. "You don't understand. The family can weather it. We have the money to assure our privacy, but Marma can't. She's the one I'm worried about. The kidnappers are still out there. If they find out that Marma caused their scheme to bomb, I'm afraid of what they might do. Not just for revenge, but from fear that Marma might use her psychic powers to help the police find them."

Steve, who doubted very much that the kidnappers had any such fears, only nodded. "So how do you propose to protect her? Hire a bodyguard?"

"I doubt if she'd stand for that. But I do have a plan. The trick is to get her to cooperate. Since she works for me, I was going to insist that she take a vacation. I've already checked with her superior and she has five weeks free time coming. Now with this publicity business, I'm going to suggest that she stay at my lodge at Tahoe. I think I can convince her that she'll be doing me a favor by house-sitting for me and keeping an eye on things."

He paused to pick up the brandy bottle again, but after considering its depleted contents thoughtfully, he sighed and set it down again.

"Here's where you come in, Steve—as a personal favor to me," he said. "I don't want to alarm her. God knows, she's gone through enough as it is. And like I say, I doubt she'd stand still for hired bodyguards. But what's to prevent you from keeping a close eye on her? You can rent one of those cabins near the lodge—this early in the season, there's bound to be vacancies. It shouldn't be hard for a young stud like you to get acquainted. You can always use that monster of a dog you own as bait. I have a hunch the two of you will hit it off. She's—well, she's a very special young woman. How about it, Steve? Can I depend upon you?"

MARMA WAS DOZING on the living-room couch when
Angie came home, bouncing in with her usual insou-
ciance, explaining why she was so late. She broke off
when she saw Marma lying on the couch.

"Hey, what's up? Iron Woman Marma crashing on
the sofa? Are you sick or something?"

Marma yawned and sat up. "I'm great," she said
automatically, and then discovered it was true. "I
really do feel great."

"You don't say. There wouldn't be a man involved
in that statement, would there? Like that gorgeous
hunk who brought you home from the banquet last
week?"

She giggled at the surprise on Marma's face.
"Danny wanted to fix some popcorn and we were all
out, so I made a quick trip to the corner store. I was
still in the lobby when you and the hunk pulled up out
front in that black station wagon. I figured you'd invite him up, so I made a wild dash upstairs to tidy up
the living room a bit before you got there. But then
you came in alone and since you didn't mention him,
neither did I. I just caught a glimpse of his profile, but
he looked like a real dish. What's he like, Marma?"

"I have no idea. He was just someone I met at the
banquet. He offered me a ride home and since it saved
me the hassle of getting a cab, I accepted. He didn't
ask for my telephone number. He wasn't interested, I
guess."

Angie made a rude sound. "I don't believe that, not
for a moment. What did you do—freeze him out?"

"I don't know what you mean by 'freeze him out.'"

"Oh, yes, you do. The temperature drops twenty
degrees when you're putting distance between you and

some guy you want to discourage. I just hope you're never on the receiving end of that kind of freeze, Marma—not that it's ever likely to happen to you. You could get just about any man you want."

"I don't know where you get the idea that I'm some kind of femme fatale," Marma said crossly. "I don't lead men on. I don't even flirt."

Angie sighed in exasperation. "Okay, you don't flirt. Big deal. Maybe you should. Flirting is harmless and fun and it keeps the old blood circulating and— okay, okay. Don't give me that look. Subject closed." And then she added, "If you're interested in the guy, why don't you call him?"

Marma didn't ask which guy she meant. "Indeed I won't. If he wants to see me, he knows where I live and also where I work."

"You're hopeless. And old-fashioned. How do you think I got my first date with Danny? I met him at a party. He was with this blond gal who had so many teeth she looked like a shark when she smiled. As soon as I saw him, I knew this guy was for me—and much too good for the shark lady. When she went to the powder room, I moved in on Danny. When he didn't ask for my phone number, I asked for his. I called him the next night and invited him to a party. He said, 'Yeah, sure, it sounds like fun,' and then I had to put together a party in a hurry. Which wasn't easy on such short notice—you remember the time my cousin Luigi had that surprise birthday party for you and it wasn't your birthday?"

Marma began to laugh, and couldn't seem to stop. The laughter turned to sobs and suddenly she was crying on Angie's shoulder. The tears stopped as abruptly as they'd begun. Too embarrassed to look at Angie, she blew her nose with a tissue that had somehow found its way into her hand. "I'm sorry," she said awkwardly.

"What are friends for? You needed a good cry. You hold it all in too much, Marma. That's why you're always so tense. And why don't you tell me what's been bugging you lately? I might not be able to help, but I can listen."

Even though they were good friends, Marma hesitated. Did she really want to confide in Angie? And if she did, would her friend understand? What if she turned away from her, stopped being her friend?

Not willing to take a chance, she started to say something light and off-putting, and then she caught the hurt in Angie's eyes and knew that this time evasion would be a mistake. Angie had proven her friendship a dozen times over. To pretend that nothing was wrong would only make her feel that she wasn't trusted. Besides, if the whole story came out in the news, as it very well could, Angie would find out anyway. *Better that she hear it now than from some sensationalized newspaper report,* Marma thought.

She took a deep breath for courage—and began talking. It was easier than she had expected.

"It started a long time ago," she said. "Ever since I can remember, I've known that I was different than other people. I have this gift—or maybe it's a curse. I—I see the future sometimes, things that will happen."

"You mean you've got second sight?" Angie said; although her eyes were bright with interest, she didn't seem especially surprised. "I suspected something like that. You can go right to things I've misplaced. That's part of it, isn't it?''

"I'm not really sure. I have no idea how it works. But sometimes I do seem to know instinctively where lost things—and lost people—are.''

She discovered her headache was back; it was sending pulsating stabs of pain through her skull. She pressed her fingers against her eyelids, praying it was only eyestrain this time.

Angie got to her feet. "We're both going to get into our robes and slippers, and then I'm going to fix us some of that new rose-hip tea I bought at the natural food store. When we're all relaxed and comfortable, then we can have a real heart-to-heart," she said, her tone brisk, and Marma knew that Angie was giving her some space—and a chance to change her mind.

But she didn't change her mind, and later, as they sipped their tea, Marma told Angie about Papa, about his hatred for the thing that set her apart. She told her about their final quarrel—and what had precipitated it.

"And that's why he didn't answer your letters? Because he thinks of you as some kind of witch? What is he, a religious fanatic or some kind of bigot?''

"He isn't either, Angie. He's really a very good man. People in our valley come to him when they need help—and they always find it. But the church is his life. He told my sister once that before he accepted the Bible as literal truth, he had been heading for damnation. Anything that smacks of—well, what he calls the devil's work is abhorrent in his eyes. He was furious when I accepted that scholarship to Brown. He told me that I'd never be safe away from my own people. He said I'd inherited the thing I'd been born with from my grandmother. I never knew my mother, of course, but I often wonder if she had it, too, because Papa never talked about her, never mentioned her name."

"And knowing it wasn't your fault, your father still punished you?"

"He wasn't really punishing me. He thought it was his duty, as my father, to suppress the second sight, to tear it out by the roots because it was evil. Well, I believed that once, too, but I don't now. It isn't evil any more than being born color-blind is evil. But it does set me apart. All my life, I've felt—different. Which is why I've fought so hard against it."

"Is that what causes those migraines you get sometimes?"

"I'm sure there's some connection. Luckily, I stopped having the visions after I left home. Maybe when Papa had the congregation pray for me, they really did go away."

"Or were scared away for a while. And now they're back. They are, aren't they?"

"I've had three visions in the past few days. I really hate them, Angie, even though they probably saved Lisa Montgomery's life again."

Angie listened, totally fascinated, as Marma gave a brief account of her part in finding Lisa. "Thank God it's all over now," she added.

"I'm not so sure it is over," Angie said, looking troubled. "Some jerk had a ghetto blaster going on the bus coming home, and I heard part of a news bulletin about the kidnapping before he switched channels. The police think the kidnappers are still in this area, and if they've been listening to the radio, they must know how they got caught. They didn't give your name, but they talked about the police getting help from a psychic. I think you need police protection, Marma. What if they find out who you are and come looking for you?''

"Why would they do that?"

"To shut you up. Maybe they're afraid you'll conjure up another vision and learn where they're hiding out.'' She paused, looking thoughtful. "You'd think this would occur to the police, wouldn't you? And how about this Flagg guy? Has he called you since his granddaughter was found?''

"I don't know. I took the phone off the hook,'' Marma confessed.

Angie groaned. "You need a keeper, so help me. That was pretty dumb, you know.''

Marma watched silently as Angie replaced the phone in its cradle. She half expected it to start ringing immediately. She discovered she didn't want to talk to anyone, least of all the police. Absently, she rubbed her upper arms inside the sleeves of her robe, and found them cold and clammy.

"Nobody knows who I am except Lisa's family and the police,'' she said, more to reassure herself than Angie. "Why would they talk?''

"Someone did, or the media wouldn't know a psychic was involved. Look, you told me not long ago that you had to use up some of your vacation time this year or lose it. Why don't you take a long vacation, get out of town for a while? Go on a cruise or something. I'm sure Mr. Flagg would arrange things for you and pay your expenses.''

Marma shook her head. "I wouldn't take his money, even if he offered. It would be wrong to benefit from—the second sight."

"Now why aren't I surprised that you said that? Okay, pay for it yourself. You need a rest, judging from the way you've been dragging around here the past few days. I've been knocking myself out trying to make you laugh, and half the time you don't even get the point of my naughty little jokes."

"Naughty! I have a different word for those little zingers you bring home. Who do you get them from, anyway? Surely not from Danny."

Angie sighed. "Danny doesn't tell risqué jokes. In fact, he turns red as a beet when I tell him one. I get them from my cousin."

"Shame on him," Marma said with mock severity.

"Him? Who said it was a him? I've got girl cousins, too."

Marma groaned. "You're bad. Really bad, Angie."

Angie gave her a cocky grin, looking pleased with herself. "And don't change the subject. How about it? I think a nice cruise where you'd be incommunicado for a couple of weeks is just what you need."

"It isn't that easy. There are complications—such as the way our office designates vacation time. We have to bid for it several months in advance. Besides, this is the busiest time of the year for mortgages, what with so many people buying homes in the spring. Charlotte would have a fit if I asked for time off now."

"So let her have a fit. You can always go to your friend, Mr. Flagg, and tell him you need a favor."

"Go over Charlotte's head? She'd never let me live it down. I just can't do it."

"Oh, yes, you can."

Marma knew her friend's intentions were good, that she was genuinely worried about her, but she was suddenly tired of the subject.

"I'll think about it," she promised, and then, as a diversion, she suggested they order Chinese food and pig out. Angie called in their order, and when she left the room to take a shower, Marma quietly disconnected the phone again and laid a newspaper over it to hide the evidence. Danny was out of town on a construction job, she reasoned, and anything else could wait until morning.

So that was why it wasn't until early the next morning, when she plugged the phone back in, that she heard from Arnold Flagg.

CHAPTER SEVEN

AFTER STEVE LEFT Arnold Flagg's house, he didn't get back into his station wagon. His brain was overloaded with unanswered questions, and he needed to do some serious planning. Since he'd always done his best thinking on his feet, he decided to take a walk before he drove home.

He strode down the steep hill that fronted his uncle's property, taking long breaths of air into his lungs. The night air was crisp and fresh, thanks to the previous night's rain. Indeed, the tangy air was only one of the blessings of living in San Francisco, Steve thought. The city, located on a peninsula, was naturally air-conditioned by rejuvenating ocean winds. The other thing Steve loved about San Francisco was the pride of ownership that kept most of the neighborhoods, even the less prosperous ones, clean and attractive.

When he'd first returned to the city, he'd been unable to find an apartment that suited him. So he had spent a portion of the more-than-sizable trust fund he'd inherited from his father on a Nob Hill condominium, not only as a favor to its owner, an old friend who had moved to Italy, but because both the neighborhood and the building suited his own taste and needs.

The cost had been exorbitant—the high price of living in paradise, he'd thought at the time—but its advantages were well worth the money. For one thing, his living-room windows offered a panorama view of the bay. At night, one could see an enchanting line of lights along the curved expanse of the Golden Gate Bridge, and sometimes, in the early morning, white fog hung low over the bay, and the red spires of the bridge seemed to float on air. At those times the bridge looked like a Chinese temple, as exotic and other-worldly as San Francisco itself.

Not that San Francisco didn't have its warts. It had all the problems of other major cities: overpopulation, crime, too much traffic, aging public transportation systems and conflicting cultures. But like most natives, Steve blandly ignored such things and went on thinking his city was the loveliest of all worlds.

Today, however, he was blind to the wonders of the tree-lined streets and the colorful bay-windowed houses that someone had once called "painted ladies." He barely took note of the breathtaking views and the crooked streets that played strange tricks on unwary motorists.

His thoughts were on Marma Duncan—and they weren't pleasant thoughts.

Not only did he not believe that she was a psychic, he had no reason to believe such things as clairvoyance, second sight and precognition even existed. What he did have was contempt for those charlatans who preyed upon vulnerable people. During his thorough research into parapsychology, he had followed every lead he could find, and had interviewed a multitude of believers and debunkers, as well as a dozen or more so-called psychics. All this had only deepened his conviction that the whole psychic phenomenon was pure myth.

Not that he'd made the mistake of trying to convince Arnold. Once his uncle made up his mind about something, it was a waste of time trying to change it. It was a trait that ran in the family, Steve thought as he turned into another tree-lined street. Not that he was knocking it. It was his own stubbornness that had earned him what success he'd achieved in life. Not once had the offers of bribes or other persuasions ever turned him off a story—and this time, he had a personal reason for proving that Marma was a fraud.

During his research, Steve had found that many people who were taken in by the so-called psychics were gullible, ignorant or superstitious. None of these words described Arnold. But even the shrewdest person had his vulnerable points—and Lisa, his granddaughter, was Arnold's. No wonder his usually impeccable judgment had failed him. And whatever else Marma Duncan was, her act was very convincing.

For a moment, Steve felt a rush of warmth. The memories of dancing with Marma, of holding her in his arms when she'd had that fainting spell, had destroyed his sleep for more than one night. Okay, she was a charmer, with all the feminine equipment needed to turn a man's head. Her air of innocence and vulnerability seemed so real. But he had to keep remembering that hers was a calculated charm—one she undoubtedly used to advantage.

How much of his uncle's lapse in judgment had originated in his glands, not his brain? Maybe his first assumption that Marma Duncan had some kind of sexual hold on Arnold hadn't been so far wrong, after all....

Whatever the truth, it was his duty, his obligation, to see that Arnold didn't become victimized by the woman. His uncle was already hinting that he might change his will again to increase her legacy. What would come after that? Courtship, followed by marriage? Would she eventually be a very rich young widow?

Steve frowned as he stopped to wait for a traffic light to change. Was that the purpose of the whole elaborate kidnapping scheme? To snare a very rich older man into marriage? Most scams, he knew from his research, were complicated, with all kinds of red herrings thrown in to obscure their true purpose—to separate the victims from their money.

This particular scam had probably started by happenstance. Marma had been so young when Lisa had fallen down that mine shaft that Steve doubted she'd had a hand in the accident. But that didn't mean she hadn't taken advantage of the situation. She could have heard the child crying at the bottom of the mine shaft, realized this was the missing child and concocted a story about having had a vision—yes, that could well have been how it had happened. She must have expected a reward, although a girl that young, raised in a rural slum, probably had pretty low sights. When her father, whom Arnold had described as a sanctimonious bastard, had refused a reward, she must have been disappointed—and furious.

The scholarship Arnold had arranged for her hadn't been the same as cash, of course, but it had served to release her from poverty. Had she been disappointed when, after being recruited for Arnold's bank, she had learned that she would have to earn her own promotions? Was that what had prompted the kidnapping scheme?

The trickiest part of a kidnapping was collecting the ransom without getting caught. Most schemes failed at that point. In this case, it hadn't gotten that far, which meant the risk had been minimal. As for Marma not accepting a monetary reward, Arnold was probably right about her. She—and her cohorts— must have realized that a reward, unless it was enormously large, couldn't compare with winning his gratitude and trust. But just what was she ultimately hoping for? Did she really intend to become a rich widow by marrying Arnold and waiting for nature to take its course? Perhaps she even planned to hurry nature along a bit....

A cold chill crept over Steve, despite his rapid pace. How complacent she must be right now, snugly installed in Arnold's good graces, knowing that eventually, one way or another, he would find a way to put a great deal of money into her hands.

Well, the little bitch wasn't going to get away with it. Somehow he was going to scuttle her whole rotten scheme—whatever it was. He owed Arnold that. Arnold had saved him from being raised in boarding schools; maybe, finally, he had found a way to repay his uncle. He was certainly going to give it a try.

ARNOLD'S CALL, although Marma had expected it, affected her in a strange way. She knew even before he spoke that he wouldn't try to offer her a reward for her part in Lisa's rescue, but she also knew that more subtle pressure would be put upon her. So when he asked her for a favor, she tensed, wondering what was coming next.

"If I can," she said warily.

"It's Lisa. She wants very much to meet you. It's really important to her to thank you in person. She's also very curious about you."

Marma hesitated, not sure of her own feelings. She did want to meet Lisa, but if the teenager was going to overwhelm her with gratitude—well, that would be too uncomfortable.

"Are you sure she's well enough for visitors?" she asked.

"Oh, yes. She's still a little weak from the tranquilizers, but I think your visit is just what she needs."

"Is she in the hospital?"

"She's at home. After the doctors examined her, they thought she'd be better off in familiar surroundings. Millicent's fussing over her like a hen with one chick, of course. My daughter is something of a nurturer—gets it from her mother."

"Or from you?" Marma suggested slyly.

"Most people consider me a pretty crusty old fellow."

Marma smiled at his plaintive tone. If ever someone was fishing for a compliment, it was Arnold Flagg. "Nobody who works for you thinks that," she said.

"Hm. That's good to hear. So what about it? How about a visit with Lisa—and lunch as well?"

"This is a workday, Mr. Flagg," she reminded him. "I was just getting ready to leave for the office when the phone rang."

"My friends call me Arnold," he said. "And you've earned a day off. In fact, I've already arranged it with your supervisor. She isn't expecting you in today."

Marma stifled a groan. Charlotte was probably seething—and just what had he told her, anyway? Presidents of big banking firms didn't personally arrange for minor employees to take the day off without arousing a lot of gossip. Maybe she would find out the details from Mr. Flagg—no, from Arnold—before she reported in to work tomorrow morning.

She started to ask what he'd told Charlotte, but he was already going on. "Shall we say—in an hour? Is that enough time?" he asked. "Why don't I send the car to pick you up at nine o'clock?"

"I can take the muni," she said, referring to San Francisco's public transportation system.

"My daughter lives in Burlingame. It's far too much trouble for you to get out there on your own."

"In an hour, then," she said, giving in.

"Good—and don't worry. Millicent and Lisa both understand that an excess of gratitude is pretty hard to take. You won't be bothered along those lines."

Marma hung up with mixed feelings. She did want to meet Lisa. She almost felt as if they had been friends for a long time. On the other hand, she seemed to be getting in deeper and deeper with these people. Maybe Angie was right. Maybe it was time to spend the money she'd been saving for a car on a vacation....

SHE HADN'T EXPECTED Mr. Flagg—no, she had to remember to think of him as Arnold!—to accompany her to Burlingame, but of course she should have known that he'd be eager to check up personally on his granddaughter. Any initial fears that the ride would be uncomfortable were quickly dispelled when they fell into a conversation about food. It seemed that Arnold was a devotee of southern cooking, with a preference for Cajun. Caught up in the heat of the argument, she offered to prove to him that her own Tennessee cooking was as good as Cajun anytime, and he accepted her challenge on the spot.

He had a knack—one she'd noticed before—of drawing her out, and she found herself telling him about her friendship with Angie and relating some of her roommate's most outrageous adventures.

"We're such a contrast in personalities," she said, ruefully, encouraged by his interest. "I'm sort of reserved, a regular sobersides sometimes, and Angie—well, she positively bubbles."

"A female odd couple," he said, nodding his understanding.

Marma thought about the contrast in their bedrooms, too, hers so obsessively neat and Angie's a perpetual disaster area, and she had to laugh. When Arnold wanted her to share the joke, her description of their bedrooms got him laughing, too. He had, she noted, a particularly nice laugh.

By the time they reached Burlingame, they were chatting together like old friends, and she was sorry that the ride had to end.

The Montgomery house was a surprise. Subconsciously Marma had been expecting a duplicate of the

Flagg mansion, but this house, while obviously expensive and imposingly large, was contemporary in style. Surrounded by spacious, well-kept grounds, it sported a tennis court, a pool that she knew instinctively was Olympic size, plus a large wooded area and an impressive rose garden that Arnold told her was his daughter's special pride. Inside, the house was the antithesis of Arnold's antique-furnished Victorian in Pacific Heights. With its open plan, high, timbered ceilings, starkly modern furnishings, bold colors and spacious floor-to-ceiling windows, it would have been right at home in a copy of *Town and Country*.

Leaving Marma in the care of his daughter, Arnold disappeared, saying he'd pop in on Lisa for a few minutes and then make some phone calls. Mrs. Montgomery, whom Marma was soon calling Millicent, insisted on showing her around the house. She must have sensed Marma's curiosity because she explained that she'd craved something more modern for her own house after growing up in a historical landmark.

"Luckily, Phillip feels the same way," she said. "Of course, Daddy growls about living in a fishbowl every time he comes here. He loves that old mausoleum in Pacific Heights."

Marma, who loved rambling old houses with odd corners and nooks and crannies and well-used furnishings, murmured something polite. She asked about Lisa, and Millicent's cheerful facade developed a crack. To Marma's embarrassment, the other woman reached for her hand and squeezed it tightly.

"I know I promised Daddy I wouldn't make a fuss over you, but, oh, I am so grateful. Lisa means the whole world to Phillip and me—she's our only child, which makes her doubly precious. If you ever need anything—anything, you understand?—you just have to ask."

She wiped her eyes on the sleeve of her expensive jacket, and Marma found her own eyes were a little moist.

"There—that's the end of that," Millicent said briskly. "I promise I won't get sentimental again. Lisa was dozing when I left her, but she should be awake by now. Why don't you go up to see her while I check up on lunch preparations? Daddy will be on the phone for ages—he's a workaholic, you know—and you can have a nice visit, just the two of you. Lisa was so excited when Daddy called to say he was bringing you for lunch. She's been feeling a little depressed, but—well, seeing you will cheer her up."

She gave Marma directions to Lisa's room, then hurried off toward the back of the house.

Marma found Lisa's room easily. The door was open, but she rapped softly anyway. At Lisa's invitation to "Come on in," she went in the room, stopping just inside the doorway.

Her first reaction was one of surprise. She'd seen Lisa in her visions, of course, but she hadn't realized how lovely she was. And while it wasn't strange that Lisa seemed familiar to her, Lisa had never seen her; so why was she getting such a strong impression that the girl recognized her?

"Hello, Lisa," she said.

Lisa didn't answer right away. She stared at her fixedly, her pink lips parted slightly. When she smiled, Marma felt relief, knowing that it would be all right, that there wouldn't be any awkwardness between them.

"So it *was* you," Lisa said.

Since her remark didn't make sense, Marma asked, "What do you mean?"

"I don't remember much of what happened after I was kidnapped—the police say my kidnappers used chloroform and then tranquilizers to keep me out of it most of the time—but I do remember waking up and seeing this woman standing by the bed, watching me. It was you—I was sure it was you. There's this old folk song, the one about 'Dark is the color of my true love's hair,' that kept going through my head—you know the one I mean?"

Marma, who knew the song very well because it was one of her favorites, nodded.

"As long as I kept saying those words to myself and thinking about you, I wasn't afraid." She paused, and for a moment, Marma caught a haunted look in Lisa's dark eyes. "Well—maybe I was a little scared, but don't say anything to Mom. She's really freaked out about what happened. Anyway, I was sure you would tell the police where to find me—you know, like you did the other time. I guess it sounds pretty weird, seeing you there and hearing that song, huh? My cousin was here last night, and he told me there had to be a logical explanation. I don't think he believes in psychics."

"He's probably right about there being a logical explanation," Marma said cautiously. "Your parents probably described me to you. Then when you were in danger again, you looked to me for help. It was only natural."

"It was more than that," Lisa insisted. "How could I have known that you had cut your hair? Mom and Daddy described you as having very long hair that you wore in a braid. And I've never seen a picture of you, so I couldn't know about that deep indentation in your upper lip, could I? It was you, all right."

Since Marma couldn't think of a rebuttal to that, she let the matter drop and said, "Your grandfather tells me you have several horses, that you've won a lot of ribbons in shows. What are your horses' names?"

They were still talking about horses when Arnold joined them. For the next hour, the conversation was lively and wide-ranging. Marma discovered that Lisa shared her love of books, and that while Lisa was sweet-tempered, she was perfectly capable of defending her opinions to her strong-willed grandfather. It was also clear that the two of them loved each other thoroughly. Marma thought about her own grandparents, whom she hadn't known. Would Papa have been different if there had been grandparents to stand up for her as, she suspected, Arnold stood up for Lisa when her mother's overprotective instincts showed themselves?

Millicent appeared to announce that lunch was ready and that she was having a tray sent up for Lisa, who promptly announced that eating alone was a drag and she wanted to come downstairs. A little to Marma's surprise, Millicent nodded agreeably, her approving smile in Marma's direction indicating that she gave Marma full credit for Lisa's high spirits.

They ate on a sun-dappled terrace that overlooked a small pond. Although the conversation included a brief discussion of Lisa's experience, to Marma's relief, nothing was said about her part in Lisa's rescue. Arnold, who had a robust appetite despite his size, alternately teased and argued with his granddaughter. The excellent rapport between them became increasingly obvious, and Marma discovered that she was envious. Although she'd become resigned to being estranged from her family, there were still times, like now, when she wanted terribly for things to be different.

"You look so sad, dear," Millicent said in a quiet aside. "Is something bothering you?"

"No—I was just thinking about—" Her voice faltered.

"About what?"

"About my family."

"You have quite a large one, don't you? Do you get back to Tennessee very often to see them?"

Marma hesitated. "Not as often as I'd like," she said, earning Millicent's sympathetic smile.

She had already decided that Arnold was a dear, and that Lisa's natural friendliness was endearing. By the end of lunch, she had also come to realize that Millicent was that rare thing, a person unaffected by the possession of great wealth. Her main interests, aside from her family, seemed to be her garden, the charities she was deeply involved in and the camping trips that seemed so incongruous with her family's social position.

As well as heading charity committees, Millicent Montgomery did such volunteer grub work as delivering Meals On Wheels to housebound elders, chauffeuring patients to cancer clinics for treatment and visiting the infirm at local nursing homes. When

Marma found herself hoping that she would see more of the Montgomery family, she caught the thought up short. Pleasant though this visit might be, it was a one-time thing. She would call Lisa a few times to see how she was getting along, of course, but even if there were further invitations, she'd make excuses to turn them down. There was no way to return their hospitality. It might not be so apparent to the Montgomerys or to Arnold Flagg that the rich were different, but she wasn't going to kid herself. The gap between someone who earned her living working in an office and Mr. Flagg and his family was just too wide to cross.

Arnold was so quiet on the trip back to the city that she wondered if he was still worried about Lisa. She might have thought he was napping, except she caught him watching her from under the brim of his pearl-gray homburg.

"Have you thought about taking a vacation until this thing blows over," he said abruptly. "I understand you have quite a bit of vacation time piled up."

"About five weeks," she said, hiding her surprise.

"Good. That makes it easier to ask you for another favor."

"A favor?"

"I have a lodge on the California side of Lake Tahoe. It's a bit rustic, but very comfortable. It's only a short walk from the lake and isolated enough for complete privacy. Ordinarily, a caretaker looks after it, but the one I had quit a few days ago. I'd like someone there in case of rain damage or a busted pipe. How about house-sitting for me until I can arrange for someone else to take over?"

Marma wasn't fooled by his studied casualness. He needed a house sitter about as much as she needed a dozen more cats. But she was touched by his concern for her safety and his careful effort to protect her pride. It wasn't until much later that it occurred to her how cleverly he'd sprung his trap. He had known she would see through his scheme, and had counted on her accepting for the very reason that she *was* touched.

It was inevitable that she would agree to his proposition. Marma even pretended to believe that the well-stocked pantry and freezer at the lodge were for the convenience of his caretaker. After all, his offer did kill two birds with one stone. It allowed Arnold to assuage his desire to reward her—and it also solved the problem of where to go on her vacation.

MARMA WAS AWARE of the trilling cry of a bird even before she opened her eyes. She lay there for a few moments, wrapped in a warm down comforter, happily conscious that she could stay in bed for the rest of the day if she liked. *I'm going to be so spoiled I won't ever want to go back to the city,* she thought hazily.

Her mind cleared when a dog started barking frantically nearby—if that sharp, coughing sound really was a dog's bark. She turned onto her side to find herself staring at the back of a sofa. The quilt slipped off her feet, exposing them to the cold morning air, and only then did she remember why she was curled up on the living-room sofa and not installed in the king-size bed in the lodge's master bedroom. Magic. She'd fallen asleep on the sofa while waiting for that wretched cat to come in from the cold.

She sat up and slid off the sofa, wincing at the bite of the cold morning air on her bare arms and feet, but she didn't stop to put on a robe before heading for the door in a run. She'd had her doubts about turning Magic loose in a strange place, but since she'd gone to bed without first preparing a kitty litter box, she'd had no choice when, in the middle of the night, Magic had started tapping her mistress's cheek—not so gently— to let Marma know in no uncertain terms that she wanted out.

So Marma had opened the patio door and watched the cat scamper out into the night. She had waited by the door for a long time, finally going out on the veranda to call Magic's name until the night chill drove her indoors. She'd curled up on the sofa in the quilt to get warm, trying to convince herself that at least there was no traffic in the vicinity to worry about. But that hadn't worked; she was only too aware of other dangers—dogs and wild animals and traps. Magic was, after all, a city cat who had no defenses against such terrors....

Noting that the dog had stopped barking—was that good news or bad?—Marma crossed the wide veranda, calling frantically. "Magic—where are you, you crazy cat? Here, kitty, kitty...."

As if her words were a signal, a new commotion started up. This time, she noticed that the coughing bark definitely held pain. She spotted a large white dog then—if it was a dog and not a skinny goat. It was cowering against one of the veranda posts, its eyes rolling so widely that white crescents showed underneath. A drop of blood oozed from a scratch on the tip of its nose. Magic, her fur ruffled so that she

looked twice as large as usual, was stalking back and
forth in front of the dog, her tail twitching omi-
nously. Although she wasn't uttering a sound—not
even a growl—the message was unmistakable. She was
about to make mincemeat of the dog.

"Magic—come here this minute," Marma scolded.
"That dog is at least ten times your size!"

"If that creature of yours was another dog, Leggs
would swallow him in one bite," a male voice said.
"But he's afraid of cats, and don't ask me why. I
found him on the highway and I know nothing about
his sordid past."

Marma gaped at the newcomer, recognizing him at
once. What on earth was Steve Riley doing here? She'd
been thinking of him just last night, wondering why he
had bothered to ask her out when he hadn't even asked
for her phone number. It seemed that every time she
thought of the man, he popped up out of nowhere....

A flush warmed her all-too-mobile face as she realized why he was examining her with more than casual interest. Aware that she was standing there in a
short, thin nightie, she instinctively crossed her arms
over her breasts. Instantly annoyed with herself because the gesture was like something out of an old-
fashioned melodrama, she turned and retreated into
the house. She snatched up her robe and put it on before she returned to the veranda.

"Do remove that—your dog from my property,"
she said. "I wouldn't want to see any animal, even a
cowardly one, get hurt."

Steve eyed Magic. "The creature *is* rather formidable. A trained attack cat, I presume?"

Was he making fun of Magic—or her, she wondered crossly. "She's just defending her own territory. Cats do that, you know."

"No, I wouldn't know. I'm not a cat person."

"I wouldn't admit that if I were you," she said loftily. "Some people claim it's a sign of an inferiority complex not to like cats."

"That's not one of *my* problems."

His smile irritated her. "I'm sure you're right about that," she agreed.

Obviously unruffled by her tart tone, he bent over to pat the dog on the head. "Come off it, old fellow. That cat won't hurt you. She's just—uh, defending her territory."

The dog's white tail quivered, then thumped against the ground. The huge animal kept a wary eye on Magic, who was ignoring him now and devoting herself to her morning toilet.

"What kind of dog is that, anyway?" Marma asked, studying its spindly legs and long, narrow head.

"A borzoi. Most people call them Russian wolfhounds. They're the second tallest dog in the world—or so my veterinarian tells me."

"He must be very valuable. Why would anyone abandon him on the highway?"

Steve gave the dog's silky white head a final pat and rose. "I doubt he was abandoned. He may have jumped out of a car. It's possible there was an accident and his owner lost track of him. I advertised daily for a month in the classified ads, but no one came forward to claim him, so I adopted him." He studied Marma lazily. "I meant to call you, you know," he said.

"Oh? Why on earth do you say that? Have we met somewhere?"

His face relaxed in a smile. "You recognized me, all right, even in these country style clothes." He gestured toward his jeans and wool jacket. "In case you're curious, I'm renting a cabin just down the road. How about asking me in for a cup of coffee? I'm chilled to the bone."

Marma discovered it was almost impossible to maintain aloofness in the face of his good humor. She gave up and waved him inside the house. "Make yourself comfortable. I'll be back in a minute—I have to get dressed."

"Don't do it on my account," he said. "I've been enjoying the view."

Marma gave him a dark look and disappeared into her bedroom. After she'd changed into jeans and a sweatshirt and ran a comb through her tousled hair, she went into the kitchen where she found Steve taking down a can of coffee from a cupboard shelf.

He whistled softly. "Even in a sweatshirt, you are something special to look at," he said.

"Sit down," she said, flushing. "I'll make the coffee."

Dammit! The man was obviously an experienced flirt, so why had she let his compliment fluster her? From their first meeting, he had intruded on her space—and blown hot and cold. What was his game anyway? It seemed too much of a coincidence that he'd turned up again in her life. This was one of those rare times when she wished her second sight was available when she needed it. What she wouldn't have given to know what was going on behind that cool smile, those dissecting eyes....

"Is this your place?" he said, looking around the well-equipped kitchen with its sunny walls and rattan table and chairs.

"I couldn't afford anything nearly this nice," she said. "It belongs to a—to an acquaintance."

"Man or woman?" he said, his eyes glinting, and she remembered he'd asked the same question when she had told him she lived with a roommate.

"Man—but it isn't what you think."

"How could you possibly know what I'm thinking?"

"I'm making an educated guess. I suspect you're thinking the worst."

"As it happens, you're wrong. If this place belonged to your lover, he'd be here with you—if he had any sense at all."

Was that a compliment—or a subtle dig? She decided that no matter how she responded to it, it was a no-win situation. "Have you had breakfast yet?" she asked instead.

"I was hoping you'd ask. What's on the menu this morning?"

"Ham and eggs, fried grits, red-eye gravy and soda biscuits," she said.

He groaned. "I've been doing my own cooking. It isn't fit for man nor borzoi. For a meal like that, I'd sell my dog."

"Not to me, you wouldn't. And before you make foolish statements, you'd better taste my cooking. It could be worse than yours."

"Nothing could be worse than mine," he said so wryly that she smiled as she measured coffee into the coffee maker, plugged it in, then got out the ingredients for biscuits.

Steve settled down at the counter to watch her.

"Where did you learn to cook like that?" he said as she deftly cut some butter into a bowl of sifted flour and baking soda, then added buttermilk and rolled out the dough on a floured board.

"My mother died when I was born and Papa never remarried. I was helping my older sister with the cooking by the time I was six. I'm not a fancy cook. All I know is—well, my roommate calls it my down-home vittles."

"Tell me about your family," he said, and to her surprise, she found herself doing just that for the next few minutes.

"So you're the youngest of five kids," he said. "Are they all married now?"

The question brought her up short. She still thought of her family members as they had been when she'd left home, but of course they were almost seven years older now—including Papa.

"I don't know," she said. "There was a quarrel when I accepted a scholarship for Brown University. Papa doesn't believe in higher education for women. I haven't heard from my kin since I left home seven years ago."

"That must be rough on you, being cut off from your family like that."

To her chagrin, Marma felt her eyes smart. She turned away quickly and took down some cups and saucers from the cupboard. "Do you use sugar and cream?" she asked over her shoulder.

"Black," he said.

She poured two cups of coffee, set one in front of Steve, then took the other with her, sipping it as she finished cutting out her biscuits.

"We have a lot in common," Steve said. "I lost both my parents in a boating accident when I was fourteen."

But at least you had your mother for fourteen years, Marma thought. "What was your mother like?" she asked, and listened as Steve described a quiet, patient woman with warm eyes and a great smile.

"Like yours," she said without thinking.

"Thank you—but believe me, there's no comparison. Mom's smile lit up her face like—like some people's do. She wasn't pretty, not in a conventional way, but she was beautiful inside. My dad was a great guy, too, but he ran a big investment company and was gone a lot. Luckily, Mom was always there when I needed her."

"What happened to you after they were—gone?"

"My aunt and uncle took me in and gave me a real home. They never had a son, so I was more than welcome. Their daughter, my cousin, was quite a bit older than me. She's like my older sister. I was lucky—very lucky. That's why—"

He broke off, looking so disconcerted that Marma wondered if he was embarrassed because he had talked so much about himself. She pointed out the cupboard where the plates and glasses were stored, and told him breakfast would be ready in ten minutes. While he set the table—the rattan kitchen table rather than the formal dining-room table—she frizzled some ham, then used the drippings to make the red-eye gravy that had been a breakfast staple when she'd been growing up.

When the biscuits, golden brown and flaky light, were ready, she put the food on the table, then had the pleasure of watching Steve make a hog of himself.

When he reached for his sixth biscuit, he looked up and caught her smiling. He looked embarrassed, but he buttered and ate the biscuit anyway.

When he was finally full, he pushed his empty plate away with a sigh. Leggs, who had been sitting on his haunches in a corner, watching them eat with a quivering nose and anxious eyes, seemed to take Steve's gesture as a signal. He gently eased himself upward on his long, thin legs. As silently as a ghost, he insinuated his way across the room until he could almost, but not quite, touch the table with his nose. It was Marma he fixed his golden eyes on, his plumed tail waving gracefully back and forth.

"Is it okay if I feed the table scraps to your dog?" she asked Steve.

"So you're a sucker for dogs as well as cats?"

"I was raised on a farm. Our animals had to earn their keep," she said. "But he's such a—a gentlemanly dog," she added.

"Characteristic of the breed. He has better manners than most of the people I have to deal with at work," he said.

"Oh? I don't believe you told me what you do for a living."

"I'm in public relations," he said. "And yes, you can feed Leggs if you like."

Marma found two aluminum pie pans in a cabinet drawer. She filled one with water and the other with scraps of ham and eggs, and one lone biscuit, then dumped left over gravy over it and set it down on the floor. Before Leggs could reach it, Magic stalked over to examine the food. She kept a wary eye on the dog as she hooked a piece of ham with her paw. Leisurely, she ate it, then returned to her perch on the kitchen stool. Only then did Leggs streak across the floor to demolish the food in a few frantic gulps.

Steve shook his head. "Talk about pecking order. She's a beautiful cat. Does she have a pedigree?"

"I have no idea," Marma said. "I found her in the laundry room of our apartment building during a rainstorm. She was so thin her ribs were sticking out and her feet were all cut up, as if she'd been walking a long way. Sometimes I have the feeling she's just staying with us long enough to get her second wind."

"Sort of a feline version of *Lassie Come Home*?"

"I keep expecting her owners to turn up."

"If they did, would you let her go?"

"Of course—but I'd hate it."

"So we have one thing in common—we're both supporting freeloaders."

"Oh, pets pay their way. Who else loves you and yet never gives you advice?"

"And who else can be spoiled rotten and never talk back?" he said, grinning.

Marma laughed, and for a while they sat over coffee, swapping pet tales. Steve finally admitted to a fondness for cats, and when Magic, as quixotic as ever, chose to perch on the extreme end of his knee, he didn't push her off, nor did he make the mistake of stroking her until she invited it by rubbing the side of her head against his hand.

By the time Steve finally rose to leave, it was almost noon, and Marma found herself wishing he would stay a little longer. She felt ridiculously happy when he asked if she'd like to go on a picnic that afternoon.

"My treat," he added.

Marma's nod was deceptively cool; it didn't match the warmth she felt inside. After Steve was gone, the kitchen seemed very empty. An involuntary thought—that she wished he had kissed her goodbye—made her wonder if she'd made a mistake, accepting his invitation.

She struggled with the problem for a while, then shrugged philosophically. It was only this one time, so what difference could a few hours in his company make? If he asked to see her again, she'd make an excuse, which should discourage him. And that should be the end of that.

CHAPTER EIGHT

As STEVE STROLLED down the road toward the cabin he'd rented two days earlier, Leggs ranging back and forth in front of him, he congratulated himself for thinking of bringing his dog along on what he had come to think of as a fishing trip. There was nothing better than a pet to strike up a conversation, and Leggs, with his irrational fear of cats, had performed beautifully. He'd thought Marma might have been a little piqued that he hadn't phoned her after he'd taken her home from the banquet, but it obviously hadn't bothered her. Which was what he wanted—wasn't it?

So why had it rankled a little that she hadn't recognized him immediately? Or maybe she had. She had looked pretty startled when he'd first spoken, but then she'd been dressed in that thin nightgown, which had shown an inordinate amount of skin. So had she or had she not been playing games? It was hard to believe that he hadn't made enough of an impression that she'd forgotten him so quickly.

The conceit in that thought made him grin. He stopped to watch Leggs, who moved like a white ghost in and out of the shadows under the trees that lined the road, occasionally pausing to investigate an interesting beetle or to lift his leg against the trunk of a tree.

The chemistry between a man and woman, Steve reflected, was a strange and irrational thing. It seemed to have a life of its own, impervious to common sense or reason. There was no doubting that it existed between Marma and himself—at least on his part. He'd felt it today, just as he'd felt it the first time they'd met. The night of the banquet, he'd had the devil's own time not kissing her, which would have been a big mistake. She was already suspicious of him. Wariness had radiated from every inch of her enticing body this morning, at least at first. Had she recognized the unlikelihood of three chance meetings in such a short period of time?

Maybe—and this was more likely—she was wary of everybody at present. If she had plans to lure Arnold into marriage, she would have to be careful not to get involved with another man, however casually. And yet she had accepted his invitation for a picnic without hesitation. It didn't make sense unless—well, maybe she was a woman who needed the company of men. There was something undeniably sensual about that lush, lush mouth....

Steve discovered his mouth had gone dry. He licked his lips, angry with himself and his lack of control. God, if he could be aroused just by thinking about that mouth, that husky voice, what effect would kissing her have? He'd have to be careful to keep his distance. One thing he couldn't afford to do was to get sexually involved with Marma Duncan.

Anyway, it was time to think of something else—where to get together a picnic lunch on such short notice. Luckily, there was a New York-style deli in Tahoe City. He could get everything he needed there.

He whistled for Leggs and started on. When he reached his cabin, a small but well-furnished cottage nestled with several others in a grove of pines, he put Leggs in the back of his station wagon, the only vehicle he'd found that had enough space to accommodate the dog's long legs. The drive into Tahoe City took half an hour, and he spent another half hour browsing through the deli.

After surveying the wares offered, he bought corned beef and pastrami, both sliced paper thin, a quarter pound of Petaluma Swiss cheese, cartons of potato salad and coleslaw, sourdough bread from a San Francisco bakery, a cheesecake topped with strawberries, and a six-pack of Coors. Then, remembering that Marma drank mineral water when he'd accepted her offer of a beer that morning, he added a six-pack of Calistoga mineral water.

During their conversation, she'd said something about being a chocoholic, and he wondered now if he shouldn't have chosen a chocolate cake for dessert instead of the cheesecake. Rather than make the change, he compromised by picking up a couple of candy bars from a rack and adding them to his cart.

When he returned to the cabin, he took a shower and changed into clean chinos and a dark blue sweatshirt. Although the sun was warm, now that the morning fog had lifted, spring in the Sierras came much later than in the lowlands and he knew from experience that any warmth from the sun could disappear in a minute if the wind rose.

As an afterthought, he tossed a blanket into the wagon before starting off.

Marma was waiting for him when he pulled up in front of his uncle's lodge. She was wearing a pale pink sweater that complemented her unusual coloring, and there was definitely a sparkle in her eyes as she smiled down at him from the veranda.

"Can I provide anything?" was her greeting. "I baked yesterday—how about cookies?"

"I bought a cheesecake, but maybe I should have made that a chocolate cake. I did toss in a couple of candy bars to feed your habit."

Her face stiffened. She bent to pick up the thermos at her feet, but not before he caught the sudden brightness in her eyes.

"Hey, what's wrong? Did I say something wrong?"

"No, no—of course not," she said, blinking furiously.

"Look, Marma, I obviously committed some kind of faux pas. How about letting me in on it?"

"It has nothing to do with you. It's just that—well, I had a rather bad experience once that involved a chocolate cake that didn't appear as expected. It was my sixth birthday and I thought for sure Papa would—well, no matter. And thanks for the candy bars. I've been known to pig out on them on occasion. Disgusting, isn't it?"

"I have a weakness for those big fat doughy pretzels you eat with mustard, so pig out all you want."

Marma laughed, and to his chagrin, he found that something was happening to his breathing again. What *was* there about the woman that got under his skin? He'd had relationships with New York and Washington women who made her look like Little Orphan Annie. But that husky laugh got his glands all stirred up, and that wasn't good. If he wasn't careful, the hunter would become the hunted, and then what would happen to his objectivity?

"I hope you don't mind my bringing Leggs along," he said. "He needs a good workout, and he can run all he wants where we're going."

"Of course not. Where *are* we going, anyway?"

"To a secret place, known only to thousands, which I discovered when I was a kid. My uncle had a lodge in this area and I spent part of my summers here every year. This place is located at the edge of a grove of Tahoe pines. It's reasonably private, and sheltered from the worst of the wind. It also has a grand view of the lake."

As they drove toward the picnic site, they talked of inconsequential things. Steve discovered that Marma had lost her heart to San Francisco, although she admitted that she'd been too busy to see much more than the usual tourist spots, and he promised that when they returned to the city, he'd show her sights few tourists ever saw, such as the road that ran along the top of a Marin County ridge from which one could see the entire, breathtaking San Francisco skyline.

When she asked how he came to choose public relations for a career, he gave her a brief, evasive answer, and then asked how a nice girl like her had gotten involved with a stuffy business like banking. To his surprise, Marma gave him a serious answer. In fact, she spoke of statistics and interest rates and other related subjects with such enthusiasm that he decided she either loved her work or was a damned good liar.

Probably the latter. If she had such a fabulous job, why had she become involved in kidnapping and extortion? Anger washed over him as he remembered Lisa's pale face, those dark eyes that would never again view the world with total innocence. The fear his cousin had sustained, believing that any minute she would be killed by her kidnappers, was unforgivable. She hadn't been physically mistreated, thank God, but she'd had a scare that would give her nightmares for a long time. No, Steve couldn't relax his guard for one moment and forget that this woman with the angel's face and the offbeat humor that matched his own had not only had a hand in Lisa's kidnapping, but had probably been the instigator.

"Are we almost there? I'm getting a little hungry," Marma said, and he realized that he'd been silent too long. He put a brake on his thoughts, and asked her how she could be hungry after that down-home breakfast, making her smile.

The picnic spot he'd selected was just what he'd promised—private and protected from the wind, with a view of the lake. The stand of Tahoe pines that acted as a windbreak was already surrounded by subtle traces of spring greenery, and the lake, an incredible shade of blue under the sunny sky, seemed close enough to touch, even though it was several hundred feet below, down a sloping hillside.

Several boats, their orange-striped sails braced against the wind, were skimming over the surface of the water, and a squat steamer, carrying tourists on a tour around the lake, wallowed slightly as it made a long, slow turn and headed back to its dock on the Nevada side of the lake.

Marma surveyed the scene in silence for a while. "I wonder what European explorer first stumbled upon the lake," she said. "I envy him."

"Why do you assume it was a white man?" Steve asked. "The Indians knew about this area thousands of years before the first white man appeared."

"Okay, I wonder which native American saw it for the first time. He must have thought he'd found the—uh, happy hunting grounds. Imagine climbing up a hill, expecting to see more trees or maybe a valley, then suddenly seeing a lake as blue as if the sky had fallen down."

"It could have been a dreary gray day," Steve teased. "Or maybe he stumbled onto it at night and almost drowned."

"No, I'm sure it was a day just like this. Maybe he climbed this very hill."

"So, you're a romantic, are you, Marma Duncan?" he said.

The glow in her eyes dimmed. "Actually, I'm a very practical person—not romantic at all," she said.

They ate an hour later, and between them, they consumed an inordinate amount of food. Leggs, his nose at full quiver, waited not so patiently for any scraps that might come his way. Although Steve did not usually feed Leggs table scraps—he knew that animals as well as humans needed a balanced diet—he weakened and tossed the dog a piece of pastrami when Marma wasn't looking, only to catch her slipping Leggs a piece of cheese on the sly.

"My vet would have a fit if he saw that," he commented.

Marma smiled at him, and he caught his breath, a habit he couldn't seem to break. "You should do that more often," he said, his voice uneven.

"Do what? Feed your dog tidbits?"

"No. Smile. Or maybe not. It could get you in a whole lot of trouble with susceptible guys like me."

To his surprise—his tone had been teasing—her eyebrows knitted into a frown. "Are you really susceptible?" she asked. "Somehow, I find that hard to believe."

"Explain that, please."

"You have a way of—well, standing back and weighing everything I say before you answer me. Are you sure you aren't a lawyer?"

"Very sure. And if you aren't going to eat that last sweet pickle you're holding, which is dripping juice all over your jeans, I will."

Promptly, she popped the pickle into her mouth and chewed it with exaggerated enjoyment. The juice ran down her chin and she ran her tongue around her lips to lick it off. Her pink tongue was incredibly provocative, and yet Steve would have sworn she hadn't done it intentionally. Or was he being naive? His uncle, a shrewd judge of people, would see through most feminine wiles. But this woman, with her mixture of sensuality and innocence—yes, she might easily fool Arnold, fool anyone who wasn't already suspicious of her tricks.

And you'd better be very careful, Steve old boy, that you don't get caught by the same lure....

AS FAR AS Marma was concerned, the afternoon was as near perfection as an afternoon could be. She found

Steve wonderful company for the simple reason that they had such an uncanny liking for the same things. They both loved ice cream—any flavor—sauerkraut on their hot dogs, all forms of music (although Steve favored classical jazz and Marma, country music) and both were avid Forty-Niners and Giants fans. Their taste in mystery novels, even mystery writers, meshed almost perfectly. When Steve told her he was crazy about science-fiction movies, the cornier the better, Marma confessed that she was an old-movie buff—the older the better.

"I'd never seen a movie before I went away to college," she told him. "Papa thought they were a bad influence on us kids. My first movie was *Key Largo*. I went because the art department at Brown was sponsoring a Humphrey Bogart festival, and it was free. I thought I was in heaven. For over an hour, I was lost in this place where exciting things happened to fascinating people, and there was drama and romance and—a whole world I hadn't known existed." She laughed ruefully. "I was so mesmerized that I went right on sitting there after the lights went up, too stunned to move. I remember feeling so—so angry at Papa for denying me so much pleasure, and yet I understood for the first time why he thought films were a bad influence. They made real life seem so dull, you see."

"And that's why you're an old movie freak?" Steve was watching her closely, a strange expression on his face.

"I'm still catching up on the movies I missed during the first eighteen years of my life. Angie is always laughing at me for staying up late to see some black-

and-white oldie on the classic movie channel. She thinks I'm crazy." She gave a little shrug. "I guess I am. They're pretty bad, the majority of them."

"You must be a cheap date. A couple of tickets to one of those North Beach movie houses that show old classics, a bag of popcorn, and mineral water and a piece of chocolate cake on the way home."

And then he smiled at her, a twisted smile that didn't seem to match his teasing words.

There was another reason the whole afternoon seemed so special, although it wasn't one she liked to admit. It concerned the strong physical pull between them, something she didn't need second sight to know Steve felt, too. When he touched her arm accidently while reaching for the mustard, the pupils of his eyes darkened almost to black. And once, when she laughed so hard at one of his terrible puns that she fell over backward on the blanket, Steve lost his smile and he suddenly was very still, as if listening to a voice she couldn't hear.

As for her—her senses seemed incredibly acute. She was aware of every nuance in Steve's voice, of the subtle shading of his hair, which she'd thought was a uniform rusty brown, only to find that in the direct sunlight it was really a dozen shades of rust and cinnamon, all the colors of autumn leaves.

It was when she found herself wishing he would kiss her that she knew it was time to put some distance between them. Not for her were the casual relationships experienced by other women her age. She'd never had a lover and didn't want one now. How could she possibly expose herself to that kind of temptation, knowing how disastrous it could be?

And Steve? What was he thinking, feeling, when he looked at her so intently sometimes, as though he were trying to get inside her skull? Generally, though, their conversation was light and full of laughter. When it did drift into something more serious, Steve was quick to shift it back to the impersonal. It seemed obvious that he was as wary of getting involved as she was. Surely, then, it was safe to give herself a little slack, to take him up on his offer to show her the sights of Tahoe and environs....

FOR THE NEXT three days they were together constantly. They took a ride on the sturdy little steamer that plied the waters of the lake, spent an evening at Caesar's Palace watching Johnny Cash perform and ate dinner at a Basque boardinghouse where ruddy-cheeked Basque waitresses served them thick vegetable soup, chicken cooked in a rich tomato sauce and picon punch to wash the food down with.

When Steve learned that Marma had never been to a casino, he drove her to one of the clubs in Reno and taught her the intricacies of baccarat, which he told her was the favorite of die-hard gamblers because it was a simple game in which the odds slightly favored the players.

She had a run of beginner's luck and didn't want to leave, but he coaxed her into cashing her chips, and told her sternly that winning big the first time out was the worst thing that could happen to a novice. She promised meekly to give up baccarat, not because she thought she was in any danger of becoming a compulsive gambler, but because it pleased her that he really seemed concerned. She didn't tell him that she'd always been lucky at games of chance, especially Old Maid, which she'd played with her brothers when she'd been a kid.

On the fourth day, she invited Steve to dinner. She realized by now that he knew his way around the fanciest of menus, so she fixed crisp and golden brown southern fried chicken, mashed potatoes and gravy, baked yams and succotash—Tennessee-style, with string beans and corn—and crusty hush puppies made from cornmeal, which she assured him would replace sourdough bread as his favorite.

After he'd stuffed himself, he groaned and pushed himself away from the table. "Why do they call them hush puppies?" he asked.

Leggs, who had been watching with anxious eyes, edged closer and gave one of his coughing barks.

Marma tossed the dog a piece of the crusty corn bread. "Hush, puppy," she said, and Steve laughed so hard that he almost upset his chair.

When he could speak again, he said, "You know, of course, that this meal, which tasted like ambrosia, was chock-full of such things as cholesterol and sodium?"

"So how do you explain all the old people, some in their nineties, who live in Duncan Holler?" she said— a little defensively because she knew he was right. "They've been eating this kind of food all their lives."

"Duncan *Holler*?" he said, his eyebrows twitching.

"Duncan *Hollow* to outsiders and Yankees," she said huffily. When Steve grinned, she tossed a hush puppy crumb at him. Before it had a chance to reach him, Leggs snatched it out of the air and swallowed it.

"Oh, you wanna play, do you?" Steve growled at Marma. He got out of his chair and advanced upon her, his eyes intent, and she shrieked with mock fear. But before he could reach her, Leggs was there in front of Marma, growling, his teeth bared at Steve.

Steve looked so disconcerted that Marma couldn't help laughing, and Leggs gave his master a look that could only have been described as sheepish. With his tail tucked between his legs, he slunk back to his corner. Steve didn't seem to notice. He was staring at Marma so fixedly that she stopped laughing. As if he were moving in slow motion, he pulled her to her feet and kissed her.

It was a gentle kiss that seemed to ask a question. It made her lips tingle, but it wasn't intrusive or demanding. She felt a warmth at the base of her throat, which spread to her face, and then to her breasts, until it finally enveloped her whole body. Her knees threatened to give way, and she put her arms around his neck, clinging to him instinctively. His thigh was pressing against her, so intimately that an ache, a need blossomed within her. It was a feeling so new to her that she felt disoriented and confused. She knew she should pull away, that she was playing with fire, but it felt so good, so right, being in his arms, knowing that he was sharing the heat in her blood.

The kiss deepened. His tongue, soft and supple and very hot, invaded her parted lips. She hadn't known how erotic it could be, this slow, relentless probing of a man's—of Steve's—tongue against the soft inner tissues of her mouth, that it could start a slow trembling in her thighs, and a need to move convulsively against the evidence of his own arousal. He groaned, deep in his throat; his hand moved—over her throat and down her arm, and with an instinct as old as time, she changed position, giving him access to her breast.

He caressed her breast, stroking it gently, but she didn't want gentleness. She wanted him to bare her breasts, to fondle them, suckle them—

And then he was turning away, moving out of reach, and she was standing there alone, bereft. What was wrong? Why had he stopped? Having kissed her, had he discovered that he really didn't want to make love to her, after all?

Her face flamed again, but this time it wasn't the flush of passion. She wanted to call him a bastard and tell him to get out of her life, but most of all she wanted to hide her face, to sink through the floor. But her pride came to her rescue, as it so often did, and when Steve finally turned around to face her, she was able to smile coolly.

"I didn't mean to lose my head like that," Steve said softly. "I couldn't resist that kiss, but I had no intention of taking advantage of the situation. I realize you hardly know me, that I was moving too fast. Am I forgiven?"

He sounded contrite—and he was taking all the responsibility for what had just happened. There had been an expertise to his lovemaking that was unmistakable, even to a novice like her. She hadn't resisted him, hadn't tried to escape, so it must have been apparent that she had wanted him to kiss her and had wanted more, as much as he had. So why had he stopped—and how was she supposed to interpret the expression in his eyes right now?

"Forgiven," she said lightly, playing his game—whatever it was. She told herself that she was relieved. Steve's kiss—a kiss and a few caresses was all it had been, after all—had taken her by surprise. If she'd been prepared, she could have handled it much better. And it wouldn't happen again. She'd make sure of that.

But oh, it had felt so good, being locked tightly in his arms, his warm mouth possessing hers, his hard body pressing into her softness. It had been so good to feel the strength, the gentleness of his hand on her breast, to taste his mouth, to inhale the musky male odor of his body....

Afraid that he might read too much on her face, she turned away and began clearing the table. Steve gathered up the cutlery and loaded it into the dishwasher.

"So how about a game of cards?" Steve said easily. "And just to make it interesting, I'll make you a little wager. Winner fixes breakfast tomorrow morning."

Marma eyed him carefully. She discovered that her pique had disappeared with his challenge. "Okay," she said, then added slyly, "how about making that the next *three* breakfasts?"

"Agreed. I think I can manage three more of your down-home breakfasts," he said amicably. "What's your pleasure? Poker okay?"

"Old Maid," she said, and went to get a deck of cards.

CHAPTER NINE

MARMA COULDN'T GET OVER how carefree she felt. After so many years of fighting against depression, self-doubt and, yes, guilt, she found it hard to accept the change. Every morning for the past five days, she had awakened with a feeling of anticipation, knowing that in a little while, Steve would be tapping at the door, loaded down with food, ready to fix another of the breakfasts he owed her because she'd really skunked him at Old Maid. When she answered his knock, he would greet her with a quip, then chastise her for cheating at cards, the amusement in his eyes matching the smile she found so devastating.

They would spend the rest of the day together, and when they returned from whatever excursion he had planned, he would drop her off at the lodge, only to return in a couple of hours. Then they would spend the whole long evening together, either going out for a dinner show at one of Tahoe's or Reno's fine dinner theaters or staying home to linger over a dinner she'd prepared, talking and laughing—always, always laughing. Or they might play cards. He taught her poker and rummy, and then groused because she always won. And when the card playing palled, they would end the evening sitting quietly and listening to jazz, country or light classical music from Arnold's eclectic collection.

And all the time, the sexual tension was building and building until sometimes Marma was afraid she might explode. She wouldn't let herself think of where it all might lead. It was enough to be with Steve, to enjoy the mornings, the sparkling air washed clean by night showers, the golden days, the cool evenings, all the other wonders of a Sierra spring.

That she might be falling in love, she wasn't ready to admit. Instead, she credited her high spirits to being on vacation, to the perfect weather, to her deep relief that Lisa Montgomery was safely back with her family—to anything and everything except the truth. Because once she admitted that Steve was the reason for her euphoria, then she would have to leave, retreat to the city, and she was having far too much fun. Indeed, she was quickly becoming addicted to happiness.

For this short period of time, until she returned to the city where numerous decisions about her future awaited her, she would relax and enjoy being with Steve. Later, she might regret letting down her guard, but for now, he made her feel cherished, wonderfully alive and carefree. *To hell with worrying,* she thought. *The future will take care of itself.*

To her relief, there had been no more visions. She was even beginning to hope that their appearance after a long hiatus had been a temporary aberration, that Lisa's second plunge into danger had simply been an echo from her childhood. Sometimes Marma did feel the initial dizziness, the scintillating light at the corner of her eye that heralded an attack, but by concentrating very hard, she managed to thwart an attack. These episodes always left her with agonizing migraines, but it was worth the pain not to have another hateful attack.

As she told Angie during one of the daily calls her roommate insisted she make, "I think I'm finally cured. I haven't had one of my spells since I came here."

"You make them sound like epilepsy," Angie said crossly. "It could be a mistake, fighting them the way you do."

"I know what I'm doing," Marma said.

"Okay, Ms Independence, but I still think you should learn to cope with them instead of denying them." Angie paused, then asked, "Have you heard from Mr. Flagg?"

"He's called several times," Marma said. "There's still no news about the kidnappers. I guess they were scared off. The police seem to think they left town."

"That's what the newspapers say, too. Mr. Flagg denied the psychic angle, and it dropped out of the news. But you be careful. I still don't think it was wise, going off on your own."

"I'm not on my own," Marma said impulsively. "I've met someone who—well, he has a cabin down the road from the lodge and we've been seeing a lot of each other."

"Hallelujah!" Angie exclaimed. "I thought it would never happen."

"Nothing's happened. He's just—well, Magic had a run-in with his dog and we started doing things together. It's nothing serious. We've been on a couple of picnics, took in some shows, had dinner together, that sort of thing."

"So tell me about him. What does he look like? Fill me in, please."

As Marma described Steve's rust-brown hair and brown eyes, it occurred to her that she sounded like a teenager, describing a boy she had a crush on to her best friend. Was that what it was, some kind of post-juvenile crush? After all, she'd never gone through that phase. She'd always been too reserved, and too aware of the dangers of getting involved with a man. Was she making a mistake, letting any kind of relationship with Steve develop when she knew it couldn't go beyond a certain point? Was she being fair to Steve? To herself?

She started, realizing Angie had asked her a question. "Say that again? I didn't catch it—"

"I asked when you were coming home. I miss you, Marmalade. I even miss that miserable freeloading cat of yours."

"Oh, come now! You know you're having a ball, playing house with Danny! 'Fess up—am I right?"

Angie giggled. "It's been a blast. Sort of a prenuptial honeymoon. Not that I've let him stay over, you understand. I have my reputation to consider. I intend to be a proper Italian bride and come to my wedding-night bed a virgin."

Marma laughed. She couldn't help it. She had been her roommate's confidante too long, and she knew Danny and Angie couldn't keep their hands off each other, that her friend hadn't been a virgin since shortly after she and Danny had met.

After she hung up, Marma was ashamed to admit that she was envious. Life was so simple for Angie. She'd had a wonderful childhood with a family that had loved her and spoiled her, followed by four years at a college that was far away from San Francisco. She'd known, while having her fling at independence, that she could go back home anytime she wanted to, that her family would always be there, solidly behind her. And then, after she'd worked just long enough for the business world to begin to pall, she'd met the man she wanted and he had fallen right in line. Marriage, the next phase, would present no obstacles. Angie would be the perfect wife and, in time, the perfect mother.

So yes, she did envy Angie—but not totally. Because if disaster ever came—God forbid—or if Angie's luck ever ran out, Marma wasn't sure her friend would be strong enough to weather the storm....

Marma shook her head, repudiating her own thoughts, and went to get dressed. In a few minutes, Steve would arrive for their evening walk and she was eager to see him, even though they'd been together most of the day. Somewhere up ahead, she knew, there would be a reckoning, and then she would have to pay for taking this detour from real life, but for now—well, she'd take her chances. After all, it might be safe. Steve hadn't tried to kiss her again, not even before saying good-night. Maybe he had reasons of his own for keeping the relationship cool, on the level of a friendship between two adults who just happened to have a few things in common....

WITH LEGGS, a huge white shadow, roaming far ahead, Steve strolled down the road toward his uncle's lodge. He enjoyed these twice-daily walks with Marma when he put aside his suspicions and simply enjoyed himself. It was surprising how comfortable he felt with her, as if he'd known her all his life. There was a playfulness behind her reserve that always managed to surprise him. Those Old Maid games she'd suckered him into, for instance, had honed his skills as a cook—at least as a breakfast cook. And how on earth did she manage to win so much at cards, even the games he had taught her? If she ever took up gambling as a profession, that kind of luck would get her barred from every casino in the country. And then there was that offbeat sense of humor—he'd laughed more with her than with any woman he'd ever dated.

Steve winced suddenly. Was that what they were doing? Dating? Yes, he took Marma places, showed her sights that seemed new to him because he was seeing them freshly, through her eyes. Sometimes it was difficult to remember that he wasn't there to have fun. In fact, it was becoming increasingly hard to reconcile the person his logic told him Marma had to be with the woman whose eyes shone when she watched Willie Nelson perform and who cried over a dead kitten they'd found in the woods. Was it possible that he'd been mistaken, after all—that there was some unknown factor to explain how she'd become involved in a nasty business like kidnapping? And where were her cohorts, the couple that had carried out the actual kidnapping? Waiting somewhere safe until she hit the jackpot and married Arnold? Were they blackmailing her into going along with their scheme?

Steve shook his head, suddenly angry at his continual attempts to find excuses for her, the very thing he'd warned himself about. It was disturbing as hell for a man who prided himself on his logic. In his world, two and two made four, and he was, if not a cynical man, certainly one who had been around the barn a few times.

Being a reporter had taught him to look beneath the surface of events, of people. Hell, that was what he was noted for, wasn't it? His exposés went far beyond what other reporters considered adequate. That was why his pieces invariably commanded attention—and often caused controversy. He'd never been sued for slander or libel, which proved that he was careful about his facts. And the facts in this case added up to one conclusion: that Marma was part of a gang of swindlers. And if he was harboring doubts, well, that only proved how effective she was.

Leggs's frantic barking aroused Steve from his thoughts. He laughed when he saw what the commotion was all about. Leggs was running in circles around Marma's cat, who was ignoring him disdainfully. With finicky feet, Magic was threading her way between the small pools of rainwater that filled the potholes in the road, and when Leggs, emboldened by the feline's lack of aggression, ventured too close, one velvet paw, claws retracted, reached out and gave him a warning tap on his long nose. Leggs retreated, but just a few feet. He sat down on the wide haunches that always reminded Steve of an old man's breeches, and stared at the cat with bewildered eyes, as if wondering why she was being so agreeable.

"You're something else," Steve told Magic. "An enigma, just like your mistress—and just as lovely."

Magic's tail twitched and she opened her mouth in a soundless meow. When she came up to Steve and began forming figure eights around his feet, Leggs whined jealously and pranced around the cat, emitting coughing little barks.

"I think it's time you two became friends," Steve said.

To his surprise, Magic deserted him, and in a leisurely manner, approached the wary Leggs. When she rubbed up against one of the dog's long, thin legs, emitting a rusty purr, he gave a yelp, collapsed on the wet ground, looking like a white-faced clown who had just taken a pratfall, and rolled over on his back, his spindly legs extended straight up in the air.

"Better watch it, fellow," Steve told him. "It's when the ladies start coming on to you that you have to be careful."

His words struck an unpleasant chord. For the past few days Marma had been surprisingly open with him. Maybe *he* was the one who should be watching it, he mused.

He walked on, followed by both Magic and Leggs. Marma, who was standing on the lodge veranda, waiting for him, eyed the animals as they came up. "Is the war over?" she asked.

"Maybe yes, maybe no." He pointed at the sky. "It's clouding over. I hope we can get our walk in before it starts raining."

"Oh, we've got half an hour before it starts. If we make it a short walk, we won't get wet," she said.

Steve eyed her quizzically. "Why half an hour? Do you have a hot line to the local weatherman?"

She flushed and said, "Just a hunch," then went into the lodge to get a sweater.

Following their favorite path, they tramped along the bank of a small creek that fed into the lake. The wind, fresh and moist and redolent with the resin odor of pine, aroused Steve's appetite. He was thinking about the joys of Marma's cooking when the first raindrop struck his face.

"Whoops—we'd better make a run for it," he said.

As they ran toward the lodge, the sky opened up and the rain came down in sheets, pounding their heads and obscuring the trees. By the time they reached the veranda, they were both wet to the skin, and Magic and Leggs, who were already there waiting for them, were soggy masses of fur.

Steve glanced at his watch. It was exactly thirty-three minutes since they'd started off. He started to comment about the accuracy of Marma's "hunch" and then, for no particular reason, he didn't.

Inside the lodge, Steve set a match to the kindling under the logs stacked in the fireplace. By the time the fire was emitting heat, both animals had been rubbed down with towels and were drying off at opposite sides of the hearth, emitting an odor that Marma called Eau de Wet Fur.

"I could use a hot shower," Steve told Marma. "And I'll need something to wear while my clothes are drying."

"I saw a man's robe in one of the closets. I'll get it for you. I'm sure Mr.—my friend won't mind if you borrow it."

She got the robe, pointed out the door to the guest bathroom, then left him to go take her own shower. When Steve returned to the kitchen, wearing a heavy silk robe that looked just like Arnold—solid and dignified and also a bit elegant—she had already started dinner preparations.

She, too, was wearing a robe, a plush maroon one that more than adequately hid her assets. Amused, Steve settled down at the breakfast bar with a cup of hot tea she gave him, and watched as she deftly turned pieces of floured round steak, which she called chicken-fried steak, in a big iron skillet. Steve's idea of a good steak was a thick porterhouse or filet mignon broiled over charcoal, but he reserved judgment. After all, he'd been wrong before. Who would have guessed that a cold, mushy concoction of cornmeal, fried golden brown, could be so delicious with a rasher of bacon?

He watched hungrily as Marma dumped grated raw potatoes and onions into a hot, well-oiled skillet and set it on a burner to sizzle while she put the finishing touches on a simple tomato-and-lettuce salad. She sprinkled the tomatoes with a pinch of sugar, and he teased her about refined sugar, but when he popped a wedge of the tomato in his mouth, he had to admit that the flavor was out of this world.

Looking smug, she poured him a glass of Chardonnay. "What—no dandelion wine?" he said. "I thought all you Southern types drank dandelion wine."

"Not at the Duncan house, we didn't. No alcohol at all, not even rum-ball cookies. Not all that many cookies of any kind, come to think of it."

As always when she mentioned her childhood, there was an expression in her eyes that he couldn't define. Sadness? Resignation? Or was it anger? He remembered Arnold's description of Marma's father, but he suppressed his sympathy. Was it Arnold's knowledge of what he'd called her "wretched childhood" that had made him so susceptible to her lies? Well, it wasn't going to happen to Arnold's nephew. Her unhappy childhood didn't excuse what she'd become. He had to keep remembering that....

"Is that why you're a teetotaler?" he asked.

"Not really. I tried alcohol a couple of times, but I didn't like the feeling of losing control, even a little bit."

Steve nodded. He felt the same way himself, which was why he seldom joined his colleagues for happy hour at the bar where they all congregated after work. Not that he didn't enjoy a cold beer now and then, or a glass of good wine with dinner.

"So you get the wine just for me?" he said. "Or is it for other guests, too?"

"I'm not expecting any visitors. The friend who lent me the lodge may drop by. Of course, he's a very busy man."

Steve's face stiffened. "I don't believe you've told me his name."

"No, I haven't, have I?" she said.

"He wouldn't be married, would he?"

A flush began at her throat. She turned away without answering him, and he immediately regretted his remark. "Sorry," he murmured. "None of my business, I know."

She still didn't answer, just cut some corn bread into wedges and arranged the pieces on a warm plate. When he asked her why the bread was white rather than yellow, she told him she'd used white corn meal.

"That's the way we do it at home," she said, so stiffly that he knew she hadn't forgotten his unfortunate remark.

But she warmed up as they ate, especially when he lavished praise upon the meal. They finished it off with strawberry shortcake, made with biscuits instead of cake, and after he'd taken his first bite of the luscious treat, he reflected that he'd seldom enjoyed a better meal—and where the hell had he gotten the impression that Southern cooking was indigestible and tasteless?

He helped Marma clear the table, and didn't argue when she told him that she'd finish cleaning up. Feeling pleasantly tired, he sighed with contentment as he sank onto one of the living room's rattan sofas. His eyes moved to the fireplace, and his laugh brought Marma out of the kitchen.

The two animals were on the same side of the fireplace now. Magic was lying inside the curve of Leggs's long legs. Her eyes were closed, and she was purring loudly, but Leggs's eyes were wide open. He was watching her with what could only be called pure terror.

"Now I know why she made up to Leggs," Steve said. "She couldn't resist his soft white belly hair."

Marma dropped a tape into the deck, then curled up at the other end of the sofa. He tensed, his nerves jangling, when her foot accidently brushed his thigh. She rubbed her temples with the tips of her fingers as if she had a headache, then yawned like a sleepy kitten and rested her head against the back of the sofa, her eyes closed. Barbra Streisand's voice, throbbing and much too sensual for Steve's peace of mind, filled the room. Was Marma or was she not wearing a bra and panties under that thick, enveloping robe?

He swallowed hard and told himself it was time to leave. Of course, it was still raining outside. And his clothes, which were tumbling in the dryer in the service room, probably weren't dry yet. A few minutes more couldn't matter—could they?

He finished off his wine—a surprisingly good wine, he noted—and tried to relax. In a little while, he'd put on his clothes again, collect his dog and take his leave. No big deal.

Later, he wasn't sure how it had happened. When Marma began to nod off, her chin dropping to her chest, it seemed only natural to pull her around so her head could rest in the hollow of his shoulder. Her mouth, slightly open, revealed a line of white teeth, and her breathing was so regular that he knew she was asleep.

Half smiling, he studied her face, so close that her breath fanned his cheek. If a face could have been compared to a flower, then Marma's was like a pansy, with the black, black hair that surrounded it, the fair skin and the blue eyes that sometimes took on the violet hue of evening shadows. Yes, Marma was like a pansy—but she wasn't as fragile, wasn't as shy.

It was her mouth that was his undoing. As if it were a magnet, he bent his head and pressed his lips against those dark rose lips....

Her body stiffened, and he expected her to pull away. Instead, she relaxed against him with a sigh, and he knew he'd made a mistake, that he'd been tempted beyond his power to resist. The kiss deepened; the pressure of his mouth forced open her lips and his tongue invaded that incredible softness, that sweet moistness.

The taste of strawberries and whipped cream mingled with a different kind of sweetness that he knew was all her own, and he took greedy possession of her mouth. He ran his fingertips along the soft swell of her throat, pausing when he reached her pulse, which leaped erratically beneath his touch. Her flesh was silky, resilient with youth; its heat burned his fingers, touching a part of him that had never been touched before.

The tenderness that quickened within him warned him he was playing with fire, but he was too far-gone to heed the cautioning voice. He wanted too much to keep touching and caressing her. He wanted to know every inch of her body intimately.

His fingers lingered at the small hollow at the base of her throat, then moved lower, pushing inside her robe so he could touch her breasts. Gently, he cupped one soft mound. *Just the right size for my hand,* he thought, and he nearly became undone at the sight of her perfect auréole, which was only a shade or two darker than her breasts.

He touched his tongue to her nipple, and she moaned deep in her throat and moved convulsively, arching her body against his. The involuntary movement excited him even more, and a surge of pure pleasure shook him. He pulled her closer, slipping his leg between her thighs, and she moaned as his hardened body pressed against her most sensitive flesh. When he kissed her again, her mouth softened and this time, it was her tongue that was the invader.

Carefully, he slid the robe off her shoulders, then pulled away slightly so he could drink in the sight of her naked body. In the light from the fireplace, her skin had a luminous glow, and he saw that a blush covered her from head to foot. Was it a sexual flush—or one of embarrassment? There was no mistaking her lack of experience. She didn't even know how to kiss properly. Not that he was complaining. Just touching her was almost enough to send him over the edge, and it was all he could do not to take her without preliminaries or foreplay.

But it was too soon. Although she trembled from wanting him, instinct told him that she wasn't yet ready, so he set about preparing her for ultimate intimacy.

Gently, he caressed her breasts until she was moving frantically against him. He left her breasts and brushed her body with butterfly kisses, moving downward, tantalizing her by lingering at her navel for a long time before finally reaching the soft, dark mound below. She gasped as he probed the sweet mysteries of her body with his tongue, and then she was writhing beneath him, her eyes glazed, her swollen lips the color of ripe plums. And still he played with her, seducing her with his fingers, his mouth and tongue. Only when she reached out to touch his swollen shaft, uttering small, inarticulate sounds, did he finally spread her thighs and position himself above her.

As he stared down into her passion-drugged eyes, he was sure he'd never seen anything lovelier or more alluring. How could he have thought that she wasn't as beautiful as some of the other women he'd been intimate with? She surged upward, opening herself fully to him, and finally he took her with a growl of triumph.

He had known she was inexperienced but he hadn't expected her to be a virgin, not at twenty-four, not with that mouth, those eyes, that body. By the time he realized what the barrier that thwarted his invasion was, it was already too late. He was out of control, plunging, sinking, sheathing himself in the moist heat of her body. Even when she gave a small, mewling cry of pain, he couldn't stop. For a moment, she lay quietly, as if stunned, and then she was matching him thrust for thrust, her face contorted not with pain but with passion, the very awkwardness of her movements incredibly erotic because he knew no man had ever possessed her sweetness before.

But when he finally collapsed on her, spent and weak, he knew that she was still unsatisfied. Although his own hunger was appeased, he didn't roll away from her. Instead, he kissed her gently, letting his facile tongue speak for him, saying without words that he recognized her frustration, that he would not leave her until she was satisfied, too.

For a long time, he fondled her breasts, then suckled them gently, before he slipped lower down on her body to stroke her soft belly and the spongy thatch below. Using his mouth, his hot tongue, he brought her to the peak of passion, and when she was writhing against him, her eyes wild, he discovered that he was aroused again, too. He sank into her enveloping softness, moving slightly forward and upward, using his knowledge of women and their needs to bring her the ultimate pleasure. Only when he heard her keening cry and felt the vibrations of climax deep inside her did he allow himself his own peak of ecstasy.

And it was sweet, so sweet, that when they both were finally spent, still holding each other tightly, his eyes were moist with tears.

It was the sweetness, the feeling of rightness, that dissolved something hard and cynical and too wise in him. Suddenly, he didn't give a damn about evidence or facts or logic. Whatever the real explanation, he no longer believed that Marma was a predator who preyed upon other people's credulity and weaknesses.

"Did I hurt you?" he murmured against her ear. She shook hear head, her eyes dark. Because of passion or regret, he wondered.

"Am I too heavy for you?"

A tiny smile lifted the corners of her mouth. "I like you there," she said.

"Then I'll stay a little longer," he said.

He stroked her incredibly thick, ebony mane, then her eyelids and her lush, full lips. He tried to memorize the feel of her high, flat cheekbones and the hollows beneath, under his fingertips.

Shyly, she touched him back, her fingertips feather-light against his lips, his jawline and his thick eyebrows. Now he was sure it was stars, not dark shadows, he saw in the depths of her eyes. How was it possible that she had been on her own so long and yet hadn't experienced sex before, he asked himself again.

But who was complaining? He was a lucky man to have been the first to taste her sweet honey....

He kissed her, and she opened her lips to admit his agile tongue, letting him explore the soft, moist depths of her mouth to his content. Then he slid his hands under her hips, and though he was still inside her, he was too satiated at the moment to feel anything but tenderness.

In response she ran the palms of her hands over the relaxed muscles of his shoulders, exploring his shoulder blades and the small of his taut back. Then she slid out from under him, but not to leave the sofa. She pushed his side, urging him to turn over, and when he was lying on his back, she bent over him, her hair falling around his hips like threads of black silk. Like a child examining a new toy, she touched his flaccid shaft—no, not flaccid, not with her fingers playing erotic little games, fondling him as he had fondled her earlier. Did she know what she was doing to him, he wondered, or was she simply curious about the male body?

His breath caught. Now she was stroking him, her fingers enveloping him, and he realized that she was trying to return his earlier generosity. Her touch was clumsy, inexperienced, but no woman had ever aroused him like this before, making him groan with a pleasure that bordered on pain, sending him half out of his mind. When he felt himself losing control, he reached for her, and pulled her down until she was straddling him. He entered her for the third time and she was ready for him, her need as great as his.

It seemed like a miracle—no, it *was* a miracle that she wanted him again so quickly, that she moved above him without embarrassment, her eyes glowing, her lovely breasts swinging to the erotic rhythm of love....

They fell asleep in each others' arms, using Arnold's robe as a cover. When Steve awakened in the middle of the night, it was because Leggs, whining softly, had thrust the cold tip of his nose into his master's ear. Steve eased away from Marma and started to sit up, only to pause, arrested by her sleeping face.

How young and vulnerable she looked with all her defenses down, with her face softly illuminated by the dying embers of the fire. And how quickly she had become the most important thing in his life. He wanted her, but not just for sex. He wanted to come home to her at night, to share her life as well as her bed. He wanted her to have his babies, wanted the security of knowing that in the December of his life, she would still be there for him.

The question was—did she feel the same way? She obviously found him desirable, or she never would have allowed him to make love to her. To still be a virgin at twenty-four, a woman as exciting as Marma must have developed strong defenses. She wouldn't be easily seduced by a man she didn't have strong feelings for. Or would she? Maybe it was simply a case of a frustrated sex drive that had finally matured. He had to be realistic and admit that it was possible she didn't love him and—no, he couldn't accept that. He *had* to believe that she felt the same way he did. Anything else would mean pure misery.

He put his borrowed robe on and let Leggs out through the patio door. A soft touch against his ankle made him jump—until he realized it was Magic.

He let her out, too, but he didn't rejoin Marma on the sofa. Instead, he slid his arms under her shoulders and legs, carried her limp body to the bed in the master bedroom and tucked her under the covers.

He kissed her gently, unable to resist, and she opened her eyes, gave him a sleepy smile, then went back to sleep. When he crawled in beside her warm, naked body, it was all he could do not to wake her and make love to her again.

He fell asleep, her head cradled on his shoulder, and his last thought before he drifted off was that soon he had to tell her the truth, that he was Arnold's nephew, here at his uncle's request to "keep an eye" on her. He'd be honest with her, not hold anything back—including his former suspicions—or try to put his actions in a better light. And then he'd tell her that he loved her. . . .

CHAPTER TEN

AFTER ALL THE EXCITEMENT of the night before, Marma should have slept late, but she awakened as usual just as the first flush of dawn was lighting the sky. For a long time, she lay there, full of wonder and a deep contentment that was marred only slightly by a niggling little doubt. Had it really happened? Had she and Steve, a man she hardly knew, really become lovers last night?

She shifted her position and the movement made her wince. Yes, it had happened. There was definitely physical proof that she was no longer a virgin. Steve and she had made love three times, and it had been the most exciting thing that had ever happened to her. And now she had a lover—or was that the right term for a man who might very well consider her a holiday fling, a one-night stand? Did Steve, whose sleeping presence she was now aware of beside her in the bed, think of her simply as someone he'd been sexually attracted to, an easy conquest? He hadn't said he loved her, hadn't said anything to make her believe she was special to him.

And even if he did feel the way she did, there was no future for them. Because nothing had really changed—except that she'd lost her virginity. It still wasn't fair to start a serious relationship with a man who might be hurt by an affair that would inevitably end with them going separate ways. How could she possibly commit herself to anything deeper, even if Steve would want that?

But oh, she did wish it could be different! She wanted to belong to Steve permanently, to know that he really cared, to have him comfort her when she needed it, to love her, to cherish her, just as she would love and cherish him. Already, she had gone too far; she had allowed herself to be caught in the trap of a sexual drive that she hadn't known could be so overwhelming. It was so hard to think of Steve as a temporary lover. Last night had been wonderful, she thought, sighing. Had it been wonderful to Steve, too?

She sighed again and opened her eyes to find herself looking directly into Steve's dark eyes. He was leaning on one elbow, watching her, and his expression was thoughtful, distant. Was he already regretting the previous night?

Then Steve smiled, and everything changed. A recklessness, a feeling that there was no tomorrow, swept through her. He kissed her, his lips warm and firm, and her heart swelled until she was afraid it might burst. She slid her arms around his neck, arching her body against his, her fingers tangled in his thick hair. As the kiss deepened and he touched her breast, everything faded except her own aroused senses, and nothing mattered except Steve—his caresses, his masculine, virile body and his skillful lovemaking.

But afterward, when she was dressed and fixing breakfast, she discovered that the doubts were still there, nagging at the back of her mind. She was grating cheese for an omelet, only half listening to Steve's cheerful chatter, when he took the grater from her hand and turned her around to face him.

"Okay. Out with it. Are you worried about what happened last night?"

She wouldn't look at him. "Of course not."

"You're a terrible liar. Good thing you're not a lawyer. You'd lose every case you took."

"I really don't know what you mean, Steve."

"Come on. A woman loses her virginity only once. It must be a traumatic—well, crossing over. And you're not a teenager. You're a beautiful, mature woman who has never known a man, which must have been a conscious decision. So it must be particularly difficult for you. I just want you to know that I am honored—deeply honored—that it was me you chose."

She looked up at him and tears clouded her sight. Suddenly, everything slipped into place and was right—at least for now.

"So am I," she said, and then she was in his arms, and he was hugging her tightly, and kissing her passionately.

After breakfast, they went for a walk, and she made the discovery that something strange had happened while she'd slept. Everything looked different— sharper, clearer. The sky was bluer and the clouds whiter. She felt exhilarated, euphoric. Did other women get this same high after they lost their virginity to the man they loved?

"God, I feel good this morning," Steve said, echoing her thoughts. He took her hand and smiled down at her. "If I didn't think it would scare you, I'd thump my chest like a gorilla and howl like a wolf."

Marma laughed, her doubts fading. She also made a decision. For these few precious days, she would put everything except Steve out of her mind. She would live for the moment—and let the future take care of itself.

DURING THE NEXT FEW DAYS, they took advantage of the wonderful playground that is Tahoe. One afternoon, they rented a speedboat and explored the lake from end to end. The next, they borrowed fishing tackle from the lodge and fished off a rickety pier. Steve caught a large bass, which Marma promptly insisted he return to the water.

They picnicked twice at their favorite place amid the pines, played tennis at a public court in Reno and snuck into a hotel swimming pool to splash around for a couple of hours. Steve, whose swimming was smooth and masterful, laughed at Marma's erratic stroke, but she got the last laugh when she almost beat him in a race.

When they passed through one of the gambling rooms on their way to a casino's dinner club, Marma stopped to watch a blackjack game and finally coaxed Steve into letting her try her luck. He found a two-dollar table with two empty seats and taught her the fundamentals. But when she had a streak of luck and he decided she was in danger of catching what he called "gambler's fever," he dragged her, protesting, off her perch at the blackjack table.

As she gloated over her winnings, he told her it was beginner's luck and that she wasn't even to look at a blackjack table again or he'd have to do something drastic—such as keeping her busy in bed day and night.

They ate at the Basque boardinghouse again, feasting on ham and beans and crusty kettle bread, and when the diners who shared the long, communal table took them for newlyweds and toasted them with picon punch, Marma only blushed and didn't correct them—and neither did Steve.

When Marma tried to sum up these golden days with one word, the first that occurred to her was *fun*. But other words were in the running, too: euphoria; happy; love. . . .

She had always been a sober person, but it seemed to her that she and Steve were always laughing at something. He even laughed at the jokes she stole from Angie, though, more often than not, she messed up the punch line. And she was convulsed by Steve's atrocious puns. But when they ducked into a casino to get out of a sudden shower, the sight of a row of little old ladies sitting at the slot machines with piles of coins in front of them, their winkled arms relentlessly working the levers, didn't make her laugh. Instead, it made her want to cry.

All those lonely people, she thought with the insight of someone who had been on the outside of things most of her life. How sad that they should try to find consolation for the love and companionship they'd lost—or never had—in a slot machine or at a blackjack table.

She looked at Steve and saw her own pity reflected in his eyes, and she knew that no matter what happened in the future, she still had this, a taste of what it meant to have someone with whom to share her feelings, her view of life.

Time passed by quickly. During the days they played, and at night they made love. Sometimes they moved in a leisurely fashion as they explored their sexuality to the limit, learning how to please each other, while at other times, their lovemaking was almost frenzied, and left them exhausted and shattered afterward.

Marma had never thought of herself as a sensual person. Now she was discovering a different Marma, one with an incredibly strong sexual appetite that even Steve's most casual touch brought to life. She considered it a good omen that since she and Steve became lovers, she'd had no nightmares, no visions and no migraines or panic attacks. It was as if loving Steve had made her immune to the terrors that had once haunted her.

Afraid to break her emotional high, she wouldn't allow herself to think of the future, of her decision to never become seriously involved with a man. Even so, she was practical enough to be glad when, after their first night together, Steve matter-of-factly started using protection when they made love. If she'd been afraid that it might make their lovemaking less spontaneous, she'd been wrong because Steve made it a part of their foreplay. Only in the deepest recesses of her mind, at those times when she awakened late at night, did a cold little voice warn her that in the end, she would have to pay for these days of happiness, of letting go.

One thing that she never doubted was the depth of Steve's passion for her. Every time he looked at her, his eyes darkened almost to black, and when he touched her, his hands trembled slightly. For all his fierce sexual drive, he was a generous lover, and when they made love, he taught her things about herself she hadn't known: that the soft spots behind her ears were erogenous zones, that the small, dimple-like depressions behind her knees were so sensitive that a kiss there made her whole body quicken. And when he stroked, ever so lightly, the hidden bud of sensation, the essence of her sexuality that she'd known existed only in an academic way, she grew weak and trembly and moist, ready for the act of love.

And then, a week after they became lovers, her happiness, her whole world, collapsed like a burst soap bubble.

THAT MORNING, Steve had declared that he would be chef, host and general flunky for dinner, that it was time he showed off his cooking skills. Since he added loftily that he didn't need her help, she luxuriated in a long, leisurely bath, and took her time washing and blow-drying her hair and putting on a new dress that she'd bought at a Reno boutique—a long, silky shift that clung to her body, creating a graceful line from her shoulders to her ankles.

Steve had bought her what he called an "unbirthday gift" at a hotel gift shop, a large bottle of Joy perfume, an extravagance that made her wonder for the first time about his financial situation. He never seemed to worry about money, she noted, although some of the places he took her to were extremely expensive. On the other hand, he was just as apt to stop at a diner or a truck stop for lunch, declaring that it had the best hamburgers or chili or tacos in Nevada.

His station wagon, although not flashy, was new, and looked like a very expensive model—she knew this because she'd been saving for a car for a long time and was constantly checking out prices. His daytime clothes were invariably casual—jeans and boots and open-necked shirts—as were the sport jackets he wore out to dinner, but she couldn't help noting that the boots looked handmade, and the jackets were cashmere or English tweed—and impeccably tailored.

So which was the true reflection of his bank account—the jeans that could be bought in any chain store, or the expensive sport jackets and boots? She hoped it was the former. The suspicion that he might possibly be rich troubled her because it seemed to put a distance between them.

As she dabbed some Joy behind her ears, she pushed the uneasiness out of her mind. She touched the stopper to other pulse points, not neglecting the valley between her breasts, which she knew would get lots of attention before the night was over. Smiling to herself, she added an extra dab to her insteps and the dimples behind her knees.

Since there was a moon, she decided to walk the few hundred yards to Steve's cabin. With Magic trailing behind on noiseless paws, she strolled through the lambent moonlight, enjoying the sounds of the wind rushing through the pines, and an owl's haunting cry. The night breeze caressed her flushed cheeks, reminding her of Steve's touch when he made love to her. Did he know how exciting it was to a woman to be touched lightly, to be seduced instead of simply being taken?

Was the way he made love instinctive, she wondered, or had some woman—women?—taught him love skills, as he was teaching her?

What did it really matter? He was with her now, and the past was the past. They were good together, she who had no sexual history and Steve, who may or may not have been with many women before he met her. If he had loved other women, he never mentioned them—for which she was thankful. Not because she was jealous. How could she be when it was so obvious that he wanted only her—at least for now. But talking about other lovers would surely mar the perfection of their time together....

Up ahead, the lights of Steve's cabin spilled out into the night. As she ran up the front steps, she heard his cheery, off-key whistle in the kitchen. Rather than interrupt him by knocking, she opened the door and let herself in. It had delighted her when she had realized that Steve, who loved music, wasn't capable of carrying a tune. Somehow, this imperfection made him more lovable, more human. As she stood in the kitchen doorway, watching him, she thought how familiar, how beloved every inch of that lithe, well-formed body was to her already.

A familiar warmth startled her, and when Steve looked up, finally aware of her presence, she found herself blushing. He laughed softly and then he was holding her, kissing her as if he never meant to let her go.

She broke away finally. "I'm famished. What's for supper?"

"What a greedy little gal you are. How do you stay so thin?"

"Metabolism. I was born with the right kind."

"Does it run in your family?"

"No, my older sister and brothers are all inclined to be stocky."

"They're all older than you?"

"I was the youngest by several years, which is probably why I was never close to them." She turned away from his searching eyes and went to the range to lift the cover on a pot. "Mmm. Smells good. Looks good. What is is, anyway?"

"Escargot stew," he said blandly.

She looked at him in dismay. "Snails? I—are you kidding me?"

He cocked his finger at her. "Gotcha! Snails stewed for several hours, my naive friend, would be an abomination. It's a ragout. I got the recipe when I was living in New York. My landlady was Hungarian and she was always taking pity on her poor underfed bachelor tenant and inviting me for dinner. Of course, she also invited all her friends' unmarried daughters, but it was worth it because she was famous for her ragouts."

"Sounds like Angie. She keeps parading her bachelor cousins in front of me."

"But it's never worked? No sparks?"

"Not until lately," she said, smiling into his eyes.

"If you keep looking at me like that, you'll be sorry," he said, his voice uneven.

She widened her eyes in mock surprise. "Why on earth would I be sorry?"

He laid down the wooden spoon he was holding, turned down the heat under the stew and swept her up in his arms, all in the space of a few seconds. He had her dress unzipped before they reached the bedroom door, and by the time he laid her on the bed, she was naked except for her sandals.

He knelt by the bed and took them off, paying homage to her toes in a most delightful way by spreading them and touching his tongue to the sensitive flesh between. When he moved his attention to her instep, she was glad she'd dabbed perfume there because he breathed in deeply and gave an exaggerated groan.

"Smart you," he said, his warm breath sending little sensory signals up her legs to her thighs, "not to wear a bra."

He slid out of his clothes and then joined her on the bed. He touched her in the ways she had come to crave, stroking and fondling her, kissing her in unorthodox places like her nape, which she had recently discovered was incredibly sensitive.

"The Japanese know how seductive the nape can be," he'd told her once.

As he went on kissing her, never lingering too long at any one place, the tension building inside her became unbearable. Only after he'd brought her to the peak of ecstasy did he take his own pleasure. His thoughtfulness, as always, touched her, and afterward, she kissed him on each cheek, then on his mouth, and told him that she loved him.

It was the first time she'd said it out loud, and for a long moment, he stared at her, his eyes unreadable, as if her words troubled him. And then he kissed her back, a hard, fierce kiss, and told her that she was his joy, his passion, his obsession. As they made love again, she told herself that his choice of words didn't matter, that they were just the same as saying he loved her, too.

It was the delicious odor of paprika and stewing meat that finally returned them to reality. When they had dressed and gone to the kitchen, Steve handed her a paring knife and got a salad spinner, loaded with green vegetables, from the refrigerator.

"Here, make yourself useful, woman. I just remembered that I forgot something very important—the dessert. I have to get it from the station wagon. I want this to be a particularly memorable dinner because afterward, I have something to tell you that—that needs to be said. So don't go away."

As if I would, she thought, staring after him. *No, Steve, I won't go away....*

She fixed the salad, then checked the table, which was already set. The dishes and cutlery that came with the cabin were utilitarian, but Steve had picked a handful of violets and had put them in a blue cup; the makeshift centerpiece added a festive look to the table.

The lad's okay, she thought, smiling to herself. Then: *I wonder what he has to tell me that "needs to be said"?*

She was wondering what was taking Steve so long when a cold draft from the door reminded her that she wasn't wearing panties under her shift. For some reason, that embarrassed her. How odd: when they made love, she forgot all her inhibitions. So why did she feel so uncomfortable just because she'd dressed so quickly afterward that she'd forgotten to put her panties back on? Was it because leaving them beside Steve's bed reminded her of a dozen bad jokes she'd heard during her college years? Maybe she hadn't changed as much as she'd thought. Was that good or bad? she asked herself.

She went into the bedroom and picked up her panties from the floor. Grimacing a little, she slipped them on. Her arm brushed a sheet of thick, creamy paper that was lying on the corner of a chest of drawers and it tumbled to the floor. As she bent to pick it up, her own name, written in a tight, neat handwriting, caught her attention.

She didn't make a conscious decision to read the letter. The words seemed to leap off the page at her, burning themselves into her brain.

Why the devil haven't you called me, Steve? And why didn't you rent a cabin with a phone so I could get in touch with you without writing a blasted letter? You know I hate writing letters!

I hope you're keeping a close eye on Marma, as promised. I feel responsible for her, even though the danger is over now that the kidnappers are in custody. And I think it's about time you told Marma that you're my nephew. She's going to find out eventually anyway—and then she's going to know it wasn't an accident that you two met.

She's a very sensitive and vulnerable young woman, you know—and you happen to be an attractive man. It's just possible she might have read too much into your attention. Since you harbor suspicions about her, this could lead to trouble, so I hope you've been careful not to give off any false signals. And I hope to hell she never finds out about your ridiculous suspicion that she's involved in a scam to extort money from me—"

There was more, but the letter fell from Marma's nerveless hand and fluttered to the floor. She bent stiffly to pick it up and her eyes moved to the bottom of the page. The letter was signed only with the initial A, but it didn't matter. She already knew who had written it.

She was still standing there, holding Arnold's letter, when Steve returned to the cabin.

"Where are you, honey?" he called from the living room. "Would you believe I dropped my key and had to root around in the grass for it? Leggs wasn't any help. He thought I was playing a game and—"

His voice broke off as he came into the bedroom. He stared at the letter in her hand and his eyes filled with consternation. "I'm sorry, Marma," he said quickly. "That was what I was going to tell you tonight."

His words released her from her paralysis. A storm of rage swept through her. She raised her hand and slapped him—hard. Although his head rocked backward and she knew the blow must have stung, he didn't retaliate, didn't defend himself—not even when she slapped him again.

"Now that you've got that out of your system, are you ready to listen to me?" he said.

"I don't want to hear anything you have to say, you bastard," she stormed. "I want you out of my sight, out of my life. Your uncle was right. I did read too much in your—your attention. I'll never make that particular mistake again."

He flinched at the venom in her voice, but his eyes never wavered. "Yes, I did lie to you. Arnold Flagg is my uncle, the one I told you about who raised me. I owe him more than I can ever repay. When I found out he'd put you through college, that he was convinced you'd saved Lisa's life with paranormal powers, that you had done it again when she was kidnapped, it was natural I'd be suspicious of you."

"Oh, yes, very natural. A young woman and an older man: what did you really think was going on between your uncle and me?"

His jaw tightened, but he went on doggedly. "I admit something like that occurred to me. And yes, I wrangled an invitation to the banquet for the sole purpose of looking you over. And it wasn't an accident that I wandered into your office, pretending I was looking for the personnel department. I'd heard someone call you Marma on the elevator and I was curious to see the woman my uncle was—so impressed with. Later, when Arnold told me you were staying at his lodge and asked me to keep an eye on you, I jumped at the chance, hoping that I could find a way to discredit you in Arnold's eyes."

He paused, and when he went on, his voice had lost its dispassion. "Then everything changed. I got to know you, and you were nothing like I had expected. I knew someone who cried over a dead kitten couldn't deliberately set out to victimize Arnold. Whatever those people did to get you involved in their scheme, it doesn't matter—"

"What are you talking about?" Marma interrupted. "Surely, you don't think—but you *do* think I was part of the kidnapping scheme, don't you?"

"You have the wrong tense. I did think it was possible, but now I'm not sure. I do know you couldn't hurt anyone, much less a helpless fifteen-year-old girl."

Marma stared at him; something he'd said earlier didn't make sense. "Why did you say Arnold put me through college? I went through Brown on a scholarship that came from the Pershing Foundation. He had nothing to do with it. He did ask his recruiter to offer me a management trainee's job after graduation, but I filled all the requirements and I've earned my promotions, too. My work record is proof of that—and why am I standing here, defending myself, anyway? I don't owe you any explanations—"

"Are you telling me you didn't know that Arnold set up the Pershing Foundation, that he arranged for you to get that scholarship?"

"I wouldn't try to tell you anything. You can believe what you want—"

She broke off for the reason that her words sounded hollow, even to her own ears. No wonder her adviser had commented more than once that the scholarship seemed tailor-made for her, down to requiring that the recipient came from a "religious" home. How could she have been so naive? She had suspected nothing. But why would she have, when she hadn't even known that Arnold Flagg existed, much less that he was Lisa's grandfather?

"Okay," Steve said, his tone so reasonable that she wanted to scream. "I believe you. You never suspected that Arnold arranged for your scholarship. But surely you suspected something when you were recruited by his bank. It must have seemed too much of a coincidence—''

"Why would I think that? I had no idea the president of Flagg Banks was related to Lisa Montgomery, not until a couple of weeks ago when he told me his granddaughter had been kidnapped and asked for my help." Despite herself, her voice rose. "Her name is Montgomery, not Flagg—how could I possibly associate her with Arnold?"

"Look, I'm handling this all wrong. You're on the defensive, although God knows I'm not accusing you of anything. Why don't we give ourselves time to—to cool down? I don't happen to believe in ESP or clairvoyance or any of the rest of that mumbo jumbo, but I'm willing to believe that *you* do. The details of how you got involved in Lisa's kidnapping aren't important. What you decide to do now that the guilty parties have been caught is up to you. If you want to tell your story to the police, okay. But if you decide not to, there's enough evidence against those two to put them behind bars without your testimony. Either way, I'll do everything in my power to back you up—including getting you the best lawyer in the country. And when the record is clear, then we can put it all behind us and go on from there. Is it a bargain?"

Marma's disillusionment was complete. She stared into the eyes of the man who had initiated her to love, who had given her so much happiness, and she realized she didn't know him at all. He had deceived her, not directly, but by inference—by the things he hadn't told her. What else had he done or said to deceive her? That she was his joy, his passion, his obsession?

Maybe she was—but he still hadn't trusted her enough to tell her the truth *before* they had become lovers.

It didn't help that he'd never promised her anything, never really said he loved her. Okay, he wasn't a total liar, just a man who had cultivated her friendship and seduced her, all the time believing her to be part of a swindle. How much of his passion had stemmed from his determination to protect his uncle? And what did he want from her now? Now that she'd caught him out, why was he continuing the charade? Was he afraid of Arnold finding out that he'd taken advantage of her trust to seduce her?

"What about it, Marma?" Steve said. "Can we start from scratch?"

An ache started up between Marma's shoulder blades; she realized she was holding herself so stiffly that all her muscles where bunched and tense. She took a deep breath and let it out slowly.

"Go to hell," she said.

She pushed past Steve and was running by the time she reached the veranda. Only later would it register that a large chocolate cake was sitting in the place of honor in the middle of the dinner table. *An unbirthday cake?* she would think painfully.

She reached the veranda and paused only to scoop up her cat, then hurried down the road, knowing she was fleeing not only from disillusionment but from temptation as well. Steve still had so much power over her, God help her, that she didn't dare take a chance that he might say something, do something, that could make her weaken—and open her to more pain.

Even if she could convince him that she wasn't involved—innocently or not—in Lisa's kidnapping, she knew she could never fully convince him that she was clairvoyant and prescient. His reservations would always be there—and she had lived with distrust and intolerance most of her life because of what she was. She couldn't—wouldn't—do it again.

Steve didn't come after her, not then. Later, she would wonder why he hadn't followed her immediately. When she reached the lodge, she began packing, ruthlessly wadding up her clothes and thrusting them into her canvas suitcase. She had already changed into jeans and a sweater by the time Steve came. She'd locked the door upon reaching the lodge, and he pounded on it for several minutes, finally calling to her that he would come back later when she'd had a chance to calm down.

As soon as his station wagon was gone, she tossed her luggage into her rented car, stuffed a protesting Magic into the back seat, then took off at a reckless speed, not caring about safety or traffic tickets or anything except escape.

She spent the night in a small motel on the outskirts of Truckee. The bed was comfortable, the silence restful and the temperature in the room an even sixty, but still she couldn't fall asleep. Her thoughts raced in circles, around and around, full of images of her quarrel with Steve, loaded with the things she wished she'd said to him—and a few things she wished she hadn't said.

So many mistakes—why hadn't she thought of the inconsistencies of her relationship with Steve? He'd been so evasive about his work, about his past. She hadn't even known if he was a native of San Francisco although once he'd said something about living in New York. What did he do for a living, if anything? Somehow she very much doubted he was in public relations.

And the coincidence of accidently meeting him for the third time in an out-of-the-way place like Tahoe—that alone should have made her suspicious. But no, she'd wanted to believe that he was just what he seemed. Was that why she had asked him so few questions about himself? All the time, he must have been laughing at her, setting her up for a fall. Had seduction been part of his original plan—or had she made it so easy for him that he hadn't been able to resist temptation?

It was in the morning, after hours of soul-searching, of reviewing her life and listing her mistakes, some old and some recent, that she came to a conclusion. She had been incredibly stupid. No wonder Steve had shown disbelief when she had denied that Arnold had put her through college.

Why had she never questioned that oh-so-convenient scholarship with its generous living allowance? It had been so timely, and the requirements had seemed honed for her particular circumstances—and it had been offered only a few weeks after Papa had turned down the reward the Montgomerys had tried to give her. Had Papa suspected the truth? Was that why he'd been so angry when she told him she was going to accept it? It didn't do any good to say that she hadn't known of Arnold's existence then. She'd been aware that the Montgomerys were rich and very grateful. She should have put two and two together and guessed the truth.

Well, she'd accepted charity from Arnold Flagg for the last time. She'd been proud of her progress at work, but now she knew it had come, at least in part, because Arnold had directed it. Had Arnold given Charlotte orders to promote her over others in the department who had been there longer? At the time, she had thought she'd gotten her relatively quick promotion because she had worked so hard. *How naive can you get!* she thought furiously. Charlotte was probably convinced that Arnold was taking care of a mistress. How many others at work believed that?

She was sure of one thing: she could never return to her old job. Her pride—that stiff-necked pride that she'd inherited from Papa—wouldn't permit it. From now on, she was on her own, without the crutch—and curse—of other people's gratitude. And if that meant starting all over again, so be it. If she ever hoped to forget the past and go on from there, she had to clean the slate, once and for all. From now on, she meant to do things right. No more running away when things got rough—which meant that before she handed in her resignation, she owed it to Arnold, whose intentions had been good, to tell him why she was quitting. It wouldn't be fair to resign without talking to him first.

And then—yes, then she was going to set another part of her life in order. It was time to go home to see Papa and her family. He might not want to hear what she had to say, but she had to tell him she was sorry that she hadn't been honest with him, that she'd applied for the scholarship without letting him know. Not that she regretted going to college. Papa was wrong about that. But she shouldn't have shamed him by going behind his back—and she should have kept on writing to him, no matter if he did return her letters.

So it was time to make her peace with Papa—and with her family. And if she told them she was sorry and did it without recriminations or anger, then maybe she could find, if not happiness, at least a small peace for herself in her new life.

CHAPTER ELEVEN

DESPITE MARMA'S DETERMINATION to tie up the threads of her old life before she started a new one, she found herself dreading her decision to call Arnold Flagg to let him know, as tactfully as possible, that she wouldn't be returning to her job. There were so many things she couldn't say to him, not without hurting him, that she was sure the conversation would be very difficult.

Although it was tempting to blame him for creating such havoc in her life by sending Steve to "keep an eye" on her, her own highly developed sense of fairness prevented her from making that mistake. Arnold's intentions had been unassailable. He'd wanted to protect her, and so he'd done what he'd thought best: enlisted Steve's help to look after her. The fact that she'd fallen in love with Steve and had ended up with a slightly bent heart had nothing to do with his uncle.

Rather than put it off any longer and maybe lose her courage, she called him the afternoon of her return from Tahoe. As she used the private number he'd given her, she couldn't help remembering his wink as he'd told her that it would bypass the switchboard and his secretary, who was very protective of him—something she already knew.

"This is Marma Duncan," she said when his voice, always so surprisingly deep, answered on the third ring.

"Thank God—are you all right?"

"Yes, I'm fine. Why wouldn't I be?"

"I've been trying to reach you since last evening. Is the phone at the lodge out of order?"

"Not that I know of. However, I'm not at the lodge. I came back to the city early this morning."

"Oh? Then you must already know about the police picking up the couple that kidnapped Lisa. I've been trying to reach you ever since the news broke last night. I thought you'd have some questions about it."

"I do. According to the radio report I heard, they were arrested several days ago. Is there any reason why I wasn't notified?"

"When the police questioned the woman, she decided to turn state's evidence, hoping for a lighter sentence. She told them a third party was involved in the kidnapping, a man who'd once worked for my son-in-law's law firm as a clerk. They were afraid he would make a run for it if he learned his cohorts had been picked up, so Captain Wilson asked me to keep it quiet, which of course I did. I did tell—uh, my family because I thought it would relieve their minds."

"I understand," Marma said, remembering the letter he'd sent Steve. "I'm glad it's over. Now life can get back to normal for Lisa and her parents."

· "There's still the trial." Arnold's voice held worry. "I wonder if Lisa will ever get over this business. Oh, she'll shake most of it off, of course. Life does go on, and she's young and resilient. But she won't ever totally forget what she went through, I'm afraid."

Marma nodded, forgetting he couldn't see her. He was right. The past could never be totally expunged, but that didn't mean it had to ruin a person's life. Lisa would recover from her harrowing experience, just as she'd recovered from her fall into the mine shaft. In time, her kidnapping would seem a particularly bad dream. It would also leave scars. Marma, who bore a few scars of her own, knew this. But there were ways of fighting back, of facing up to what couldn't be changed.

Sometimes all it took was a complete change of scenery.

"There's something else, Mr. Flagg—"

"I thought we'd settled the Mr. Flagg business," he interrupted. "It's Arnold—remember? And why don't we continue this conversation over dinner tonight?"

"Oh, I don't want to take up your time—"

"Nonsense. I can't think of a more pleasant way to spend an evening than in the company of a lovely young woman. Strokes the ego of an old man like me."

"You're one of the youngest men I know," she said warmly.

"Thank you," he said, sounding pleased. "Then it's settled. I'll send the car around at—shall we say seven-thirty? I'll have my secretary make reservations at the Blue Vixen and we can have a long talk about your future."

Marma hesitated. Did she really want to go out to dinner with Arnold? A phone call, over quickly, was what she had intended, but maybe that was the coward's way. Besides, what better time to tell Arnold something he wouldn't want to hear than after a good dinner, when he was in a mellow mood?

"I'll be ready at seven-thirty," she said.

After she hung up, she took a shower and washed her hair, all with half a mind because she was so deep in thought. She hadn't seen Angie yet, although she'd called her at work earlier to tell her she was home, and she dreaded the questions her friend was sure to ask. How much should she tell Angie? The bare bones of what had happened, deleting any reference to Steve and the wounds he had inflicted with his masquerade? If she said too much, Angie would be sympathetic, but she would also demand all the details, drag it all out, give endless advice....

Feeling lethargic and wrung out emotionally, Marma curled up in her favorite chair. Magic, always the opportunist on the lookout for a warm lap, joined her mistress, courting her attention with a silent meow and some loud purring. As Marma stroked the cat's soft back, she made a mental list of all the things she still had to do, including making some decisions after she'd seen her family.

She started nervously when the lobby intercom buzzed. It was an impatient, prolonged sound; every instinct told her it was Steve, leaning on the bell. A rush of anger sent her jumping to her feet, causing her to drop the disgusted cat to the floor. How dare Steve come to her apartment when she'd made it so clear that she never wanted to see him again! She could just picture him, smugly sure that she'd cooled down by now and would fall into his arms. With her hands over her ears to shut out the irritating buzz, she stalked up and down the living room, brooding over her grievances with Steve —all the time aware that she was deliberately whipping up her anger as a defense against the temptation to let him in.

After a while, the buzzing stopped, and she told herself she was glad. He didn't deserve another hearing, especially when she knew what he would say—that it was only natural for him to have suspected her intentions because, after all, that psychic stuff was pure nonsense. By now, he might even have come up with a reason for having made love to her without first telling her the truth about himself—and why he'd tricked his way into her life. Not that she would believe him. No way could she risk further hurt. She already felt too emotionally battered for that.

So why would he bother to try to patch things up? That was simple. He still wanted her sexually—he couldn't have faked that part. But a man could lust for a woman and still not respect or love her, while a woman—God, what a fool she'd been! She had opened her heart to him and let him inside. Never again would she risk that kind of disillusionment....

Determined to keep busy until it was time to dress, she tidied up the living room, which looked like a disaster area after two weeks of Angie's housekeeping, and after she'd given the kitchen and bathroom a good cleaning, she called the airport and made a reservation for an early morning flight to Nashville. From Nashville, she would take a bus to Bradyville, then get someone to drive her out to Duncan Holler.

And after that? There were so many variables that it was impossible to make any further plans at present. So much depended on the reception she got from Papa. Maybe she would stay in Tennessee. Nashville,

with its large financial center, might be a good choice.
Or maybe she'd try a city farther away, like Cincinnati or Chicago or Detroit. She might even tackle New
York City. She didn't feel the same thrill of adventure
she had when she'd first decided to come to San
Francisco, but that would undoubtedly come. By this
time next year, if she heard Steve Riley's name, she'd
draw a blank and have to ask who he was. . . .

She was sitting down, listening to the voices in her
mind, when the sound of a key turning in the hall door
lock alerted her that Angie was home. By the time
Marma was on her feet, her friend was flying toward
her to give her a giant hug.

"You don't know how glad I am to see you! When
you called this morning, I almost decided to develop
a headache and take the rest of the day off. The only
thing is, we're pinching every penny for the honeymoon. I've missed you—thank God those creeps are
behind bars so things can get back to normal. How
about a celebration tonight—my treat? Danny's at a
sales meeting over in Oakland, so it'll be just us girls.
There's that new diner on Gough Street, really
funky—you know, like right out of the fifties? I hear
the food is great and the price is right."

"It sounds like fun, but unfortunately, I'm having
dinner with—with a friend."

"Let me guess. With the guy you met in Tahoe,
right?"

"Wrong. That relationship didn't work out. It's
with Arnold—Mr. Flagg. He's taking me to the Blue
Vixen."

Angie collapsed into a chair and flung her arms over
her head in an extravagant gesture. "Oh, you are a sly

one! The big, big boss. You're moving on up, sister! I figure Danny might be able to afford to take me to the Blue Vixen on our tenth anniversary. Or maybe the twentieth. So tell me everything. Is Mr. Flagg going to make you a vice-president or something?''

"Nothing like that. He's just being polite. He still thinks he owes me something. If I hadn't called him, I doubt he would have asked me out.''

"Why did you call him—or is it a secret?''

"It isn't a secret. I wanted to thank him for—for a favor he once did me that I just found out about. I also wanted to tell him that I'm quitting my job and apologize for not giving the usual two weeks' notice.''

Angie's eyes widened. "Are you insane? You've got it made there. After what you've done for him, Mr. Flagg would give you the moon if you asked for it.''

"I don't want that kind of patronage. I want to know that I've earned any promotions I get. I could never be sure of that if I stayed on at the bank. And anyway, I want to redirect my life. Which is why I'm going back to Tennessee tomorrow to see my folks.''

"You made up with your father? Oh, that's wonderful—''

"It isn't like that. I don't even know if Papa will talk to me. But I have to try for a reconciliation. It's not for him. It's for me—do you understand?''

Angie nodded slowly. "I think I do. You're getting ready to make some changes, but before you do, being the demon housekeeper you are, you want to straighten up all the drawers and clean out the closets. Isn't that it?''

"You do have a way with words,'' Marma said, smiling at her roommate. "And you're right. I think this has been coming for a long time, this feeling that I have to go back home and try to straighten out my relationship with my family. I've reached a point in my life where I want to tie up all the loose ends of my personal life before I change jobs and make a fresh start."

Angie sighed. "Well, good luck. It might not be easy, finding a job as good as the one you had. Things are pretty slack just now."

"I'm not worried. I'll take any job as long as it's honest work."

"Right. I remember the time you got that job washing dogs during school vacation. Anyone standing within ten feet of you couldn't help knowing you'd gone to the dogs."

"And I remember that bar of deodorant soap you gave me, all wrapped up in pink tissue paper and ribbon. Talk about hints."

"It was that or get a new roomie. And I've never been noted for my tact. But I'm nice. Admit it—I *am* nice."

Marma started to say that yes, indeed, Angie was rather nice, even if she did have an overactive curiosity bump, and then, to her consternation, she was making little blubbery sounds and tears were running down her cheeks. Angie, silent for once, found her a box of tissues, then lent her a shoulder, and after they'd both had a good cry, they looked at each other's ravaged makeup and started laughing.

Marma, who had been afraid that she'd never laugh again, felt a bitter relief. *See how easy it is, Steve?* she thought. *And it'll get even better. It just takes time. Like maybe a hundred years....*

When she went to her closet to select something to wear to dinner with Arnold, she realized she had nothing suitable for the Blue Vixen except the shift she'd worn the evening before—and the lapis-blue dress.

She laid the blue dress out on the bed. To give in to impulse to rip both it and the other dress to shreds would be a mistake—and set a precedent. She wasn't going to allow her disastrous love affair with Steve to ruin a very small pleasure for her. Tonight might be her last meeting with Arnold, a man she admired, and she was going to make him proud of her by looking her very best.

What was more, she was going to enjoy herself. So help her, she was.

THE BLUE VIXEN was even more elegant than she'd expected. The lights, tinged slightly pink, were more than flattering, the soft chamber music was soothing, and the sparkling crystal, delicate china and impeccable silver were impressive. As the obsequious maître d' paid homage to Arnold's importance by greeting him by name and guiding them to a well-placed table, Marma had to fight the impulse to giggle. Had they sent the man to school to learn that unlikely French accent—or had he acquired it on his own?

Arnold, who was looking very handsome and less diminutive than usual in a dinner jacket, gave her an inquiring look. "What's going on in that mind of yours?"

"I was wondering about the authenticity of the maître d's accent."

Arnold's eyes twinkled. "You caught that, did you? I have a hunch it came by way of the Bronx. But that accent probably earns Pierre more in tips per year than our governor makes. Luckily, the food here is more authentic than Pierre's accent."

The wine steward approached their table and presented a long wine list to Arnold. After a rather esoteric discussion of good and inferior years, of wineries that were over- or underrated, Arnold selected a bottle of Petite Sirah for himself and sparkling mineral water for Marma.

"How did you know that I very seldom drink alcohol?" she asked curiously after the wine steward had glided away.

"As I told you once, I know quite a bit about you, Marmalade Duncan."

She studied his half smile. "Is that because you read my scholarship application, Arnold?"

His smile slipped a little. "So you've found me out, have you? Well, you were bound to put two and two together eventually, I guess. And since this is a celebration, let's make a pact. No serious talk until after dessert. Later, I want to talk to you about taking a management course at Stanford that I recommend for junior executives on the rise, but for now—tell me what you thought of Tahoe."

Marma was telling him about her gambling adventures and her run of beginner's luck when the wine steward returned with their order. He presented a few drops of Petite Sirah in a glass with a flourish, and after Arnold had given it serious consideration, he nodded his approval. Looking as gratified as if he'd blended the wine himself, the steward poured some of it for Arnold and some mineral water for Marma, then glided off again.

They ordered dinner—mussel soup, pike quenelles and lamb with remoulade sauce, followed by Grand Marnier soufflé for dessert—and while they waited, Marma listened as Arnold talked about his first trip to Paris as a young man.

Marma didn't have to pretend her interest. She had never lost her thirst for knowledge, and Arnold's anecdotes were witty, urbane and also so lacking in conceit that she had to keep reminding herself what an important man he was. If she and Steve had met in a different way, at a party or a friend's house, it was possible that she might have become part of Arnold's family—and how the devil had that thought crept in? More likely, Steve wouldn't have given her a second look. Or she, so determined not to get involved with a man, would have rejected his attention—if he had directed any at her.

"You're very quiet tonight, Marma," Arnold said. "Are you tired after all the excitement of the past three weeks?"

Marma looked into his kind, concerned eyes, and suddenly she wanted to pour out her hurt and anger. But of course that was impossible. How could she confide in Arnold, Steve's uncle, when she hadn't even been able to talk about her hurt with Angie, her best friend?

And wasn't it ironic that the person she found easiest to talk to had broken her heart?

"I *am* a little tired," she said. "And I also have a lot of things on my mind—which I'll tell you about later.

Right now, I'm famished. Isn't that our waiter coming with our soup?''

As they dipped into bowls of steaming mussel soup, redolent of fennel, garlic and saffron, their conversation ranged from Arnold's disdain for nouvelle cuisine to Marma's first experience with non mountain-style cooking.

Earlier, she had wondered if she could do the meal justice, considering her mental state, but she discovered that she was famished. Only now did she remember that she hadn't eaten anything since lunch the day before. As she dug hungrily into her soup, she reflected that it wasn't true, after all, that a disappointment in love took away the appetite. What other misconceptions did she have about love? That once broken, a heart couldn't mend? Hers was already mending, developing a hard new shell. In time, she would be just the way she had been before Steve had come into her life, only much, much wiser. . . .

When they had finished dessert and were sipping cognac from long, fluted glasses, she knew it was time to tell Arnold she was quitting her job. As a lead-in to the subject, she rummaged in her purse, found the key to the lodge and gave it to him.

"This is yours. I know you said to leave it in the flower pot where I found it, but I forgot and walked off with it."

He took the key, his quizzical smile reminding her of Steve's. "It isn't like you to forget details. Was your mind on other things?"

"Yes, primarily on your nephew. We had a quarrel and I left in a hurry."

Arnold nodded. "I know. Steve called me this morning. I advised him to tell you who he was as soon as possible, you know. I suppose that's what you quarreled about. You do understand that I asked him to get acquainted with you only so he could watch out for you? He usually isn't into deception. A little sleight of hand is required once in a while to get a story, but he's one of the most honest people I know."

"A story?"

"For his job—he's an investigative reporter. He does exposés and special features for *World Beat*. He didn't tell you?"

"He told me he was in public relations."

His chuckle had an indulgent sound. "Well, he is—in a way. He's quite well-known in his field. His articles get a good deal of attention and sometimes cause a lot of controversy."

Marma stared at him with bleak eyes, so many things suddenly becoming clear. "He wrote a series of articles on psychics, didn't he? He did a real hatchet job. According to him, they—we are all crooks. I just wish the author's name had stayed in my mind."

"I hope that won't prejudice you against Steve, my dear. He's a bit single-minded at times, but his heart is in the right place. When he sees an injustice, he tries to do something to change things. He cares, you see, about the victims. And he doesn't give a damn about bureaucracies or power structures. All that is what makes him so good at his job."

Marma was silent. His words echoed in her mind. So Steve cared about victims, did he? That hadn't stopped him from deceiving her in the worse way possible. She was tempted to tell Arnold exactly what she thought of his single-minded nephew, whose heart was in the right place and who used a little sleight of hand sometimes to get a story, but since she had no desire to hurt Arnold, she changed the subject.

"I also wanted to thank you for arranging that scholarship for me," she said.

Arnold looked uncomfortable. "You seem to know all my little secrets. And no thank-yous are due. What you did for my family has no price tag. And besides, you've been paying back the grant—not that it's necessary."

"But it is necessary. We Duncans always pay our debts."

"I understand. Well, you'll be happy to know that every cent of that money goes back into the foundation to help other recipients of scholarships. I found the whole setup so rewarding—and needed—that it's now an ongoing process. At present, eighteen young women from Tennessee are enrolled in various colleges they couldn't have afforded without the scholarships. Some will return to Tennessee, hopefully to teach. So you see, a lot of good has come from that special talent of yours."

"I'm glad—very glad," Marma said, deeply touched.

"You must have figured out why I felt I had to keep my involvement with the foundation a secret from you. That pride of yours is admirable, but we all need a hand up at some time or other in our life. And I'm delighted it's finally out in the open because I've been wanting to change the name of the foundation—if you have no objection. How does the Marma Duncan Foundation sound to you?"

Marma fought for composure. Only when she was sure she could speak in a reasonably steady voice did she answer his question.

"I have no objections as long as it's clear that the Marma Duncan being honored is my mother, not me. We have the same name, you see."

She stopped, lost in the past. How strange that she'd picked up so much information about her mother when no one had ever spoken about her directly. Or maybe it wasn't so strange since she'd been so quiet as a child that adults sometimes forgot she was in the room when they were exchanging gossip.

"She never did learn how to read or write," she went on. "There were six kids in her family, you see, and her mother—my Grandmother McCann—was in very poor health. My mother, being the youngest girl, stayed home to help out instead of going to school. There may have been another reason that they kept her at home. My name isn't the only thing I inherited from my mother."

"I see—yes, I do see," Arnold murmured.

"Papa was raised in another valley—Duncan Holler. The Duncans and the McCanns didn't get along, so I don't know how she and Papa met. Maybe while he was hunting. I do know she was only fourteen when he got her pregnant. When her father found out, he disowned her and she went to live with Papa's family. After my oldest sister was born, Papa married her. I don't think Mama had ever been off Duncan Mountain until Papa took her into Bradyville to get married. So you see—" she gave Arnold a tremulous smile "—I'd be honored if you named your foundation for her. I never knew my mama, so I don't know what she was like, but I'm sure she'd be proud to know that other mountain women will get the education she never had from a foundation that bears her name.''

Her voice was wobbling a little at the end, but she made it without crying. Arnold patted her hand, and then he said briskly, ''Well, this has been a memorable evening—one I'll never forget. And wasn't there something you wanted to tell me? Or have we already covered it?''

Marma took a long time answering; the words didn't come easily. ''I've decided to quit my job. I want you to know that it's a personal decision that has nothing to do with you.''

''But you're doing so well! You have such a splendid future with us—'' He broke off, studying her face. ''You've already made up your mind, haven't you, and nothing I can say is going to change it. So I'll just tell you that any time you want to return, a job is waiting for you. And anything I can do to help you get established elsewhere—''

''That won't be necessary. I have to do it myself or it won't mean anything. I hope you understand.''

''Oh, yes, I do understand. I remember having a similar conversation with Steve when he graduated from Stanford.''

''Steve?''

''I wanted him to join the firm and eventually become my successor. But no, he wanted to do his own thing—I think that's the expression young people used ten years ago, isn't it?''

At her automatic nod, he added, ''He made the right decision although I still hope that someday he'll change his mind. And what is it you want to do with *your* life, Marma?''

"I haven't figured out all the details yet," she said evasively.

"But you will keep in touch? Lisa would be disappointed if you dropped out of sight. Your visit did wonders for her. She seemed much more—oh, not cheerful. It's too soon for that, but she is looking forward to returning to school next week. My daughter says she talks about you all the time. You made quite an impression, you know."

"I'll call her in the morning before I go to the airport—"

"Airport? You're taking a trip?"

"Yes. I'll probably be gone a couple of weeks, but as soon as I get back, I'll go see Lisa again."

"I appreciate that," Arnold said. Since he seemed to have more questions, Marma was relieved when their waiter appeared with the bill.

Later, when she let herself into the apartment, she was so wrung out emotionally that she was glad Angie had already gone to bed. As she packed her suitcase, she was careful to move around her bedroom quietly, knowing Angie would be sure to want to talk if she woke. When Marma was finished, she set her alarm, then crawled into bed.

Magic, who had been carefully watching her owner pack, jumped into bed and curled up at Marma's feet. She was glad to have the cat's company. Already, she felt lonely, cut off from everything familiar to her. Which was stupid; she was going home, wasn't she? What could be more familiar than Duncan Holler? Yes, she would be burning a few bridges behind her, but not totally. Even if she decided to settle in some other city, she would still be returning to San Francisco for her things. And she certainly intended to attend Angie's wedding in August. Her friendship with Angie would remain a constant all her life. But with Angie busy with her new life, there was certainly nothing to keep her, Marma in San Francisco. Maybe she'd just burn all those bridges at once, after all....

CHAPTER TWELVE

IT HAD BEEN late summer when Marma had left Tennessee. She had held off telling her father that she'd applied for a scholarship and had been accepted at Brown University, dreading the quarrel that was sure to erupt. Although she was determined to get an education, she was well aware that if she left home, she would be turning her back on all that was familiar to her. She had never really been close to her family, but they were all she had—and to an eighteen-year-old girl who had never been farther away from home than Bradyville, the world seemed very large, very strange and very frightening.

But the day had come, in late August, when she couldn't put it off any longer. Registration day at Brown was just ahead, and to turn up late would be a terrible way to start this already terrifying venture. When a neighbor relayed a phone message—when Papa was working out in the fields, luckily—that Mr. Walters, her school adviser, wanted to see her on an important matter, she knew that things had come to a head.

The next morning, she waited until Papa was busy in the barn before she walked down to the highway and hitched a ride into Bradyville. She found Mr. Walters at home, and he gave her a bus ticket to

Maryland, then told her a room had already been reserved for her at a boardinghouse near the campus,
where she would stay until she could move into one of
the freshman dormitories. He also gave her a check for
her first month's living allowance with a remark about
not spending it all in one place.

Marma didn't laugh at his little joke. To someone
who had so little experience with money, the amount
of the check seemed like a small fortune.

That night, after the supper dishes were done, she
told Papa she had something to tell him. Standing very
straight, she told him about the scholarship, and that
she'd be leaving for Maryland in a few days.

The quarrel was even worse than she'd expected. His
face livid, he quoted from the Bible about an un-
grateful child and a serpent's tongue, then told her to
pack her things and get out because she was no longer
his daughter.

She spent the night with a neighbor and took the bus
to Nashville the next day. She hadn't seen or heard
from her family since.

And now she was going back to Duncan Holler,
again on a sunny summer day. As the laboring old bus
came to a stop in front of Bradyville's lone drugstore,
she had to force herself to get off. The driver, a gar-
rulous man who had kept up a running conversation
with another passenger since they'd left Charleston,
the county seat, unloaded her suitcase and wished her
a cheery "Good luck, miss!" A minute later, the bus
took off in a cloud of dust and exhaust fumes, leaving her standing alone on the sidewalk.

Marma looked around, and was surprised at how
small the town looked. There had been a time when it

had seemed large to her. But that had been a long time ago, and now the place looked shabby, run-down and very, very small.

The drugstore hadn't changed, she noted, except that it had gotten a little dingier. It bore the same faded sign—William's Drugs—above the front door. Across the street, the Stop 'N Dine lunchroom was still in business. But two of the stores on the block, which had formerly been a Sears catalog store and a hardware store, were now boarded up. The gas station on the corner must have changed hands because it sported an unfamiliar sign: Brotski Service Station, and a large notice, tacked on the door of the feed store across the street, announced that the place was now open only on Monday, Wednesday and Saturday.

A tall, gaunt-faced man, wearing jeans and a soiled sweatshirt, came out of the drugstore. He looked familiar, but if it was someone she knew he obviously didn't recognize her. He eyed her curiously, then sauntered across the street to disappear into the diner. A small boy came barreling out of the post office next door to the drugstore, holding a fistful of mail. When he saw Marma, he skittered to a stop to stare at her, but when she smiled and said, "Hi, there," he took off at a run, followed by a small white terrier.

It had been a long time since she'd had breakfast in Nashville, so she was tempted to get a cup of coffee and a sandwich at the Stop 'N Dine, but changed her mind almost immediately. Mrs. Brady, who owned the café, was a gossip, and Marma didn't want to draw any attention to herself. In a town so small, everybody knew everybody else's business. Why stir up unnecessary talk about Papa and the family—especially if she left on the next bus out?

Carrying her suitcase, she set off down the sidewalk. When it ended a block and a half later, she moved to the side of the road, glad that she'd had the foresight to bring only the minimum of clothing. Even so, as the sun got hotter, the small suitcase seemed to grow heavier every minute. She had covered a mile or more when a rusty farm truck, its engine laboring, pulled up alongside her.

"You need a lift, miss?" the gray-haired driver asked.

Although she'd forgotten his name, she recognized him immediately as a livestock dealer who lived in the valley beyond Duncan Holler. Gratefully, she slid the suitcase onto the floorboard and then climbed onto the passenger seat.

"Where you headed, lady?"

"Duncan Holler," she said.

He gave her a long, measured look. "Ain't you Dan Duncan's girl, the one who went East to college?"

She nodded, resigned to a barrage of questions, but to her surprise, he busied himself with getting the truck rolling. For the next few miles, until they reached her turnoff, he spoke about the weather, which had been hot even for July, and about a TV show he and his missus had seen the night before. He didn't ask her any questions, and she didn't volunteer any information. When they reached the junction where the county highway crossed the gravel road that wound up the side of Duncan Mountain, he brought the truck to a shuddering halt.

"I'd take you on up to your Pa's place, but this ol' truck can't take them steep grades anymore. It's wearing out in the joints, jes' like me," he said.

Hesitantly, she offered to pay him for the ride, but he looked offended and told her, "Why, I don't want your money, girl. Me and Dan Duncan went to school together. You take care now—and give your folks my best. I'm right sorry about your Pa."

He was gone before she could ask him what he meant. As she watched the truck disappear around a curve in the road, she suddenly felt cold, even though the afternoon sun was hot against her skin. Afraid that she was in for one of her attacks, she sat down in the shade of a chestnut tree by the side of the road. When nothing happened, she picked up her suitcase and began trudging up the narrow road.

It was almost an hour later that she caught her first glimpse of the house she'd lived in for the first eighteen years of her life. Like Bradyville, it looked much smaller than she remembered. It sat on a small plateau, surrounded by fields. Marma recalled that on the day she'd left, the corn patch had been ready for harvesting, and the fields behind the house had been golden with the summer's second crop of hay. The pockets of earth around the house had been rich enough to support three generations of her family, but now, the land lay fallow, its only crop weeds.

Was Papa sick, Marma wondered, or had he given up farming now that he was old enough to draw social security? Maybe he'd moved in with her sister or one of the boys. People in the mountains married young; the other Duncan kids had to be gone now, with homes of their own. Those last few years, Papa had suffered with arthritis—not that he'd ever complained. It would have hurt his pride if anyone had been foolish enough to comment on what was so obvious: that his knuckles were becoming distorted and his back wasn't as straight as it once had been.

As Marma climbed the porch steps, a dog barked inside the house. The porch boards, some of them half rotted away, creaked as she crossed to the front door. When she knocked, there was no response, so she knocked again, louder this time. Inside the house, a querulous voice called out, "I'm coming, I'm coming. Hold your horses, I'm coming as fast as I can."

The door swung inward, and the odors of wood smoke, unwashed dishes and dog assaulted her nostrils. It took her a moment to realize that the elderly man standing there was a stranger.

"What you want, lady?" the man said. "If you're selling something, I ain't interested."

"I'm looking for my—for Dan Duncan," she stammered. "I'm his daughter."

"Old Dan's daughter? What you up to? I know Dan's daughter, and you ain't her."

"That must be my sister, Louise," Marma said.

"Say, you're the one that up and left home and never came back. A little late, ain't you? And it won't do you no good, snooping around. I bought this place from your folks, all legal and clear."

Marma felt a deep ache under her ribs. She probed the spot with her fingertips, forcing herself to breath normally. "Where's my father?" she said carefully.

The man stared at her for a long moment before he jerked his thumb upward. "Your pa's buried up on the mountain in the old graveyard, alongside the rest of your kin. Maybe you should talk to your sis. She's living at the old Burleau place with her man and kids.''

"Who are you?"

"Why, I'm Morry Davis," he said, as if surprised she didn't know. "You go talk to your sis. She'll tell you everything you want to know."

He shut the door in her face.

Marma didn't move for a long time. Papa was dead. Like the man said, she had come too late. She would never get the chance to make her peace with Papa. How was it that she hadn't been notified? And when had it happened? If she'd still been in school, the family could have contacted her easily through the registrar's office. Even later, after she'd graduated and moved to California, they could have traced her; the university kept a record of their graduates' addresses for their fund drives. So why hadn't her family contacted her? Was it more of the same old thing—that they hadn't wanted her around? And why was she so surprised that Papa's death hadn't changed the way things were?

She heard a snuffling sound at the bottom of the door, then a low whine. She turned away, feeling very cold again. If she were lucky, she'd get a ride back to Bradyville—but first, there was something she had to do.

When she reached the road, instead of turning right, toward Bradyville, she turned left and headed up the mountain. Half an hour later, she stood at the wooden gate of the cemetery, trying to find the courage to go inside. The graveyard she remembered had been neat and well-tended, but now the ivy that covered the graves was ragged and unkempt, and several of the older gravestones tilted at a precarious angle where the roots of the sycamores that shaded the plots had pushed up through the ground.

Surely, seven years shouldn't have made such a difference—but then, she remembered, Papa had been the one who had organized the clean-up picnic every year, at which the neighbors gathered to trim the ivy, straighten any stones that were tilting and cut back the undergrowth. How angry he would be, she mused, if he knew the old graveyard, where he and Mama were buried, was so neglected.

She found Papa's grave where she'd expected it to be, next to her mother's in the Duncan family plot. Their gravestones, simple gray granite shafts, gave only their names and the dates of their births and deaths. It was then she discovered that Papa had been dead for almost two years.

For a long time, until the shadows that lay across her parents' graves grew inches longer, she knelt there, thinking about Papa and the mother she'd never known, the woman he'd remained faithful to all his life. When she finally rose, her legs were so numb that she had to flex them several times to restore circulation. She pulled some of the weeds that had grown up around their gravestones, then picked an armful of black-eyed Susans that grew wild near the fence and divided them equally between the two graves.

"Goodbye, Mama. Goodbye, Papa," she said before she turned and left the old graveyard.

By now, she had lost her desire to see her sister and brothers. That they hadn't notified her about Papa's death hurt deeply. It also proved to her that they were still following Papa's edict that she no longer was part of the family. But something stronger than hurt, a question that needed answering, sent her walking up the road toward the old Burleau place rather than back to Bradyville. She had to know how Papa had died.

As she approached the old Burleau homestead, she discovered that her feet were lagging, that she was having second thoughts about intruding upon her sister's life. As at Papa's place, the walls of the frame house were badly weathered, the paint stripped away where it faced the prevailing northwest winds. Although the yard was neat, with a few beds of marigolds and four-o'clocks, it had a run-down, neglected look. Even so, someone had attempted to make the place look cheerful. Unbleached muslin curtains, gayly embroidered with morning glories, hung at the long, narrow front windows, and now that Marma was closer, she could hear the sound of children's voices at the back of the house.

The man who had bought Papa's farm had said that Louise lived here with her husband and kids. How many nieces and nephews did she have? Marma wondered. The oldest couldn't be more than six. Was Louise happy, married to slow-moving, good-natured Charlie Burleau? Had she really loved Charlie—or had she married the first man who asked her to get away from home?

Marma felt a stirring of shame. That question hadn't even occurred to her seven years ago; she'd been too wrapped up in her own plans of escape to wonder how Louise had felt about marrying Charlie Burleau. She had seemed happy enough, but hadn't there been a quietness about her those last few months?

Marma reached the front porch, but it was a few minutes before she got up the courage to knock. Maybe she should have gone around to the back. That was expected of friends and neighbors, but then she wasn't either. In so many ways she was as much a stranger as some peddler or Bible salesman.

The door opened and a woman, short and stocky, looked at her. Marma was shocked at how much Louise had changed. Her sister's hair, once so glossy and thick, looked dull and neglected now, held back carelessly from her face with a rubber band. And she'd gained a lot of weight—too much for even her sturdy frame to carry gracefully. Louise had never been beautiful, but she'd had a freshness, a radiance about her. Now, she looked at least ten years older than the thirty Marma knew her to be.

For a long moment, the two sisters stared at each other, and then Louise was smiling, holding out her arms, her eyes very bright. "You've come home, Marma. You've finally come home."

"THEN PAPA'S ARTHRITIS got so bad he couldn't work the farm, so he sold off all the cows and got by with his social security and his garden. Then he got that bad case of flu, and it turned into pneumonia. We tried to get him to see the doctor, but you know Papa. He always was so stubborn. Said there was nothing wrong with him that a little rest wouldn't cure. When he got worse and worse, coughing and wheezing and not able to catch his breath, we moved him over here and got the doctor to come out from town. He needed someone with him all the time and with the youngsters, I just couldn't stay over there with him."

They were sitting in the kitchen, drinking tepid tea. Louise had apologized for not having any ice; their fridge had given out, wouldn't you know it, and they hadn't had a repairman out from town to fix it yet. The room was very warm, filled with reflected sunlight that showed all too clearly the worn spots on the linoleum, the rust on the ancient cooking range and the chips on the porcelain sink with the water pump at one end. But the room was immaculately clean, and there was a yeasty odor of bread in the air that made Marma sniff hungrily.

"Papa seemed to mellow those last few days. At least, he never complained when the kids made a racket." Louise's smile was rueful. "I guess I'm too easy on them. I used to hate the way Papa was so strict about us talking at the table and all, so when I had my own kids—well, Charlie and me are both too easy. The funny thing is that Papa was different with them than he was with us. He let them get by with murder, especially my oldest. She was his favorite, you see."

She smiled at Marma, tilting her head in a way Marma remembered. "I've thought of you so often, wondered where you were, what you were doing and if you was happy. When Papa died, we tried real hard to find you. Mark called that school in the East you went away to, but they didn't know nothing about you. Did you quit to get married?"

"There must have been some kind of clerical foul-up," Marma said, surprised how relieved she felt at learning that her suspicions had been unfounded. "I'm not married. I did get my MBA degree at Brown, and now I'm living in San Francisco—"

"San Francisco? So far away—it's right on the ocean, ain't it? I always wanted to go there. One of these days, Charlie and me mean to take a trip out to California. 'Course that will have to wait until Marma Lou and the boys are on their own."

Marma fought a sudden lump in her throat. "You named your daughter for me?" she asked.

"You and Mama. Hope you don't mind. I always liked your name." Louise studied Marma for a long moment. "Marma Lou looks like you. She's got the same black hair and the McCann eyes. She has your disposition, too. She's always got her nose in a book, so curious about everything. Right now, she can't wait to start school in September. Remember how you pestered me until I finally taught you how to read and write? Papa would've had a fit if he'd known how much time we spent up in the attic, playing school. It's a wonder he let you and me finish high school, the way he felt about educating girls."

Marma digested this in silence. Strange—she'd almost forgotten that it was only due to Louise's tutoring that she'd been permitted to start school in the third grade. Otherwise, she would have had an extra strike against her, being three years older than the other first graders. Louise had always obeyed Papa without argument, and yet she'd gone behind his back to teach her sister how to read and write, even to do simple arithmetic. Why had she forgotten that? How many other things had she forgotten through the years?

"Did you ever hear the story about how Mama got her name?" Louise asked suddenly.

Marma shook her head.

"Grandpa McCann gave it to her. He had a sweet tooth, so he had marmalade every morning on his biscuits. Said he had to have a sweet to finish off his meal or it didn't set right. The first time he saw Mama, just after she was born, he thought she was the sweetest-looking young 'un he'd ever seen. So he called her Marmalade."

"No one ever told me that," Marma said.

"Well, we never had much truck with the McCanns. I heard about it from Charlie's mom. Did you know the last thing Mama did was to make Papa promise to give you her name? So he'd still have a Marma to give him comfort, she said. I was only six when she died, and I remember thinking he'd name you something from the Bible, but no, he kept his promise to Mama."

"And yet he never called me Marma. I guess because he resented me so much," Marma said, her voice tight.

"Resented you? Why, you was always Papa's favorite. I used to be so jealous of you because you looked like Mama. I thought he'd pay more attention to me if I had her black hair and those McCann eyes. It about broke Papa's heart when you went off like that and never came back to see him."

"I wrote him every week for months, but the letters came back marked 'refused' in his handwriting."

"I didn't know that, not at the time. Papa always collected the mail. Well, he did have his pride. It hurt him real bad when you left home. I don't think he ever got over it."

"All he had to do was write. He must have known that. And I think you're wrong about me being his favorite. Papa was always much harder on me than he was on the rest of you."

"That was because he was afraid for you, Marma. It was—well, because you're different, having the second sight and all. He was afraid of what could happen to you around strangers. As long as you were here with your own folks, he knew he could protect you. I guess it was because he had such a hard time with it himself. He hated it—fought it all his life. But you know, at the end, he began to change his mind. Said maybe it was a gift, not a curse."

"Papa had visions?" Marma said incredulously.

"All his life. Not that he ever talked about them. But then, just before he died, he had one where he saw our youngest—that's Jimmy—in the Youngs' pasture where they keep their bull. Papa yelled to me to run and look. Sure enough, that boy had crawled under the fence and was playing with some rocks he'd found. If I hadn't got him outta there quick, that old bull could've killed him. After that happened, Papa changed."

"I thought—" Marma broke off.

"You thought what, Marma?"

"That it was Mama I inherited it from."

"No, it runs in Papa's family. Caused his grandma a peck of trouble—almost got her killed. People were scared of her, wouldn't go near her, and then they blamed her for a twister that touched down in the valley and about wrecked it. Things were a lot different back in the old days, especially in these mountains."

"Have any of your children—?"

"Marma Lou. She's got it—and I'm gonna raise her so she ain't ashamed of it, too." She paused to study

Marma's stiff face. "You don't have to tell me if you haven't got a mind to, but do you still get them spells?"

"Very seldom. I guess I'm like Papa—I try hard not to have them. Most of the time, I can head them off before they start."

"Well, it's your own business. I'm not surprised you feel that way, with Papa so down on you all them years. None of us thought it was right, the time he shamed you before the whole church, but we were all too scared to say anything."

"I wish I'd known that. I always felt so alone, you know."

"I'm sorry about that. But you were always so quiet, kind of standoffish, and it was hard to know what you was thinking. And we were just kids, too, you gotta remember. We were so fond of you, especially me and Mark. Still are, if it comes to that."

Marma stared at her, trying to digest Louise's words. All those wasted years, she thought. Could she have had the love she'd craved all those years simply by reaching out for it?

"What's new with the boys?" she asked when the silence became awkward.

"Well, Matthew is working over near Falmouth Ferry at a dairy. He's been married about five years now, got two boys. Same old Matthew—always complaining and blaming others for things that happen to him. Guess he'll never change. Luke's got three kids— two boys and a girl. He's farming for his in-laws. They're just holding on like the rest of us, but the old man's promised Luke the farm in a few years. Mark's done right well for hisself. After he married the

Thomas girl—that's Irene, the middle one—they moved to Taswell County, over in Virginia. He's assistant manager of the A & P there. Got two kids—a girl and a boy. They don't get over here too often, but we keep in touch. 'Course, Irene does most of the letter writing, but she's real faithful. She sent some snapshots with her last one—wait here and I'll fetch them.''

Marma felt a little numb as her sister bustled out of the room. It was hard to adjust to suddenly having so many new relatives. The sound of children's voices drew her to the window. Four children were playing with a Frisbee in the field behind the house. Three were boys—all towheads like the Burleaus—but the oldest, a girl, had hair as black as her own.

She was very slender, a wraith of a girl, and as she laughed and leaped high into the air to catch the Frisbee, Marma suddenly thought of another little girl, this one playing alone under the willow tree in the corner of the yard. The lower branches of the willow drooped onto the ground, forming a small pool of privacy underneath, and the girl sitting there, crooning and rocking a doll, seemed oblivious of her brothers, who were kicking a tin can around the yard.

Had it always been her own choice to never join in their games? Would she have been welcome if she'd tried? It was a new concept, one she found hard to believe despite Louise's words. To her, they had seemed so much older, so remote and uninterested in her. But maybe they had felt rejected because she had gone off to play on her own....

Louise returned with a scrapbook full of snapshots. For a while, they pored over them and Louise told her more than she could absorb about the family. When Marma questioned her again about the second sight, Louise told her that as far as she knew, none of their brothers' children had inherited it.

"I'm only sure about Marma Lou. It's the things she says sometimes that makes me think she's got it." She sighed, looking restive. "I used to envy you, you know. I wanted to see things other people couldn't see, maybe look into the future, but of course I was just ordinary."

"And that's what I wanted to be—ordinary, like everybody else. I was sure Papa hated me for being different, just as he blamed me for Mama's dying in childbirth."

"Why, Marma, Papa didn't blame you for Mama's death. He blamed himself. The doctor in town—you remember old Doctor Wells, don't you?—told him Mama shouldn't have no more kids after Mark was born. She had some kind of—well, she wasn't built right for it, I guess. Childbirth was really dangerous for her, especially after she got older.

"But Papa said that was hogwash. She'd had four young 'uns without much trouble. He believed what the Bible said, that we were put on earth to multiply. Mama always did what he said, so after a while she got pregnant again with you. After she died, Papa almost went crazy. I think that's why he babied you so, never wanted you to roughhouse with the rest of us. I remember the day he brought you home from the county hospital, right after Mama died. He got us all together and put you in my lap. 'I don't ever want to see this baby wet or hungry or dirty,' he told us. And that's the way it was. Later, he kept you home from school till you was nine, saying you was too delicate to go. He was worried about the things that could happen to you once you left the holler.''

"But—why didn't someone tell me this?"

"I guess we thought you already knew. And then we wasn't a family that talked easy about our feelings. Papa was out of his head a lot when he had the lung fever there at the last. Kept saying how sorry he was that he sent back your letters. But by the time he got over being sore, the letters had stopped coming and he was too proud to write and make up. At the end, he thought I was Mama and he kept asking me to forgive him for not taking care of you like he'd promised. I wish—'' She stopped, looking embarrassed.

"You wish I'd kept writing," Marma said dully. "So do I, Louise."

"Well, it's all water under the bridge now. And I'm glad you've finally come home. Everybody's going to be so glad to see you. We haven't had a family reunion for a long time. It's about time we did." She smiled, looking like the sister Marma remembered. "There's so much to tell you, I don't know where to start."

"And I have something to tell you," Marma said. "It's about a man, a banker, who set up a foundation to provide scholarships for East Tennessee women, but it's also about Mama—''

DURING THE NEXT FEW DAYS, Marma got reacquainted with her family. In so many ways, she was seeing her siblings with the eyes of a stranger, and it was a bittersweet experience. It was obvious that times were hard in the mountains. There were few jobs and with farm prices so low, it was a constant struggle to keep afloat. Not that folks seemed to worry too much. Maybe that was because, Marma decided, times had always been hard in this isolated pocket of the country, even when the mines had flourished. And since they all seemed to accept it as being normal, as she once had, why did she feel guilty about her own comparative prosperity?

After all, they wouldn't accept any financial help from her, even though they were her family. Help with the nursing when someone in the family was sick or sitting with a croupy baby so the mother could get some sleep—even laboring in the fields when fall rain threatened to ruin the hay crop before harvest—these things were acceptable, even expected, from family or neighbors. But to offer money—that would shame them. They'd be as insulted as the man who had given her a ride had been when she'd tried to pay him.

So Marma held her tongue and pretended not to notice the telltale signs of bare-bones living. Later, she promised herself, she would find some acceptable way to help out, certainly help the children get an education. Meanwhile, she didn't make the mistake of trying to play Lady Bountiful. These were proud people—and she knew all about their kind of pride.

I'll ask Steve's advice about this, she thought. *He'll have some ideas....*

When she realized how insidiously the thought had come to her, she gave herself a mental shake and went to help Louise prepare vegetables from the garden for supper.

By now, she had grown fond of all her sister's children, but secretly her favorite was her namesake, who

was a strange mixture of tomboyishness and feminin-
ity. She watched for signs that Marma Lou had inherited the second sight, but the girl seemed a perfectly
normal child, always doing something daring, the opposite of her aunt at that age.

And then while she and the children were picking
blackberries in the thicket at the edge of the woods
above the house, Marma Lou asked her in a matter-of-
fact voice if she was still mad at that nice man she'd
had the fight with. Before Marma could get over her
shock, Marma Lou popped her hands over her mouth.

"What is it, Marma Lou?" Marma asked quickly.

"I'm not supposed to talk about things I see to
outsiders. It scares people," she said.

"I'm not an outsider, and anyway, it doesn't scare
me. I see things, too."

"You do?"

"I really do."

Marma Lou regarded her with solemn eyes. "Why
don't other people see them, Aunt Marma?"

"I suspect a lot of them do. I don't know why
everybody doesn't. That's just the way it is." She hesitated, choosing her words carefully. "Why did you
say you weren't supposed to talk about the visions?"

"Is that what they are—visions?"

"That's the proper name for them."

"Uncle Matthew told me not to talk about them or
people would think I'm crazy." There was uncertainty in her voice.

"You're not crazy. But he's right about one thing—
it's best to keep them to yourself. Not that they're
something to be ashamed of, you understand."

"Oh, I'm not ashamed of them. When I grow up, I'm going to make a lot of money, telling people about things I see."

Marma felt a chill. "Where did you get that idea?" she said sharply.

"From Uncle Matthew. I heard him and Papa talking the other night, and he said Papa oughta set me up as a fortune teller 'cause we could make a lot of money. Is that what you are—a fortune teller?"

"No, I'm not. And neither are you. And Uncle Matthew was wrong. It isn't right to take money for being able to see things other people can't. I want you to promise you won't ever do anything like that."

Marma Lou regarded her with thoughtful eyes. "Okay, I promise," she said agreeably. She spotted a cluster of berries at the edge of the thicket and ran off to pick them, leaving Marma uncertain how she felt. It seemed that her niece was perfectly able to cope with her second sight. Even so, she meant to have a talk with Matthew very soon about being careful what he said around the impressionable child.

The Duncan family reunion was held the following weekend in Louise and Charlie's backyard. From the beginning it was a success. With so many new nieces and nephews to get acquainted with in such a short time, Marma was finally forced to give up trying to keep the various lineages of her sibling's in-laws straight. Not that anyone seemed to notice how often she avoided calling someone's mother-in-law or great-aunt by name. Everybody was too busy exchanging family news and devouring the mounds of fried chicken, potato salad, raw vegetables in lime gelatin, and pies and cakes and cobblers that, Marma reflected, really did deserve to be described with Angie's favorite superlative—awesome.

By late afternoon, she was wondering if anyone had ever noticed that she'd been away. To her surprise, no one, not even Louise, asked her anything but the most superficial questions about where she had been and what she'd been doing during the past seven years. The women, it seemed, were far more interested in why she wasn't yet married.

But, despite her feeling so comfortable among her own kind, something was coming clear, something that saddened her. She didn't really belong in Duncan Holler. Not any more. Its ways were no longer her ways, and while she loved her family and would never lose touch with them again, she didn't fit in. Maybe her horizons had expanded too much and she had become too aware of how narrow this valley, which had once encompassed her whole world, really was. Already, she felt restless, aware that there were things she wanted to do with her life that wouldn't be possible here.

So it was true, it seemed, that you could never go home. And wasn't that a pity?

The Saturday following the reunion, she rode into Bradyville with a neighbor who was going in for supplies. She used the public phone in the drugstore, reversing charges, to call Angie, guiltily aware that she'd neglected her friend. Angie pointed this out in no uncertain terms, and then went on to ask so many questions that Marma had a hard time answering them.

"Hearing about your father must have been a terrible shock, but I'm sure it felt good, making up with the rest of your family," Angie said finally.

"It wasn't a question of making up," Marma told her. "It was a question of—rearranging my feelings about them."

"You aren't going to stay there, are you?" Angie said, sounding alarmed. "I'll never forgive you if you do. For one thing, I need you to see me through the wedding—what would I do without you?"

"Uh-huh. What about that Italian tribe of yours? You have a couple dozen aunts and cousins to call upon, not to mention your mother, two grandmothers and a future mother-in-law. But okay, I promise I'll be there. That's one thing I'm calling about. I'm going to spend a couple more days here, but then I'll be heading back to San Francisco."

"For good?"

Marma hesitated. If she stayed in San Francisco, there was always the chance she would run into Steve. On the other hand—why should she let him chase her away? She loved the city—and to hell with Steve Riley....

"For good," she said firmly.

Angie's sigh of relief rustled in Marma's ear. "I was afraid you'd do something totally uncool, like move to L.A."

"No way," Marma said with the typical northern Californian's scorn for the southern end of the state.

Angie giggled. "Well, you did say you wanted to make some changes. Oh, something else—you've been getting calls from a man with a great voice: Steve somebody or other."

Marma's heart gave an extra beat. "Steve Riley?"

"That's the one. I told him you were away on a trip, that I had no idea when you'd be back, but I don't

think he believed me. He kept saying how important
it was to contact you. Is that the guy you met at the
lodge? If he calls back—and I have a feeling he will—
what do I say?''

"Yes, it's the guy I met at the lodge. Tell him I don't
want to talk to him. Tell him to get lost.''

"Wow! What did he do to you?''

"He lied to me—and worse. Just tell him I said not
to bother to call again.''

"Maybe you should tell him yourself. I don't think
he's going to pay any attention to me. You know, I felt
sorry for him. He sounded so—so desperate.''

"I don't want to talk about it.''

"Okay, so let's talk about the wedding. Wait until
you see the loot that's beginning to pour in! Danny
and I won't have to buy a thing when we set up
housekeeping. Mom and Dad told us to raid their attic, take anything we wanted, and we unearthed
enough good stuff up there to furnish two places. And
Danny's parents—you won't believe this!—are making the down payment on a house for us. How about
that?''

"You sure that isn't why you're marrying him? To
get all that loot and a house of your own?''

"I'd marry Danny if he didn't have a dime to his
name." Angie's voice was unexpectedly serious. "I
love the guy so much, it scares me sometimes. I just
wish that you—'' She broke off abruptly.

*You wish that I should be so lucky, my generous-
hearted friend.* "I suppose you're depending on me to
keep track of all those wedding gifts and probably
write your thank-you letters to boot,'' she said aloud.
"It'll cost you—say, one of Wong Yee's Cantonese

specials when I get back. I've had just about enough stewed chicken and dumplings.''

"It's a deal. We'll have one of our infamous Chinese pig-outs—and it can't be soon enough for me.''

"Nor me," Marma echoed. "I'm eager to get home.''

After assuring Angie again that she'd be back the next weekend, she hung up, but it wasn't her friend she was thinking about as she wandered over to the candy counter to buy some treats for the kids. It was her own self-revealing words.

Just when had San Francisco, not Tennessee, become home to her?

CHAPTER THIRTEEN

IT WASN'T UNTIL the morning after his quarrel with Marma that Steve discovered she had left the lodge and had gone back to San Francisco. He knew he should have expected it, should have gone after her immediately and insisted that they have it out, but his own feelings had been too ambiguous, teetering between righteous anger and the desire to smooth things over. And because he hadn't been sure that he could trust himself to be convincingly conciliatory, he'd decided to give both of them time to cool off.

Another thing that had stopped him was his uncertainty about apologizing. He wasn't even sure which of the things he'd said had set Marma off. After all, he'd made it clear that he was convinced she'd been hoodwinked into her involvement with the kidnappers, that he was willing to stand by her and do anything in his power to help her. God knows that offer was sincere. Now that he'd come to know Marma, there was no way he could believe that she'd deliberately become involved in a kidnapping scheme in order to ingratiate herself with Arnold. Whatever the truth, Steve was sure she'd been as much a victim as Lisa.

Okay, there were some troublesome questions, such as how she had miraculously come up with the address of the place where Lisa was being held. That needed to be explained. Maybe she'd overheard something that had sunk into her subconsciousness, only to surface later as one of her "visions." Whatever the explanation, he knew she wasn't capable of cruelty or deliberate deception—he'd pointed out that belief to her just before she'd had that fit of temper. Yes, he was in love with Marma, which would make his partisanship suspect to some people, but he was a mature man, the very opposite of gullible, not some adolescent kid in love for the first time.

And having made all this plain to Marma, why had she called him a bastard and then run out of the cabin? Why had she packed her things and left the lodge? Right now, he was madder than hell—and also very scared.

Yeah, admit you're scared. What if she's walked out of your life for good? What if, through some bone-headed thing you said, you've lost the one woman you want to share the rest of your life with?

His anger at Marma's flight didn't amount to much next to the possibility that he'd lost her for good. It was this fear that sent him to his cabin to toss his things into the station wagon, get Leggs settled in the back and head for the city.

And when he got there, he was going to swallow his pride and apologize convincingly to Marma for whatever it was he'd done wrong.

FIVE HOURS LATER, having swung by his condominium to drop off Leggs, Steve was cruising the streets near Marma's apartment, looking for a parking space. He finally beat out another car for a spot near a mom-

and-pop deli, five blocks from Marma's apartment. He found himself walking quickly in his eagerness to talk to and—he hoped—make up with Marma. When he reached her apartment building, he pushed the intercom button under the mailbox labeled "Duncan and D'Marco" but there was no welcome buzzing sound to tell him to come on up.

It was ten minutes before he finally gave up. Marma was there—he'd swear that—but it was obvious she wasn't going to let him in.

At least, not today.

The next morning, Steve tried to call Marma at home a dozen or more times. But no one answered the phone. He dialed her at her office next, only to be informed by a female voice that she was on vacation, and it wasn't known when she could be returning to work.

It was past five, after he'd rung her apartment every fifteen minutes for the preceding four hours, that someone finally answered the phone. It was Marma's roommate, Angie, who informed him that Marma had left on a trip that morning, that she couldn't tell him where she'd gone or when she would be back. She sounded sincere, but Steve didn't believe a word of it.

IT WAS INEVITABLE that Steve would go to see Arnold to pump him for information about Marma, but he did manage to hold out for almost a week, during which time he talked to Angie by phone several times, still hoping that Marma would return and a meeting with his uncle wouldn't be necessary.

As Arnold, the picture of casual elegance in a raw-silk smoking jacket, ushered Steve into the den and put a glass of cognac in his hand, Steve reflected that both Arnold and his house were good examples of how to reconcile the most desirable aspects of the old with the best of the new.

The bathrooms Arnold had added when the house had last been renovated were almost decadently luxurious, with sunken tubs, Nile green tiles and gold fittings. There were spacious closets in each bedroom, and the kitchen was equipped with state-of-the-art labor-saving devices, making Arnold's cook the envy of all the other domestic help in the neighborhood.

The rest of the house was filled with priceless antiques. Interestingly, each piece, whether a Hepplewhite writing table, a Sheraton chair, or an art-nouveau amber-and-green Tiffany lamp, had been chosen for its beauty rather than its value. But it was Arnold's den, Steve thought, that really epitomized his uncle's character. Like Arnold, it was quietly elegant—and every down-stuffed chair, sofa and hammock was the ultimate in comfort.

Steve took a sip of cognac and studied a Remington bronze on a pedestal, then the ceiling-to-floor bookcases stuffed with books, most of them leather bound and all obviously well read.

"I don't know how you do it," he said, postponing the inevitable revelation that he'd blown it with Marma. "My apartment is all Italian leather and rare wood and beveled glass, everything top quality, and it's about as interesting as a furniture-store window. This room is a regular hodgepodge and yet it oozes class."

"What brought that on? You've been in my den dozens of times and you never commented on it before."

"Just making conversation."

"That's not your style—making idle conversation, I mean."

"It wasn't idle. I really am curious to know how you managed to make this room an extension of your personality while my place looks like a lawyer's waiting room."

"Hm. I could make an educated guess. I suggest that you deliberately keep your place impersonal, whether you realize it or not, because you've never been willing to commit yourself to anything or any place for long. Subconsciously, you want to be able to pack up and leave on a minute's notice. Does that sound plausible?"

"It sounds like dime-store psychology to me," Steve growled.

"Then how about this? Your apartment looks as if no one lives there because you really don't. You live at your office or wherever you happen to be when you're on an assignment. So naturally you don't pick up any moss—that is, possessions. Do you rent those leather and beveled-glass furnishings?"

"I own them." Steve's voice was gloomy. "They came with the condo."

"And haven't added a thing except your shaving equipment, a TV, a VCR and your clothes, right?"

"Wrong. I haven't gotten around to a VCR yet," Steve said, grinning.

Arnold didn't smile back. Instead, he pointed to a glass dome that held a battered baseball. It sat next to a graceful and priceless Chinese vase. "Take that baseball," he said. "It made the home run that won the Giants' last pennant. I was sitting in the owner's box, and I beat out a dozen younger fellows to grab it." There was a predatory gleam in Arnold's eyes that made Steve smile. "It means a hell of a lot to me, as much as any piece of art I own—including my post-Impressionist paintings and the Ming vase sitting over there. Now you wouldn't give it shelf space if it was gold plated because it would just be something to worry about when you move on. And until recently, you were bound to do just that as soon as you got bored with a job or a city."

Steve, knowing his uncle was right, wished he'd never brought up the subject. "So? This is a mobile world. Standing still too long can land you in a rut."

"You really believe that? I know you did once, but do you still feel that way? I have a strong hunch that you've recently decided it was time to settle down in one place, put down roots and take on responsibilities—provided you can convince Marma that you really aren't the sap you've been behaving like."

"What are you? Some kind of mind reader? You should charge fees."

"I don't have to read your mind to guess that you came here tonight to pump me about Marma's whereabouts. It's also obvious that you're tied up in emotional knots. What happened between you two? A lovers' quarrel? You and Marma *are* lovers, aren't you?"

Steve stared at him with chagrin—and irritation. "Why are you pushing so hard?"

"Because I'd hate to see you make another mistake. Marma's the best thing that's ever happened to you, and you let her get away. I don't know what you did, but you blew it, boy. And now you're hurting. You came here, hoping I could tell you where she was, and if I told you, you'd rush right over there and probably make an even bigger fool of yourself. So let's get down to basics. What happened between you and Marma?"

Steve had no intention of telling Arnold the whole story, but suddenly it all came pouring out. His reportorial memory going full blast, he repeated the conversation that had triggered their quarrel. Hearing those damning words again made him cringe, and he wasn't surprised that Arnold was silent when he was finished.

"You're right. I did blow it," Steve said finally. "First, I put off telling her I was your nephew and that our meeting wasn't accidental. Then, when she found out, I handled it all wrong and—well, I acted like a jerk. No wonder she called me a bastard."

"She did that?"

"She did. And then she grabbed her cat and left. I followed her back to the lodge and pounded on the door and when she wouldn't talk to me, I told her I'd be back after she cooled down and could talk sensibly."

"It's a wonder she didn't shoot you, boy."

Steve groaned. "So what do I do now? Before I can fix things up, I have to talk to her."

"If you're asking if I know where she is, the answer is no. We had dinner together the evening before she left town, but she didn't say where she was going. She quit her job, you know—or maybe you didn't?"

Steve slumped in his chair. He rubbed his smarting eyes with the palms of his hands, knowing he looked like hell.

"So she really did leave town," he said dully. "That means I'll have to wait to apologize until she comes back." He shook his head. "The thing that bugs me is, how can I pretend to believe that she has psychic powers when I don't? If I lie to her, she'll know it, and that'd really be it."

"Maybe I can help you," Arnold said. "There's someone I want you to talk to—"

"A psychiatrist?" Steve said wryly.

"A good guess, but no. Mrs. Wright sometimes seems like a good psychiatrist, but she doesn't have a formal degree. I'm not going to tell you any more. I'll make the arrangements. Just see that you turn up at the address I give you on time."

STEVE'S FIRST IMPRESSION of the cottage in Noe Valley, the address Arnold had given him, was that it was very modest—and also well cared for. It was one in a row of similar cottages that had probably been built in the twenties, but there was nothing quaint about its brown shingles or its plain, stolid lines. The grounds surrounding it were neat, almost obsessively so, with well-shaped ornamental shrubs and flower beds that didn't sport a single dry leaf or brown blossom.

Steve glanced at his watch and saw that it was exactly five o'clock, the time of his appointment with the mysterious Mrs. Wright. He pushed the bell, and although he didn't hear it ringing inside, the door opened before he could ring again.

The woman who stood in the doorway was as plain and neat as her cottage in a no-nonsense skirt and blouse and sensible walking shoes. A solid brown watered-silk scarf was knotted at her throat, and her hair, a mousy brown color, was held at the nape of her neck with a tortoiseshell clip. Sparkling clean glasses were pushed up on her forehead, as if she'd been reading when he rang the bell. She looked like someone's nanny—the kind that never hesitated to rap a few knuckles if needed.

"So you're Arnold's nephew," the woman said crisply. "He's told me quite a lot about you. Something of a rolling stone, aren't you?" Her dark brown eyes were surprisingly sharp as she studied him. "No, that's not an apt description, is it? You've decided it's time to pick up a bit of moss. How nice for you."

She led the way into a small living room. Not so surprisingly, it was very tidy. And comfortable, too, Steve decided as he sank into the large chair she gestured toward. Like the sofa and the chair that matched it, the back of this chair was covered by a multicolored afghan.

"I need something to occupy my hands when I'm working," she said, and he realized she'd noticed his interest in her handiwork. "It's a common characteristic among psychics."

Steve felt a small shock of surprise. "You're a psychic?"

"Of course. Isn't that why you're here? Your uncle said you needed help. I assumed—"

"You were wrong." His tone was short, not because he blamed this harmless woman, but because of his uncle's trickery—or sly sense of humor. He got to his feet. "I'm afraid both of us have been the victim of my uncle's little joke. I won't waste any more of your time."

"Sit down, Mr. Riley. I'll fetch you some tea and then we'll have a nice talk."

She bustled from the room, a plain, homey, middle-aged woman, leaving Steve to glower at the rug at his feet. It was a hooked rug, of course, made, no doubt, by her busy fingers while she "worked." A cozy lot, these psychics. No doubt she earned a tidy—he bared his teeth in a ferocious smile—income for her skills.

A half hour later, he was finishing off his third cup of Earl Grey tea. He had just consumed his sixth butterscotch cookie and was telling Mrs. Wright that she was an outstanding cook. He told himself that politeness was the only reason he was still there. As for the six cookies he'd scarfed down, it wasn't his fault he had a weakness for butterscotch, was it?

But he had to admit that something had happened to his irritation with Arnold. For one thing, there had been no further mention of the paranormal. They had talked mainly about cats, Mrs. Wright assuming that he was a fellow cat lover because he'd absently petted the monstrous bull cat that had taken possession of his lap. Another cat, just as large, was making love to his shoe, and from the purr that emerged from its—her?—throat, it was obvious that the animal was very much taken with him. Were these Mrs. Wright's familiars, Steve wondered. Or was it only witches who had such things?

The word witches triggered off another line of thought, and he was suddenly remembering the strange look Marma had given him the time he'd teased her about being a witch because she'd found his sunglasses so quickly after he'd dropped them in the woods. Talking to Mrs. Wright, he had almost forgotten his reason for coming to see her—which was a mistake. From the way she was staring at him, it was apparent that she had caught his inattention—and was about to comment on it.

By now, he had come to the conclusion that she was a master at reading facial expressions, so he wasn't surprised when she said, "Oh, dear. It's very bad, isn't it? You've hurt someone you love and you feel terrible about it."

Steve managed to meet her sympathetic eyes without flinching. "How do you do that? I know you can't read minds because no one can. Is it body language?"

"No, I can't read minds and it isn't body language. But I *am* a sensitive. All psychics are—to a greater or lesser degree. Do tell me what's behind this antagonism you have toward us. Has it a religious basis? We aren't witches, you know. And we don't hold black masses or stick pins in dolls. We have nothing to do with the occult, which can be very harmful, very evil. Second sight is a natural phenomenon, an extra sense that some people are born with. It might not be understood by conventional science, but it does exist."

"I'm afraid I can't believe that," Steve said flatly. "I'm sure that you do, however. I have no quarrel with you for that. But others who profess to have psychic powers are not as—as benign as you."

"Yes, there are evil people, who, given the gift, abuse it. But as a rule, we are, to use your own word, benign. We try to help people. And the talent is less rare than you'd think. Others—like your uncle—may not have true clairvoyance or the gift of precognition, but they are sensitives, whether or not they attribute their successes to hunches or lucky guesses or something else."

"Are you saying that Arnold is—"

"Oh, yes. He's a sensitive—which is probably what makes him so formidable in business. But you haven't explained your skepticism. I happen to know that you're a journalist. Surely an open mind is a requisite for someone who's constantly seeking out the truth."

"I do have an open mind. But when I did an in-depth investigation of psychics recently, I came to the conclusion, based on the evidence I found, that they—"

"—were all charlatans. Yes, I read that series of articles in *World Beat*. But then you only sought out the ones in the public eye, the ones who profit by their so-called gift. Most of those people haven't a shred of true clairvoyance. They're very clever con men—or women. You can't judge us by them."

"I did more than just investigate the ones in the public eye. I interviewed dozens of people who claimed to have psychic powers, and nowhere did I find anything that made me believe the whole parapsychology business was anything but pure myth."

"If you took that kind of skepticism to your investigation, it's no wonder." She considered him thoughtfully. "I see it's no use trying to convince you. I wish I could help you with the problem that has you so troubled, but..."

She rose from her chair and began stacking their cups and plates onto a tray. "I've enjoyed our talk, Mr. Riley. Perhaps when you're ready to listen, we can have another little tête-à-tête. Meanwhile, I have one bit of advice for you."

She raised her eyes to his face, and now there was a sharp edge in her voice. "When you find the person you're looking for, approach her with an open mind. Otherwise, you will lose her for good."

STEVE HAD A LOT to think about as he headed for home. Mrs. Wright's parting words had done something he wouldn't have thought possible, not even an hour earlier. His mind had opened a tiny crack, and he was having a few second thoughts about his convictions. Not that he had turned totally around. He still didn't really believe in the so-called psychic phenomenon. But it was just possible that certain things couldn't be explained away as superstition or delusion. And if that were true—but he couldn't think of the full ramifications of that thought yet. He needed to talk to Mrs. Wright again very soon. Maybe then things would become a little clearer....

He was passing a curbside phone kiosk when it occurred to him that he hadn't called Marma's apartment for several hours. This time, when he dialed her number, he got a busy signal. So someone was home—and that someone could be Marma. He waited five minutes and then started to dial again, only to change his mind. If he reached her and she hung up on him, it would set a pattern. So maybe it was time to storm her portals in person again. The problem was, how was he to get through that locked lobby door? He could stake out her apartment building and wait until he caught her leaving, but he didn't want to approach her on the street. He wanted to get her alone, inside her apartment....

But as it happened, getting into the building wasn't a problem, after all. When he pressed the intercom button, the lobby door buzzed, admitting him. On his way up the stairs, which he took two at a time, he prepared a speech so conciliatory that he was sure it would get him back in her good graces.

But when he knocked, it wasn't Marma who opened the door. The woman was young, plump and pretty, a strawberry blonde with a sprinkle of freckles across her nose. She looked as surprised as he did—and also a little alarmed.

"Oh—I was expecting my boyfriend. I think you have the wrong apartment—"

"Does Marma Duncan live here?" he interrupted.

"Yes, she does, but—"

"I'd like to see her, please."

The expression on her face changed from polite inquiry to wariness. "You're Steve Riley, the man who keeps calling Marma, aren't you? Well, she hasn't returned yet, and I still don't know when she'll be back."

Steve suppressed his disappointment and forced a smile. "Look, it's pretty public talking out here in the hall. Can I come in for a few minutes?"

She looked him over so thoroughly that he was surprised when she said, "I'm expecting my fiancé any minute but—okay, you can come in. Not that there's anything more I can tell you."

She opened the door wide enough to let him pass. Once inside, he looked around the long, narrow living room, his curiosity stirring. Nothing he saw was even remotely valuable, but the living room had an air of casual comfort that made him want to sprawl on the calico-covered cushions of an old wing-backed rocker—or maybe take a nap on the wicker sofa, the slipcovers on which undoubtedly hid a multitude of sins. Most of all, he wanted to circle the room and examine the quilted wall hangings, the framed crewelwork and the collection of pink-tinged shells that shared space with pots of lush plants on the windows' wide sills.

He couldn't help comparing the place with his own austere condominium. For pure livability, his place didn't even come in a close second.

"Marma was the decorator," Angie said, smiling at him for the first time. "She has a strong nesting instinct. It comes from being raised in a house where anything not absolutely necessary was considered frivolous and therefore a sin. It's a little old-fashioned for my taste, but I let Marma have her way since I'll be moving out next month when I get married."

Steve was silent. For a moment, he had a vision of a farmhouse in Tennessee with no frills, no color, nothing gay or cheerful—just the bare essentials for living. His throat tightened as he studied a patchwork cat nestled close to a tiny patchwork mouse. Were there no pets either, just farm animals that had to pay their own way, he wondered.

"Would you like a cup of coffee?" Angie asked, friendlier now. "I just made a pot."

Steve nodded, even though he had just downed three cups of Mrs. Wright's Earl Grey tea. He needed a few minutes alone to think. It was obvious Angie was hiding something. The trick was to get the information he needed from her.

But later, as they were drinking coffee in the living room, Angie was adamant about not telling him where Marma had gone or when she'd be back. "She's a private person, Steve. I've known her for almost seven years and she hardly ever discusses her personal life with me." She gave him a searching look. "From the way her voice changed when she called me from Tahoe and said she'd met someone, I thought maybe a man had finally broken through her reserve, but I guess I was wrong. She was an emotional wreck when she came home, but all she said was that it didn't work out with you. What did you do to her, anyway?"

Steve's jaw tightened. He had failed Marma, had been tried and found wanting—but if their quarrel had affected her that strongly, maybe there was still hope....

"I made some mistakes, said all the wrong things, but I really love her, which should count for something," he said. "And I did tell her that no matter how she got mixed up in that kidnapping business, I would stand by her."

Angie groaned. "No wonder she ran away! She wasn't mixed up in that kidnapping business—not the way you obviously believe. She had a vision that helped the police find the girl—"

"I am beginning to believe that now. I didn't when we had our quarrel. Even now, I'm not totally convinced—but at least I have an open mind on the subject. Which is new. I spent several months researching psychics for a series of articles in *World Beat* recently, which convinced me that no such thing as ESP exists."

"I read those articles. What did Marma say about them?"

Steve shook his head. "Nothing. I told her I was in public relations because I didn't want her to know I was a reporter."

"Why did you lie to her? It was the worst thing you could have done."

"I know that now. But you have to remember that I thought she was a fraud."

"And now you don't?"

"Now I don't know what to believe."

"What exactly did you say to get her so furious at you? That you were willing to forgive her for being a crook?"

"I didn't say that—well, not in those words."

"Men. The sensitive sex," Angie said with feeling.

"I suppose that means something profound, but I fail to see—"

"Suppose I told you that I forgave you for stealing money out of my purse. What would your reaction be?"

"What does that have to do with—"

"You'd be furious because you were innocent, right? And I'll let you figure out what the connection is." She rose. "My fiancé will be here any minute, so you'll have to excuse me. But be assured that I'll tell Marma you called—the next time I hear from her."

Steve had no choice but to leave. He sensed the futility of trying to enlist Angie's aid, but at the door, he turned back to ask, "If I write Marma a letter, will you forward it? Or read it to her over the phone?"

He thought she hesitated before she nodded. "Okay. What harm can that do? But I wouldn't count on it changing anything if I were you."

CHAPTER FOURTEEN

MARMA HAD BEEN LINGERING over a soup-and-salad lunch, reluctant to give up her seat to another customer. It was well past noon and she'd skimped on breakfast, but even so she wasn't particularly hungry. She had stopped at the small restaurant on Larkin Street only because she needed a break from job hunting. She'd been on the go all morning, running to job interviews, registering at an employment agency that specialized in finance-related jobs and answering help-wanted ads that had sounded promising. This was the first chance she'd had to rest her feet.

As she looked out the window at the busy street, she felt depressed—far more depressed than circumstances merited, she tried to tell herself. After all, her situation wasn't desperate. She had a MBA from a top university and excellent work references. And most of the interviews she'd had so far had been promising. In fact, her last interview, with a national bank, had been more than that. Her interviewer had asked her to come back that afternoon to talk to the head of the accounting department, which was one reason she was killing time.

She had no doubts that she would get a job—if not this afternoon, then tomorrow or the day after that. Also, her financial situation was far from hopeless, despite the expenses of her trip to Tennessee. During the past two and a half years, she'd saved a small nest egg, so she wasn't broke—not by any means. Also, she was debt-free except for her scholarship, the repayment of which was a moral obligation she intended to honor as soon as she was able, and she also had vacation money and a final paycheck coming.

She winced, remembering her dinner with Arnold Flagg at the Blue Vixen. Although she knew she'd done the right thing, quitting her job, she still felt a little guilty—but not enough to reconsider her decision. How could she continue to work at a place where she could never really be sure if the promotions she received were deserved or the result of patronage?

Marma pushed away the remains of her lunch. Her waitress swooped down upon her table to whisk it away and ask, with a patently false smile, if she wanted anything else.

She left a substantial tip and paid her bill at the cashier's desk, then went outside, into the warm afternoon sun. The sunny day should have cheered her, but it didn't. Despite all the reasons for being optimistic, there was something about being out of work that made her feel very insecure. If it affected her so strongly, a small voice said, it had to be much worse for a man or woman with dependants. At least all she had to worry about was herself—and one very picky cat.

She laughed, suddenly feeling much better. Wait until she told Steve how she had let this job-hunting business get her down—no, that wasn't right. She wasn't going to tell Steve anything because he was out of her life for good....

She discovered her eyes were wet, and she blinked the tears away, furious with herself. How much longer was her mind going to play tricks on her like this? Wasn't it about time she got Steve out of her system? During the past couple of weeks, she'd gone over and over what had happened, trying to put it in perspective in a very rational and objective manner, and she'd always come to the same conclusion: that there could be no future for Steve and her.

Yes, she still felt bereft at times, and she still dreamed about him at night. That was only natural. Now that she'd allowed herself to trust a man enough to fall in love with him, it was bound to take a while to get over him.

Well, no matter how much it hurt, she wasn't going to change her mind. She could never live under siege again, surrounded by distrust and censure. She understood now what had driven her father, how his fear for her had made him try to suppress in his daughter what he abhorred so much in himself. He must have suffered terribly from what he'd thought of as a curse. No wonder the church of his birth hadn't been rigid enough for him; no wonder he'd started a new one so harsh that he had found very few others willing to join him.

But understanding and forgiving him didn't mean she was willing to go through the same thing again. To love and live with a man who felt as Steve did about something that was an integral part of her makeup would be intolerable. She would end up hating him— no, not that. She could never hate Steve, no matter what he did. But she would end up resenting him: resenting his skepticism and inflexibility, resenting always being on the defensive—and that would slowly erode the love between them.

Not that she blamed Steve, now that her anger was spent. He was a levelheaded, practical man who believed only in what was provable. How could she fault him for something that was so inherent to his nature?

And yet he said he loved me. Love is an intangible thing, something that has to be taken completely on faith, isn't it?

Marma paused on the corner of Stockton and Geary streets, waiting until the traffic light changed before she crossed to Union Square, the small park in the heart of San Francisco that someone had once compared to an urban village green. It was filled with people. Some were sitting on benches and others sat on the grass as they ate their lunches and sunned themselves. Marma stifled a laugh as she noted the variety of lunches spread out on newspapers and bench seats. Only in San Francisco—and possibly in New York— did the citizens brown bag such combinations as bagels and cream cheese, cartons of kimchi, and fat Italian sausages on kaiser buns.

A woman with a small child got up from a bench, and Marma commandeered the space. The sun felt wonderful against her skin, and she closed her eyes and tilted her face upward. She still had an hour until her appointment, and it was good to sit under the sun and not think about anything, just enjoy the hiatus.

Maybe that would be enough, she thought, to live from day to day—and never look back. Perhaps sometime, way off in the future, she would meet another man, someone who would accept her the way she was. Or maybe she wouldn't. Either way, she would survive. She always had.

And how lucky that she did love her work, loved immersing herself in cost accounting and tables and charts. Was it because the orderly and inflexible work was the antithesis of the visions? Whatever the reason, she'd learned to be wary of publicly admitting to liking her work; doing so always seemed either to amuse or annoy people.

She was just remembering how Angie had thrown up her hands in disgust that time Marma had compared the clean, orderly logic of mathematics to a Mozart fugue when a familiar dizziness sent her reeling back against the bench.

Oh, no, not now, she thought. She tried to fight it, but already it was too late. The rosy light the sun had cast on her closed eyelids was fading, replaced by a gray sameness. Although she had the sensation of motion, she knew she was still sitting on the bench, leaning against its hard cast-iron back.

Then, just when Marma thought the grayness would go on forever, a light started up and she found herself staring at a middle-aged woman whose plain face was relieved by a pair of unusually fine, deep-set eyes. The woman was sitting on an afghan-covered sofa, a china cup and saucer in her hand. Judging from the teapot sitting on the coffee table in front of the sofa, Marma guessed the cup contained tea, and she had a sudden urge to join the woman in the vision, to spend a long, cozy afternoon talking to her. A fat and placid tabby cat was curled up beside her on the sofa, and as Marma watched, the woman tilted her head slightly, as if listening to someone. When she smiled, Marma wished she could share the joke, and she was sorry when the image wavered and then was gone.

Although she knew things were back to normal, that she could get up anytime she wanted to, she continued to sit there, her eyes closed. This time, at least, there had been nothing frightening in the vision. In fact, it had been strangely comforting, almost as if she'd just had a visit with an old friend. When she finally glanced down at her watch, she saw it was time for the interview and she got up reluctantly, relinquishing her place to a passing man.

The bank at which she had her appointment was located on Geary Street. It was a thriving international firm that was one of Flagg's most formidable rivals, and she couldn't help feeling a little like a traitor as she went through the revolving doors into the lobby. The odor of marble dust and paper money gave her a lift, and she wondered idly if Steve was similarly affected by printers' ink.

As she walked briskly toward the elevators, she gave herself a pep talk. It would all be over in an hour or so. As for getting the job—that was in the laps of the gods.

But it was less than an hour before she returned to the lobby. Feeling a little dazed because the interview had been relatively superficial and she'd gotten the job so quickly, she decided to celebrate by taking a taxi home instead of a bus. Along the way, she had the cabdriver pull over to the curb in front of a liquor store where she purchased a bottle of California champagne. Tonight, she, Angie and Danny would celebrate. She might even break down and have a glass herself. And then she'd settle in to make a success of her new job and never, ever look back.

AS FAR AS Steve was concerned, it had been one rough day. Having gathered most of his research, including doing numerous interviews for the photo essay on the homeless, he had been at the word processor in his office all morning, working on the first article of the series. It wasn't going well. For one thing, several of the photographs his assistant had taken had been a disappointment, and the knowledge that he would have to settle for less than the best hurt his professional pride.

For another, the words just didn't flow as easily as they should have. Usually, he could bring complete—well, almost complete—detachment to his stories, but today the faces of the homeless, so many of them women and children, were haunting him and getting between him and his objectivity.

Previously, he had always done his research, weighed the facts and then taken a position and forged ahead, following a line of reason to a logical conclusion. This time, he kept seeing multiple facets to the problem of the homeless, who were not the bums and derelicts he'd half expected. He kept telling himself a good journalist should be able to keep his own feelings out of his articles, but God, how could he not feel compassion for the children with their young-old faces and their out-of-hope parents? How could he not imagine himself in the cold, bare shelters that smelled of despair? How could he remain objective—and when had he changed? Had it happened because he'd made the mistake of letting someone inside the barricades he'd erected around his heart?

He wasn't in the mood for the banter that passed for conversation at work. Every time one of his coworkers came through his door without invitation and parked himself—or herself—on the edge of his desk for a cozy little chat about the Giants or the Niners or the latest office scandal, he had to grit his teeth. But he endured knowing his mood wasn't their fault, and got rid of them as quickly as possible. Meanwhile, his writing kept hitting snags and his temper got testier.

It didn't help that it was a perfect midsummer's day outside. Usually, the best weather was in the fall, which was when the hordes of tourists disappeared from the streets, leaving the city on the bay to its thankful natives. But today, the sky was a brilliant blue, the wind was warm and balmy, and Steve longed to escape the stuffy office and walk for miles along the beach that bordered the Great Highway, letting the sea breezes clear out the cobwebs in his mind.

He worked doggedly until almost twelve and then, when he found himself typing the same phrase for the third time, he pushed back his chair and headed for the door. Just as he reached it, his desk phone rang, and he ripped off a curse that made a passing secretary eye him with alarm. Although tempted to ignore the phone, he turned back to pick it up. After all, he *was* a professional.....

"Riley," he barked into the mouthpiece.

There was a long pause, as if the caller was startled by his voice. "Is this Steve Riley?" a woman's voice asked.

"Right. How can I help you?"

"This is Angie D'Marco. Do you remember me? I'm Marma's—"

Steve stiffened. "Marma's roommate. Yes, of course I remember you. What is it, Angie?"

"I'd like to talk with you. Is it possible you could come over to the apartment this afternoon—say, about three?"

"What is this all about? Have you heard from Marma?"

"I'd rather not say just now. I'll tell you when you get here."

She hung up before he could ask her another question. He stared at the phone in his hand as if it were alive and might sting him, his hand tightening around it until his knuckles turned white. Why hadn't she answered his question about Marma? If she had good news—but of course it couldn't be good news or she would have told it to him on the phone. No, something had happened to Marma—and she wanted to break it to him gently. God, he couldn't wait until three! He'd go crazy. He had to know now....

He wiped his hands, which were suddenly wet with sweat, on his shirt, then dialed Marma's apartment with fingers that shook alarmingly. The phone rang, and kept on ringing. Was it possible she knew he'd try calling her back and was deliberately ignoring it? Or had she called from another phone, possibly from work?

Unfortunately, he didn't have any idea where that might be. If Marma had ever told him what Angie did for a living, it had gone out of his mind. Wasn't she a teacher? Marma had said something once about Angie getting married because she wanted to stop teaching other people's kids and have some of her own. But that didn't help. There were dozens of schools in the city. He couldn't call them all.

Steve dropped the receiver back in its cradle and left the office, tension tearing at him like a raging animal. Somehow, he had to get through the next three hours. Maybe he should stop somewhere for lunch, he thought. That would take up time. And then he'd take a walk. There was no question of returning to work. He'd just have to be patient and try not to go out of his mind.

He spent more than an hour over lunch, ordering food that he couldn't eat, that he moved around his plate with his fork. To avoid curious stares, he pretended an interest in the newspaper he'd bought, and kept ordering coffee refills until he was ready to burst. But when he finally looked at his watch, he saw that he still had a couple more hours to kill. That was when he decided to try to unwind a little by walking to Russian Hill.

He took his time along the way, resisting the urge to hurry. He even stopped a few times to admire the view, although later he couldn't remember what it was he stared at for so long. Once, when he passed a small neighborhood lunchroom, he stopped for another cup of coffee, which he left virtually untouched.

But for all his delaying tactics, he was fifteen minutes early when he finally reached Marma's apartment. Sure that he'd go crazy if he waited even a few minutes longer, he rang the bell. After a long pause, the lobby door buzzed, and he pushed it open and went inside. He took the three flights of stairs slowly, deliberately not hurrying even though anxiety was building so quickly that he found it hard to breathe normally.

Angie was waiting in the open door of the apartment when he came off the landing. Even in his flustered state it occurred to him that she looked like a female Huckleberry Finn with her red-blond hair and the freckles sprinkled across her nose.

"You're early," she said, mock-accusingly. "I just got home from work—I haven't even had time to open the windows."

He ignored her words, which he recognized as nervous chatter. "What's happened to Marma?" he demanded harshly.

She looked surprised. "Why, nothing's happened to her. Oh, you must have thought—I *am* sorry. I didn't think about—look, Marma is just fine. Nothing's happened to her."

Relief surged through Steve, quickly followed by anger. "You put me through hell. Why did you hang up like that? I was sure the news was bad."

She didn't answer immediately, and a suspicion trickled into his mind. Was it possible that Angie was coming on to him? He'd only met her that once, and she hadn't seemed that kind of woman, and yet—well, he had been the recipient of female attention, most of it unwanted, all his adult life....

He looked at Angie closely, and the suspicion faded. Whatever the reason for her invitation—and her long silence now—it wasn't that. But an inward struggle seemed to be going on behind those green eyes, and suddenly he was sure of the reason for it. Suppose his best friend had asked him not to tell someone who had hurt him badly where he could be found. He would honor the request, of course, but if he became convinced that it would be in his friend's best interest to give out this information, wouldn't he try to find a way to get around his promise?

"I told you I was sorry," Angie said finally. "All I said was that I wanted to talk to you. I never said a word—" She stopped, biting her lower lip.

"Okay. So what is this all about?"

"You're early," she said again, and at his disbelieving stare, she flushed to the roots of her hair.

"I need a drink," she said, and turned and went into the apartment. Steve followed her into the living room. "Is lemonade okay?" she said over her shoulder. "Or can I offer you some wine? There's a bottle of Chardonnay in the fridge—"

"Lemonade is fine," Steve said, resigning himself to another delay. From the set of her chin, he gathered he'd get nothing out of her until the amenities had been attended to. He'd have to wait it out, even if it killed him. Any show of impatience would just antagonize her.

It took Angie a long time to fix the lemonade. Before she'd left the room, she'd opened the windows and the breeze was already clearing out the stuffiness of the room. Fighting the desire to pace, Steve settled himself in the Windsor rocker, and wasn't surprised when Magic drifted in from the another room, stopping abruptly upon seeing him. The cat gave him a long, contemplating look, then sprang lithely into his lap and settled down, purring loudly and rubbing up against his thigh. Steve discovered he was pleased, even though the animal's sharp little claws made him wince.

"This seems to be my season for cats," he said, and Magic made a small purring sound. "Are you Marma's familiar—oops! I got a lecture about witches from the amiable Mrs. Wright. But it was a natural mistake. After all, Marma did a very good job of bewitching yours truly—"

"Did you say something?" Angie said from the door. She was holding a tray, and Steve mused that it was his season for homemade cookies as well as cats; along with glasses of lemonade, the tray Angie held was piled high with them.

When he bit into one a few seconds later, he realized they were the same kind he'd helped Marma make one memorable afternoon at the lodge. Hope galvanized him—until it occurred to him that as Marma's roommate, Angie would naturally have access to her cookie recipes.

He finished the cookie, took a long drink of lemonade to wash it down, then set his glass on the coffee table and gave Angie a hard look.

"Okay, the amenities are over. I want to hear if you've heard from Marma—and if so when."

Angie seemed to find it hard to meet his eyes. "I did hear from her. She's okay. In fact, she's fine."

"Where is she?"

"I can't tell you that. I swore on my engagement ring—" she touched the ring on her left hand "—that I wouldn't tell you where she was."

There was a curious note in her voice—or maybe it was the words themselves that rang false. Was she playing games with him?

"Did she give you a message to pass on to me?" he asked, holding tightly onto his temper.

"Not exactly."

Steve made a gesture with his hand. "Let's not play games."

"I'm not playing games," she said, her voice testy.

"Then you're being evasive. Why?"

"Because—well, a promise is a promise. Marma and I always keep our promises to each other."

"Okay. You're a good friend. So tell me what you can."

She chewed on the inside of her cheek, looking troubled. When she gave a tiny shrug, he knew he had won—on this, at least.

"She went to Tennessee to see her father. She had some unsettled business with him, something that had been festering inside her for years. She wanted to clear the air—those were her own words—before she got on with her life. But it seems her father died almost two years ago. Her family tried to find her at the time but there was some kind of mix-up at the university and—well, they couldn't locate her. She found out about her father's death when she went home."

"She must have been crushed," Steve said.

"She was at first, but now she's come to terms with it. She had a great reunion with her family, which helped, I guess. She told me she realizes now that her father had been so hard on her out of fear. He was afraid *for* her, not of her, and he really loved her, which is what she always wanted to hear. Too bad he couldn't have said it to her while he was still alive."

Steve digested this information in silence. If Marma had put to rest a ghost from her past, he was truly happy for her. But that didn't help him.

"Is she going to stay in Tennessee?"

"No. She—well, she didn't really belong there, she said. She's going to make a lot of changes in her life. Did you know that she quit her job?"

"I learned that from my uncle, Arnold Flagg. Won't you reconsider and tell me how I can reach her?"

"I can't. It's impossible. I did—"

"—promise. I know. And I respect that. We all need friends like you." He stood, dislodging the cat, who gave him a reproachful look.

"If I write her a letter, will you forward it to her?" he asked.

"Of course. I gave her the one you sent me when she—"

"Then she did come back to San Francisco?" Steve said sharply. "Is she still here?"

Angie blinked. "I'll give you some privacy while you write your letter. I have to run an errand, anyway—I won't be long."

She went to a small oak desk in a corner and got out some paper, a pen and an envelope. "Sit here—and take your time," she said. A moment later, she was gone.

It was a while before Steve started his letter to Marma. There was so much to say—and how he said it was all-important. He made his living as a journalist, presenting facts and putting them together in a way that made them interesting to the reading public. Yet now that the whole course of his life could depend on his writing skill, he found himself unable to find the right words.

How could he promise Marma, who had been hurt so many times in her life, that he would never hurt her again when both of them knew it was bound to happen? Oh, not intentionally—he would die before he purposely hurt her. But because of the very intensity of their relationship, they expected so much—too much?—from each other. And because he was human, as she was, he would inevitably falter at times, fail her, disappoint her. He couldn't promise perfection, but he could declare his imperfect-but-so-deep love, and he could apologize for his insensitivity and his blindness.

That he had misjudged her at first was excusable—just barely—because he'd had Arnold's best interests at heart. But later, after he'd fallen in love with her, shared the deepest intimacy with her, after he'd come to know the person she was, he had still assumed she was guilty of being involved in Lisa's kidnapping.

And that, his lack of faith, was unforgivable.

So maybe it was too late to expect Marma to forgive him, but he had to make her understand that despite his suspicions and lack of faith, he had loved—still loved her—as he never had any other woman. He had to make her believe that his love had been genuine or, coming on top of so many other disappointments in her life, it might well leave scars that could wreck her faith in other men.

The thought of Marma in another man's arms made Steve groan out loud. He buried his face in his hands and it was a while before he finally started the letter.

He wrote steadily for almost fifteen minutes, filling several pages with his bold handwriting. He had just finished writing "I love you, Steve" when he heard someone at the door. He got to his feet, expecting to see Angie. Instead it was Marma, looking very pale and tired, who came through the door.

CHAPTER FIFTEEN

SHE LOOKED VERY THIN. That was Steve's first impression.

"What the hell have you been doing to yourself?" he blurted.

The expression on her face didn't change. She came into the apartment and closed the door behind her.

"You don't look so hot yourself," she said.

The coolness in her voice triggered anger, but somehow he managed to hold onto his temper. "I haven't been sleeping well. Why didn't you answer my letter, Marma?"

He caught a flicker of something—pain?—in her eyes and suddenly his anger, which he realized hadn't been anger at all but desperation, was gone. "God, Marma, I've been though hell. I know what an insensitive fool I was—still am, I guess—but you'll never find anyone who loves you the way I do. Doesn't that matter at all?"

For a moment, he thought her face softened. But she didn't answer him. She turned away to drop her purse and the brown paper sack she was carrying onto a chair. "How did you get in? Angie doesn't get home until four."

"She must have come home early today because she let me in. She went off on an errand somewhere." He hesitated, then added, "She didn't break her promise to you. She wouldn't tell me where you were."

"But she left you here, knowing—" She broke off. She met his eyes, and when her full lips tightened, he knew that she wasn't as indifferent as she seemed.

"We have to talk, Marma," he said quickly. "I love you, and I know you love me. Think about how it was between us in Tahoe. That wasn't some fly-by-night affair. It was very real and—"

"And flawed," she said tiredly. "You still don't know why I left, do you?"

"I didn't know then, but I do now. I admit it took me a while, and I had to have help figuring it out. It was that speech I made, forgiving you for something you didn't do. What a jerk I was!" His voice was too loud, and he forced it to a softer tone. "Can you forgive me for having offended you?" he said, aware how stiff and formal the words sounded.

Again, she didn't answer. She just dropped into a chair and closed her eyes. Her skin had a papery look, and when she pressed her fingertips against her temples, fear clutched at Steve. Had she been ill—or was it the shock of seeing him unexpectedly that made her look so pale?

Despite the possibility that she was sick, he had to go on: he knew it might be his only chance. At least she wasn't angry. Then again, he almost would have preferred rage to apathy.

He took the chair opposite her, collected his thoughts for a few seconds and then began talking....

STEVE HAD BEEN SPEAKING for a long time. At the moment, he was describing an elderly woman he'd interviewed who had lost her life savings and had been forced out on the street because of a charlatan who had professed to have psychic powers. As Marma listened silently, she wondered how she could have ever believed that Steve, with his sharp, incisive mind, would have chosen a career in image-centered public relations. He was committed to exposing injustice, getting at the truth. That series on psychics had been devastatingly convincing, even to someone who knew how wrong he had been in his total rejection of any type of parapsychology. In fact, at the time, she'd been able to see exactly how the facts he had piled up must have seemed conclusive to most people....

She realized that Steve was still speaking, his voice dogged, his eyes burning with sincerity as he told her that he loved her, that he wanted to marry her, take care of her, and have her take care of him. She didn't doubt that he meant every word he said, so why was she holding back? It had to be fear of being hurt again. God, she couldn't go through the pain of rejection again! And for all his explanations, he still hadn't told her he was willing to live with someone who possessed the gift—or curse—of second sight....

"I think I fell in love with you that day I walked into your office," he was saying now. His voice was strained, and there were lines on his face, beside his mouth and between his eyebrows, that she hadn't noticed before. Were they due to his not getting enough sleep? Had he been going through the same torment she had? And why should she be surprised? She'd never doubted that he loved her. The thing she couldn't accept was the vast difference that lay between them.

"The first time I made love to you, it was because I couldn't help it. I never planned for us to become lovers. I knew I wanted you, yes, but I thought I could control it. Then—it happened, and I realized I loved you, not just wanted you. That's when I should have told you the truth, but I kept putting it off. I was afraid of losing you. Then you read Arnold's letter and found out in the worst way possible. I had intended to tell you that night. I swear to you, I had reached the point at which I couldn't put it off any longer and still live with myself. That's why I planned a special dinner, including that damned chocolate cake. I thought it might soften you up. I wanted everything to be just right, and then when you were mellow, I was going to confess that Arnold was my uncle, that he'd asked me to look out for you—and all the rest. Crazy, huh?"

Marma studied his attempt at a smile. It made her hurt inside, and she resented the tug at her emotions, resented Steve's power over her.

"I can understand why you were suspicious before you knew me, considering the facts you had to go on," she said only because he seemed to be expecting an answer. "What I can't understand is why you didn't tell me the truth before you made love to me. And none of that really matters now. The reason I want you to leave me alone is that I couldn't possibly live with someone who can't accept me as I am. I'd always be apologizing for having one of my spells, or I'd be hiding it from you and making excuses. It would be the same as it was with my father. I can't go through that hell again. You can see that, can't you? We're on two totally different wavelengths and there's no way they can ever become reconciled.''

Steve shook his head. "You're wrong, Marma. I've changed—I swear I've changed. No, I won't lie to you. I'm not totally convinced that such things as ESP exist, but now I have an open mind on the subject. And that makes all the difference—can't you see that? We can make it. I know we can. All it takes is faith on both sides—and love.''

"How did it happen, this sudden change?" she said, unable to help the skepticism in her voice.

"Arnold sent me to see a friend of his, a Mrs. Wright. She said something that turned me around. Maybe I should have interviewed her before I wrote those articles. They might have been a little more objective.''

"This woman convinced you that she had psychic powers?''

"No, not that. She convinced me that I should keep an open mind.''

She stared at him fixedly. "Mrs. Wright—is she middle-aged and brown-haired? Is there a multicolored afghan on the back of her sofa? Does she have a brindle cat with yellow eyes?''

"You know Mrs. Wright?''

"You might say that. If I told you I saw her in a vision, would you believe me?''

His eyes met hers. "I know you don't lie, so I'd have to believe something happened that you interpreted as a vision. I told you I had an open mind about the subject, didn't I?''

"But you aren't convinced. I doubt you ever will be," she said and even to her own ears, her voice had a defeated sound.

Steve stood and pulled her to her feet. He didn't make the mistake of putting his arms around her. "I love you, Marma. Isn't that enough? The rest of it will work itself out. I'm being completely honest, you know. I could lie and say that I'm a believer now, but that wouldn't be the truth. I'm willing to admit that there are more things in heaven and earth than can be explained by pure logic. Maybe this—this thing is a highly developed empathy for other people or the ability to read body language. A month ago, I wouldn't have conceded even that much. Isn't that enough to build on?"

"I don't know," she said helplessly. "My heart tells me it's enough, but my mind says something different. I'm afraid of you, Steve, of that pragmatic mind of yours. You have the power to hurt me—and I'm sick of being hurt."

"It doesn't have to be that way. We can work it out. Maybe you could start therapy with a—" He broke off, his eyes stricken. "I didn't mean that. I don't know why I said such a stupid thing. My only excuse is that I'm half out of my mind with fear that I've lost you for good."

When she didn't answer, he made a helpless gesture. "It's no go, isn't it?" he said. "I blew it again. Well, you don't have to worry. From now on, I'll leave you alone. Just remember that I do love you, that I always will."

He turned and walked away, toward the door. She felt sympathy for him, and yet there was a dark satisfaction in knowing that he had suffered—was suffering—as much as she. He had deceived her, put her through hell. Why should she pick up the pieces for him now? As for the future without Steve, she was strong. She had coped with rejection most of her life, and had come out of it reasonably intact emotionally. So she could make it without him. Of course she could.

She heard the door close—quietly, with finality. Blindly, wanting a diversion, she picked up the champagne she'd bought, intending to put it in the refrigerator to chill. As she turned away, her eyes were drawn to the desk where Steve had been sitting when she came in. The roll top was up, and a piece of paper lay on the blotter. Had Steve been writing her another letter? She felt a rush of anger. *No more,* she thought. She had taken enough—she didn't need any more.

She went to the desk, snatched up the piece of notepaper and crushed it in her hand, then tossed it toward the waste basket. It fell short of its target, and automatically she bent to pick it up. But this time she didn't throw the piece of paper away. Instead, following an irresistible impulse, she smoothed it out and read it.

The letter was very short. Steve apologized for his lack of tact, his insensitivity, told her he loved her and didn't want to lose her, just as she had expected, but there was something else in the letter, something between the lines, that couldn't be denied: sincerity, a willingness to humble himself, to admit guilt, to ask for her understanding.

When she was finished, she found that she was crying—and that she was ashamed. How many men had the strength to humble themselves to the women they loved? Steve had done that. He had put his pride—which he possessed in abundance—in his pocket, and had come to her to apologize. And she, so arrogant and filled with her own pride, had sent him away.

The truth came to her like a burst of blue-white light. She didn't want this proud, confident, self-possessed man humbled. She wanted him the way he'd been when they were lovers, when he had argued with and teased and confided in her—and laughed with but never at her. Most of all, she wanted him any way she could get him—the devil take her fear of being hurt again.

Steve must have lagged on the way because when she came flying down the staircase, he was just leaving the lobby. He turned and when he saw her, he threw back his head in a triumphant laugh. He met her in the middle of the lobby, swept her up and whirled her around and around, still laughing. And she laughed, too, because she loved him and he loved her, and because everything was going to be all right.

He refused to let her walk back up the stairs. He insisted on carrying her all the way to her apartment, through the door she'd left wide open in her haste, across the living room and into the nearest bedroom, which, luckily, was her own. He laid her on the quilt-covered bed as if she were a piece of fragile china, and she knew that while it wouldn't always be this way, it would be often enough to make the difference.

Quickly and tenderly, he undressed her, and she didn't try to help with zippers or buttons. She knew, from the intent expression on his face, that he was acting out something he'd fantasized about during their separation. Nor did she help him undress. Instead, as he flung off his clothes, she watched without breathing, drinking in the long, lean lines of his legs and thighs, the strength in his body that was most apparent when he was naked. He came to the side of the bed and stared down at her, his need for her so flagrant that she was smiling as she held out her arms, welcoming him back.

CHAPTER SIXTEEN

THERE WAS ANOTHER Duncan family reunion four years after the birth of Marma and Steve's son. This time, it was different from the first one, which had been such a mixture of pain and pleasure to Marma. The past was gone, if not forgotten, then forgiven, and Marma's family had assembled for the sole purpose of getting acquainted with the new members that had been added during the past five years. Everybody had a good time—or if they didn't, no one complained.

The next afternoon, as Louise and Marma sat in the kitchen of the old Burleau homestead, scraping carrots and shelling peas for supper, they rehashed the reunion. Although Louise was aware that Marma was up to date on family news, she repeated it anyway.

For starters, Luke's marriage had busted up, but he was happier now. "It never was a good one," Louise said, lowering her voice, even though they were alone in the kitchen. "Abby drank and ran around, you know."

Marma did know, having heard all about it from Matthew's wife, but she listened politely as Louise related the saga of her brother's broken marriage, then moved on to say that Mark had been promoted to store manager over there in Taswell County, and that he and his wife had put the down payment on a house.

"I'm sure it don't come near what you folks are used to," she said, not noticing Marma's wince, "but it's real nice. If they keep having kids, of course, they'll have to add on some bedrooms."

Luke's oldest son, the one with all the brains, had skipped fourth grade. "The teachers say he's real smart, could maybe get himself a scholarship like you did," she commented. "You set a good example around here, you know. Folks figure if you did it, why can't their kids? My Marma Lou is smart enough to get one but she just wants to daydream in school."

"That doesn't mean she can't get a scholarship," Marma said, her interest aroused as it always was where Louise's oldest daughter—her namesake—was concerned. "How is she—you know, handling the second-sight business?"

"There have been no problems so far. We don't make the mistake Papa did. We all take the sight for granted and so do most folks around here, even the real religious ones. She doesn't think of herself as being any different than the Bradys' oldest boy, the one that's double-jointed."

Louise obviously didn't mean the comparison as a joke, and Marma managed not to laugh. "Would you let her visit us next summer?" she asked. "She'd love the cable cars and the San Francisco Zoo—she'd have a wonderful time."

"I'm sure she would. Maybe in a year or so when our finances are better."

"Her airfare is included in the invitation," Marma said—unwisely, she realized when her sister's face stiffened. "She could more than earn it by baby-sitting for us," she added, as if she hadn't noticed.

"Well, I'll have to think on it and see what Charlie says. Likely it'll be yes. It'd do her good, seeing what's outside of the holler. And she thinks the world of you folks. You've got a good man, Marma. Why, he's as common as an old shoe. Wouldn't know he was the west coast editor of that big magazine any more'n you'd guess you had an important job in a bank." She paused to give Marma a sidelong look. "That boy of yours takes after his father's side of the family, don't he? He sure don't favor the Duncans—or the Mc-Canns."

"If you're asking whether Alex inherited the second sight, I doubt it very much. He's so much like Steve it's uncanny—stubborn and sweet and full of curiosity, and he's got a habit of weighing the facts before making up his mind about things that just breaks me up sometimes. Naturally, Steve thinks he's the greatest little guy in the world."

Louise laughed, and so did Marma. Their eyes met and suddenly they were girls again, giggling over something their brothers had done.

"It's like old times—or the way old times should have been for us," Louise said softly. "I'm real fond of you, Marma, always have been. It's just that it comes hard, saying it out loud."

"And I've never said a proper 'thank you'. That comes hard, too. I remember so many things—how you taught me how to read so I wouldn't be put in the first grade with kids three years younger than me, and how you used to cover up for me with Papa. Do you remember when you brought me those hunks of johnnycake when Papa locked me up in the corncrib? Nothing's ever tasted quite as good since."

"I remember. I couldn't sleep those nights for thinking how scared you must be out there in the dark alone. Papa was wrong to do that, you know. You couldn't help that you knew where to find water. You wanted to help him—you didn't even know that it wasn't normal. It's funny, Marma Lou's found water for several folks here in the valley. The water table dropped a few years back—something to do with the dam they built over in Murphy's Valley, they say—and folks are real pleased when she can save them from digging in the wrong place."

There was an interruption when the kitchen screen door slammed and the Burleau kids and Marma's Alex rushed in, demanding food—preferably the brownies left over from the reunion. Louise shooed them out again, then followed them with a tray of brownies. Marma watched through the window as her sister doled the goodies out, warning the kids to make them last because that was all they were going to get until supper.

Louise called through the screen door to say that she was going to fetch some eggs from the henhouse. Marma returned to the peas she'd been shelling, glancing up now and then to watch the children, who had returned to their game of tag.

Alex, with his father's dark eyes and rusty hair, stood out among her sister's towheaded boys and black-haired daughter. Although he was a little small for his age, he could hold his own, even with his older cousins. Was she happy or sorry that he hadn't inherited her gift? Now that she'd learned to accept it—to a large degree due to the tutelage of her friend, Mrs. Wright—she no longer thought of it as a curse. She had even helped the police a couple more times—once to find an elderly man who had wandered away from a convalescent home and another time to look for a child who was missing on Mount Diablo. Both had been found alive, thanks to her, which was very satisfying, but still—life would be much simpler if she didn't have the visions. There were times when she wondered if Steve wouldn't prefer a more normal wife....

"What are you thinking about so hard?" Steve said. He was standing in the doorway, with Alex—a very grimy Alex, she noted—perched on his shoulder. "Alex has just discovered the delights of mud puddles," he went on, not waiting for her answer. "How about finding him some dry clothes?"

"You promised to keep an eye on him," Marma pointed out.

"I did. I had both eyes on him when he landed in that puddle."

"Okay, I'll clean him up—but next time, watch him!"

"Yes, dear." The meekness in his voice wasn't reflected in his amused eyes.

"You did it on purpose, you dork!"

"Who, *moi*?"

"Why is it that men want their boys to do all the things that are sure to get them into trouble with their moms?" she asked the air.

"Boys should be boys. Now little girls are different. Girls should be all ruffly and sweet-smelling—like their mothers."

"I never wore a ruffle in my life," she protested.

"But you do smell sweet. Yummy. Sure would be nice to have another one like you around the house."

"Are you hinting?"

"Who, *moi*?" he said again, wiggling his eyebrows.

She groaned. "Okay, we'll talk about it later. But you know how hard it is, trying to combine a career with being a wife and a mother, even with just one child. Two would be double trouble, for heaven's sake!"

"But think ahead fifty years when you'll have two offspring and all those grandkids to keep you happy in your old age."

She looked into his eyes. "I intend to have you to keep me happy fifty years from now, and don't you forget it. So don't eat too much fried chicken tonight."

He hooted with laughter. "Look who's talking! The southern-fried cook herself!"

"You know I've changed. Okay, once in a while, I still fix some turnip greens with bacon—"

"Or red-eye gravy and biscuits!"

"But most of the time, I'm a very health-conscious cook. Admit it!"

He swung Alex to the floor. "You're a whiz—in the office, in the kitchen and in bed. The demon wife, that's what you are, and if I have to sleep out in that frigging barn one more night, all cold and lonely, I'm going to drag you off into the woods and have my way with you. How about that?"

"Believe me, you wouldn't have to drag me," she said, sighing. "And it's only one more night. Tomorrow, we'll be heading home and then—"

"And then I'm going to drop Alex off at the baby-sitter's, take you into the bedroom and undress you—very slowly—kissing every inch of you as I strip off your clothes, and then I'm going to—"

"Stop it! Little pitchers have big ears."

"Little pitchers are busy playing with that box of kittens behind the range."

"Someone else might hear you."

"So what? We're married, aren't we? Married people do certain things together."

"Louise and Charlie are very—conservative."

"They didn't get all those kids by being conservative."

"You behave," she told him, trying not to laugh. She collected Alex and hustled him off to the bedroom she'd been sharing with Louise.

"Papa won't let me play in the mud," Alex complained. "He said I hafta be clean to eat supper."

"Papa's right. Isn't it fun, eating with all your cousins at a separate table?"

"Uh-huh. I like my cousins, Marma Lou best of all. She told me a secret, so I told her one, too."

"You have a secret?"

He gave her a sly look. "Yeah, but I can't tell it to you or it wouldn't be a secret anymore."

"I have no quarrel with that. Secrets are for keeping. You only tell them to people you trust."

"I trust you, Mama. You want to hear my secret?"

She suppressed a smile. Alex, the pragmatist—just like his daddy. "Only if you really want to," she said.

"You won't tell?"

"I promise. Cross my heart."

"Well—okay. I see dreams when I'm awake like Marma Lou does. I saw her in one once."

Her heart skipped a beat. "You dreamed about your cousin?"

"It wasn't the real kind. It was the other kind. 'Course, I couldn't talk to her. You can't do that in a dream."

"When did this happen?"

"Just before we came out here. That's my secret. I can't tell you hers 'cause I promised, but it's going to happen next summer and Marma Lou and me are going to go to the zoo and ride on the elephant train."

He went on prattling as Marma laid out clean clothes for him to change into. She looked up—into Steve's eyes. He was standing in the doorway; it was obvious that he'd heard her exchange with Alex, but there was only amusement in his eyes. Which answered the question she'd asked herself earlier.

"It looks as though we have a wizard in the family," he said, sotto voce.

"What's a wizard?" Alex asked, his eyes bright with interest.

"Never you mind, buster. Soon as you're changed, I'm going to take you off your mother's hands so she can help your aunt get dinner—uh, supper on the table. Us men are hungry."

"Us men are hungry," Alex repeated importantly.

Steve's eyes were on Marma. "In fact, this particular man is real hungry—got that?"

"Got that," his son echoed.

Have You Ever Wondered If You Could Write A Harlequin Novel?

Here's great news—Harlequin is offering a series of cassette tapes to help you do just that. Written by Harlequin editors, these tapes give practical advice on how to make your characters—and your story—come alive. There's a tape for each contemporary romance series Harlequin publishes.

Mail order only

All sales final

Harlequin Superromance

MORE THAN A FEELING

A powerful new Superromance from
ELAINE K. STIRLING

Andonis Sotera was the kind of man a woman might encounter in a Moroccan café after dark, or on the deck of a luxury cruise ship. In short, Andonis was the kind of man a woman like Karen Miller would never meet.

And yet they fell in love. Suddenly the civil servant from a small Canadian city was swept into the drama of Andonis's life. For he was not only her passionate, caring lover, he was *The Deliverer*, the one man who could save a small Mediterranean country from the terror of a ruthless dictator.

But Andonis needed Karen's help. And she was willing to risk her life to save their love....

MORE THAN A FEELING...
Coming in February from Harlequin Superromance

Harlequin Temptation dares to be different!

Once in a while, we Temptation editors spot a romance that's truly innovative. To make sure *you* don't miss any one of these outstanding selections, we'll mark them for you.

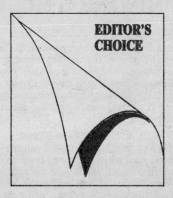

EDITOR'S CHOICE

When the "Editors' Choice" fold-back appears on a Temptation cover, you'll know we've found that extra-special page-turner!

THE

Temptation

EDITORS

Harlequin Superromance

COMING NEXT MONTH

#342 JO • Tracy Hughes
Rock star E. Z. Ellis is every woman's fantasy—a
sexy electric poet of the eighties whose songs reveal
both his passion and his compassion. Fiery
Jo Calloway is fighting to have his lyrics censored
until E.Z. teaches her what he's been singing about—
changing the world means nothing unless you first
love the people in it.

#343 GOOD VIBRATIONS • Lynn Patrick
Alyce McKenzie still lives by the values she learned in
the sixties. And when she meets lawyer Greg Holmes
at a benefit concert, she is sure she's found her soul
mate—someone who is as caring and loving as she is.
But Alyce quickly realizes that, while she shares her
love with family, friends and even strangers—Greg
wants her love all to himself....

#344 DESERT STAR • Sally Garrett
It's been twenty-five years since Caroline Noble and
Granville Kane were lovers—twenty-five years since
Caroline gave away their child. When they meet
again, their passion quickly reignites. But can
Gran ever truly forgive her? And can Caroline ever
forgive herself?

#345 MORE THAN A FEELING • Elaine K. Stirling
Andonis Sotera is the kind of exotic, mysterious
stranger a woman like Karen Miller would never
meet. And yet they fall in love, and suddenly the civil
servant from a small Canadian city is swept into the
drama and intrigue of a plot to overthrow a ruthless
dictator. Andonis needs Karen's help to free his
homeland. And she is willing to risk her life to save
their love....